Wild Lust
S.L. CARPENTER

ELLORA'S CAVE
ROMANTICA PUBLISHING

What the critics are saying...

§

STRANGE LUST

4 Rating "STRANGE LUST is an erotic collection of stories about couples coming together for sex. [...] I enjoyed the humor that SL Carpenter puts in his writing and the vivid pictures he paints with his words. This is a wonderful assortment of short stories that is guaranteed to make you laugh and sigh as you follow the characters on their erotic journey of lustful desires." ~ *Romance Junkies Reviews*

NAKED LUST

Recommended Read "NAKED LUST by S.L. Carpenter is hilariously disturbing, in a good way of course. I laughed my butt off from beginning to end. [...] Each of the stories brings their own enticements and will leave readers praying that they never experience these issues. NAKED LUST is not strong on the romance aspect, but it's definitely worth the laughter that only S.L. Carpenter can deliver to his stories."
~ *Dark Angel Reviews*

MORE LUST

Recommended Read "This is another amazing collection of far-out stories as only S.L. Carpenter can manage. I don't know how or where he gets these stories, but I'm always a little bit appalled and a whole lot entertained when I'm finished. [...] I laughed, I cried, I snorted Mt. Dew and almost threw up. It's always a roller coaster of emotions when you pick of one of these collections from this eclectically talented author!" ~ *Dark Angel Reviews*

An Ellora's Cave Romantica Publication

www.ellorascave.com

Wild Lust

ISBN 9781419957895
ALL RIGHTS RESERVED.
Strange Lust Copyright © 2002 S.L. Carpenter
Naked Lust Copyright © 2007 S.L. Carpenter
More Lust Copyright © 2002, 2008 S.L. Carpenter
Edited by Mary Moran.
Cover art by Syneca.

This book printed in the U.S.A. by Jasmine–Jade Enterprises, LLC.

Trade paperback Publication May 2008

WILD LUST

ɛͻ

STRANGE LUST

NAKED LUST

MORE LUST

STRANGE LUST

The Cabin

The sun burning into the desert glowed orange on the clouds. The open-topped Jeep raced across the sand toward their rented cabin. This was their sanctum of desire, the one place where phone calls, interruptions and life's turbulence couldn't bother them.

Even at dawn, the desert heat was intense. Stephanie, Stevie to her friends, arched back and let the rushing wind blast against her flesh. Overcome with the fever of her anticipation she pulled her skirt up, leaned back, and let the dry wind search out the moistness within her.

Don swerved on the road when he noticed that she wasn't wearing any underwear and he could see the smooth hair on her pubis blowing in the racing wind. Her pussy seemed to open to its force. She licked her fingertip, wetting it with her tongue, as she closed her eyes and envisioned sliding something else into her mouth. The way she slid the tip of her finger along the edge of her mouth and let her tongue wet it made Don adjust his suddenly tight pants.

He tried to keep his attention on the road but was distracted when she undid the top few buttons of her blouse, letting the bursts of wind flutter the fabric against her breasts. The wind stroked the lapels of her blouse against her chest. Don's hands were jealous. He reached over and slid his hand inside her blouse to grasp her breast and felt it gently mold to his hand. The hardened nipple poked between his fingers and she moaned as he squeezed the tip.

Stevie clasped his hand, extended his middle finger, and slid it between her red, lipstick-covered lips. She sucked on its length as her other hand encompassed her labial lips. Her eyes rolled back as she guided his hand down to the juncture of her thighs. She put her foot on the dashboard and leaned back, closing her eyes. Then she raised her arms above her head to pull her hair from its barrette.

Don was trying hard to watch the road but the wetness on his hand aroused him incredibly. Her hips rose and fell to his probing finger, and the muscles of her legs tightened as if they were making love. She was about to climax when Don lost control of his desires. The car skidded to a stop on the shoulder of the highway.

Stevie, shocked, opened her eyes and glared at him. Don fumbled with his pants. Stevie's hands touched his and steadied them as she undid his pants and pulled them down. She could see how excited he was and her own desires were on the edge of release. She shuffled around the stick shift then rose above him. She grabbed the Jeep's roll bar with one hand and grasped the seat adjustment to lower him backwards. As he leaned back, the fullness of her pussy slid down the length of his shaft. They were oblivious to the few passing cars, completely engrossed in the beauty and heat of their sex.

Her blouse opened to the breeze, and Don's hands reached up to finish unbuttoning her shirt and fondle her breasts. Her breasts were full and tingling from his small tugs and groping as she tightened her vaginal walls around his throbbing cock. Stevie was aroused. She shook as she forced Don deeper into her, hammering forcefully against him, needing him deeper inside. She grabbed the roll bar and leaned back, feeling his hard-on strain from the tension of the grind. When she leaned forward, her breasts swayed before his mouth and Don kissed them. She touched his face with her hands then whimpered and grabbed his shoulders. She bit her lip and closed her eyes tight. Trying to squeeze him inside her as she rose made her juice flow down between his legs. He bucked trying to remain in her grip. Stevie looked up and took a handful of his shirt in her hand as she pulled away from his chest. As a burst of air from a passing truck rushed over her, she cried out and came from the feeling of total abandon. Don lay there, still pulsing from his own orgasm.

Stevie giggled and opened her eyes. The first thing she saw was flashing lights. Then she focused on a figure walking toward her. The policeman was adjusting his belt and whistling as he strolled toward the Jeep. As Stevie buttoned her shirt up, she smiled and slid over to her seat. Don lay there smiling with his dick lying against his leg and a glimmering stream of fluid across his thigh.

"Uh, sir, could you please put that away?" the policeman sternly said, obviously holding back his laughter. "Some may consider that a weapon."

"Sorry, officer," Don said, trying to fix himself.

"A few motorists called in complaining, but I've been here for five minutes and didn't see anything to complain about. In fact, I filmed the whole thing and was going to bring it to show the wife tonight on our vacation at the cabin. I'll just give you a warning for indecent exposure and ask you to get a hotel room. And, miss, I shouldn't say this, but, you are beautiful during sex!" He gave Don the ticket and walked back to his car, adjusting his gun belt. Then he drove off.

The rest of the drive was relaxing. The sunset was beautiful. The sun seemed to set on the desert floor and melt into the sand. Stevie saw the cabin they'd rented behind a few trees, and the lights from the other tourists' cabins glowed in the evening darkness.

After unpacking and cleaning up the furnished cabin, Don lit a fire. The warmth made him feel at home. He poured drinks for them both and sat down on the couch to watch the flickering flames. Stevie came back from the bathroom wearing one of his shirts buttoned halfway up and put on some music. The slow groove of Alicia Keys echoed through the cabin and they finally relaxed.

"Dance with me?" she asked.

Don got up and stared at her. She was beautiful. Her hair was combed out straight, and the large shirt hid the curves of her body. Her almond-colored skin glistened lightly from sweat. As they danced, his hands searched, following the fabric of her shirt down to her ass and discovered she had nothing on underneath. He pulled her against him. Their mouths met and they kissed deeply.

Stevie undid his shirt as they danced. Don repaid the favor by unbuttoning hers too. Their chests pressed together and the heat from their flesh seemed to burn as they swayed together. Don kissed her again. Her hand found its way to his pants and she slid it inside the zipper flap to grasp him firmly in her hand. Her mouth opened and she buried it in his chest, licking the space between his tensing pectorals. Then she rested her head against Don's chest, and the thump of his heart was the rhythm of her dance. She didn't want to let go of his growing cock, but she also wanted to have it somewhere else.

The smooth stroking of her hand excited Don to a fever. Her long fingernails found the soft skin of his testicles and she toyed with them in her hand, giggling. Don closed his eyes and cupped her ass in his hands, feeling the muscles clench tight as his fingers traced the grooves and curves. He picked her up and she wrapped her legs around his waist. His finger found the hot, wet flesh of her pussy. Stevie was on fire and kissed Don again, deeply exploring his mouth. He moved across the room and leaned her against the cabin's center post near the raging fire.

Don lowered her back down to the floor and held her naked flesh to his. She turned around to face the post and rubbed her ass against his groin, leaning forward to push it harder against him.

"You're teasing me again, and that's not fair!" Don said.

"Awwwwww, poor baby," she laughed. "What are you going to do about it?"

Don reached over to the end table and grabbed a pair of handcuffs. He moved his hands up the length of her body, pulling her hands up around the post and locking them together. Stevie winced as he tightened the cuffs on her wrists but was incredibly aroused by Don's dominance. Her own helplessness was an aphrodisiac.

Don had an empowered moment, and he reached over to grab his drink and stood staring at his sex slave. The ice danced in his Bacardi and Coke and a wicked thought occurred to him. He took a piece of ice in his mouth, stepped behind her and pulled the shirt up. He dipped his fingers into his drink caressed her back with his wet fingertips. Leaning forward, he began to kiss her back. As he did, he poked the ice cube out between his lips and drew it along her spine, making her jolt and laugh. Don smacked her on the ass, knowing she was his toy to play with. He laughed as he chewed the ice, and Stevie asked him to release her.

Ignoring her request, he took a long slender piece of ice from his glass and knelt behind her to draw his initials on her ass. While there, he saw a glimmer on her thigh. He brushed it with his finger, brought it to his mouth, and tasted her desire. He put another piece of ice in his mouth and brushed it along the flesh of her ass, causing Stevie to moan. The small trace of her pubic hair was the treasure he wanted and the ice cube was the key.

Her knees bent and she almost lost her balance when Don grabbed her feet and forced them wider. His nose smelled the fragrance of her pussy. The fullness of the engorged labia made them purse out as if begging for a kiss. Stevie's moaning and straining from the confinement of her hands made it obvious this was driving her crazy. With his face buried in her backside, his mouth reached her pussy and he pushed the slender ice cube between Stevie's pussy lips. The ice seemed to melt as it touched the deep fire within her inner soul. As he did it, she bent her body even farther, making her sanctuary more accessible to his exploring. His mouth found its way and he licked the length of it, making her ache for him.

Stevie was frantically trying to free her hands, causing red bruising from the cuffs on her wrists—they were dangerously close to bleeding. Don's hands grasped her ass hard as he continued his journey between her thighs and began licking deeper into her. Her moans urged him on.

He stood up behind Stevie and rested one hand on her butt, playfully slapping it. He undid his pants and pulled them off with his underwear. She looked back but couldn't see him. Her body was leaning over and she looked down the length of her frame, beyond her dangling breasts and between her legs, and saw him stepping up behind her. He was stiff.

Don grabbed his dick, laid it on the cheeks of her ass, and slowly dragged it along the crease. Stevie's knees buckled and she shook her ass, trying to make him stop.

"Damn it, stop doing that. I want you," she demanded.

"Oh, is that so?" Don teased. "Tell me what you want."

"To be blunt, I want you to fuck me, you idiot."

Looking down again, she saw Don bend his knees and position his hard cock against her pussy. The tip was seeping a little fluid. Stevie pushed her ass out trying to get it angled right to enter her. Her eyes gleamed and her insides warmed as she saw and felt him disappear into her. His hands grasped her hips, and he pushed hard against them while pulling her torso toward him. He stopped when he was fully inside her pussy. The heated, slippery flesh made him breathe deeply. He felt a loosening as he slowly began to stroke within her.

Stevie raised one leg up and felt the friction of his cock rub against the base of her clit. Oh, how she wanted to use her hands, but her confinement was her aphrodisiac. The cuffs seemed to cut deeper as Don drove harder and deeper into her. The slapping sound of her ass hitting his abdomen echoed through the cabin. Again and again he plunged himself into her, digging his fingers into her flesh as he groped at her. Utterly blissful, she didn't notice when her wrists started to bleed.

He reached for her back and forced her to lean farther over and then he thrust into her with such desperate fury that his breath quivered and quickened. Don's body was dripping with sweat from the raging fire in the cabin and the raging fire in his body. Stevie's body was tensing as she grabbed the center post and started to convulse.

"Oh, fuck! I'm coming! Don't stop, don't stop."

It was too much for him to take. He felt himself erupt inside of her. Stevie came as Don thrust into her harder and harder again. As he flooded Stevie with his juices, his head felt as burning hot as if he were on fire.

In fact, he was on fire.

An ember from the fire had popped out and flown onto the carpet. And as it burned, another one had popped onto Don's hair and was starting to flame. Just then the door burst open. Something wet doused Don's head and more doused the burning carpet.

Dumbfounded, Don stood there. Dangling, naked, and wet, Stevie was helplessly handcuffed to the center post. The man laughed and his wife looked understandably shocked.

"Isn't that the woman from the movie you showed me?" the woman asked.

"Boy, I tell ya, you two just can't stay out of trouble. First on the highway in broad daylight, now in my cabin while starting a fire. What do you do for an encore?"

Turns out it was the same policeman who'd ticketed them on the highway. He'd come to the cabin with his wife for the weekend, but a reservation error had already put Stevie and Don there.

The Work Party (Peter and Susan Part 1)

ഇ

The annual Christmas party was this evening, and Peter decided to dress up real nice to see if he could make a positive impression on the higher-ups. When he arrived, the room was full of co-workers and upper management mingling. A few couples were dancing. He stepped up to the bar and ordered a Bacardi 151 and Coke to wet his whistle and help him relax. After five drinks and some terrible hors d'oeuvres, he sat alone in the corner, buzzed.

"Are you having a good time?" said a lovely voice behind him.

Susan walked up next to Peter smiled down at him. She looked stunning in a short, fitted, black crepe column gown that accentuated her petite frame. The lace back showed her slightly tanned skin.

"I hate these parties. Everyone is always so interested in kissing ass that they don't have any fun," Susan said.

Peter laughed and noticed a pleasant fragrance. As he breathed in, he remembered it. "You still wear that same perfume, don't you?" Peter said.

Susan smiled and hid her face with her hand, a little embarrassed. "Yes it is. I didn't think you'd remember."

Peter sat there next to her, watching the people as they talked and danced. He looked over at Susan, looked at the shape of her body and the curves of her features, the sloping shape of the neck. She stood tall and pulled her shoulders back, making her chest stand out proudly, like a woman with confidence. Peter was gazing so intently at her that Susan could feel his eyes. Her scent and appearance caused him to reach out to touch her. The moment he touched her side, she quivered. Peter was enthralled by the way his touch affected her, so he continued. He slowly stroked her side and then moved his hand down to her ass. She moaned quietly.

The darkness created by the dim lights made their corner almost invisible to the others. Peter looked at the front of her dress and could see her nipples harden and poke out through the fabric. As he ran his left hand down the back of her leg, he felt heat and a slight wetness. Damn, she was on fire!

Susan moved her right leg forward a little and opened her legs ever so slightly. With this cue Peter slid his hand up under the back of her dress to find she wasn't wearing any underwear. He slipped his fingers around her thigh and moved his hand against her wet, hot labia. The juice almost ran down his hand as he moved it back and forth. He dragged his thumb along the back of her thigh where her ass joined her leg. Her incredibly firm ass tightened when he touched it and her legs went weak. She dropped her purse and reached down to hold his shoulder when he inserted his index finger into her wanton pussy. He rotated his wrist and cupped her entire swelling pubis in his hand. Then he slid his finger deeper into her, grabbing her crotch harder in his hand. His hand was almost overcome by the flow of her juices. Peter pulled his hand away and put it to his mouth to suck each finger one by one.

Susan bent down to pick up her purse and gave him a full shot of her ass and hot, shaved muff. She grabbed his knee and slid her hand up to his crotch as she slowly stood up. Holding tight to his rock-hard manhood, she leaned over to say, "Let's get out of here," into his ear. She bit the bottom of his lobe and ran her tongue along it. His slacks couldn't conceal his erection so he took off his jacket and held it in front of him.

They left the party separately so it wouldn't be obvious that they were leaving together. Peter looked into the lobby outside the restaurant to see Susan in front of the elevator. The bell rang and he jogged up to catch the elevator with her. He laughed when he got there, and she turned and looked at him with a nasty grin and suggestive laugh.

Once inside, she pushed the button to close the door and he stood behind her. Susan stepped back and pressed against him. She ran her hands up the front of his legs and to his crotch. Peter moaned softly and unzipped his pants. She moved her hand into them and grasped his growing hardness. Susan slowly stroked it up and down, feeling it swell in her hand.

Ding! The bell rang and a couple stepped into the elevator.

"Hello, are you from the party in the restaurant on the roof?" the man asked.

"Why yes, we were just leaving." Susan said.

His jacket concealed her hand so she kept stroking him. This was really arousing and hot. Peter was having a hard time handling his expression. He just smiled at the couple as the elevator stopped at their floor and they got out.

When the door closed, Susan turned around, pushed his pants down, and dropped to her knees. She could tell by the twitching of his penis that he was extremely aroused. She licked the soft skin at the bottom of his penis and outlined the tip with her tongue, tasting the first sign of his oncoming orgasm. She reached around and hit the stop button for the elevator. Shyly, she smiled and moved her hands to his butt. She pulled him toward her and slowly took him into her mouth.

When she wrapped her tongue around him and sucked, the feeling made Peter's knees buckle and he leaned back. He felt like he couldn't breathe as she kept pulling him in and out of her mouth, only stopping to gasp for air and begin again.

With one of her hands she reached down and rubbed her wet pussy. The juice from her excitement had her well lubricated and she slid her finger inside and thumbed her swelling clitoris.

Peter was about to burst and he grabbed the back of her head with his hands and said "Oh, please don't stop, I'm gonna…"

Suddenly the elevator jerked and began to climb up. They rushed to compose themselves. Peter tried to hide his erection and Susan wiped away the saliva dripping down the side of her mouth.

The elevator stopped on the top floor where the party was and the CEO stepped in and asked them to push floor twenty-one.

The elevator was quiet and Susan moved against Peter, the crease of her ass pressed against his swollen manhood. She felt the flow from her passion run down the inside of her thigh. The CEO said good evening, stepped out and walked away.

Peter couldn't help himself. The door closed and he hit the stop button. He turned Susan around and pushed her against the cold steel elevator doors. He pulled up her skirt and she bent over a little. He knelt behind her and kissed her ass and the back of her legs. She bent even farther and spread her legs apart. Peter licked the back of her wet box and she reached back and pulled at his pants, begging him to free himself. She wanted to feel him so badly that she ached. The inferno of passion swelling in Susan had to be released. She grabbed the frame of the elevator doors.

Peter stood up and dropped his pants. He was so hard that he had to push his throbbing member down to get it into position. He slid it all the way in until his stomach pressed against her ass. The incredible feeling of the tight, wet flesh wrapping around Peter was almost too much for him. Susan gasped for air as he started to quicken his thrusts.

"Touch me with your hands," she begged.

He thrust deep and stopped to pull her dress higher. Then he reached around to touch her breasts. She could feel him pulsing inside of her. She reached down, took his hand, and placed it over her clit. Peter was almost out of his mind as he simultaneously stroked her clit and drove inside her. Susan's body started to shake and her knees weakened. Peter told her he couldn't hold back anymore.

Peter stood up straight, pulling her up with him, and plunged to the hilt as he gushed out his orgasm. Susan's muscles tightened around him as she came at almost the same time that Peter did. Over and over his penis throbbed, sending his hot fluids into her. He staggered back and she released him. Susan fell to her knees shaking. Peter's cock was still dripping from their experience when he tried to pull his pants up. Susan got up slowly. She helped him with his pants and gave him a kiss.

"I've missed you terribly," she whispered into his ear.

Peter smiled and laughed. "Me too. I've wanted you every day at work."

The elevator shook and started down again. When they stepped out of the elevator, ten people standing in the lobby all burst into applause, patting Peter on the back and shaking Susan's hand. Confused, they walked up to the desk.

"Nice show guys. You want a copy?" the hotel manager asked as he pointed to the hotel security camera console. They stood there in shock as they saw a bank of TV screens. Some showed people getting in and out of the elevators. Below them there was a row of screens monitoring the inside of each elevator. There was even a big screen TV...showing their elevator.

The Spotlight

ജ

The door opened. Sylvia stepped out and stood in the doorway. The light from the bathroom shined behind her. Bill sat on the bed, in awe of this beautiful creature. Sylvia slowly dropped the white satin robe over her shoulders. It cascaded down her body and onto the floor. The light accentuated her silhouette. From the curvature of her breasts to the shadows on her inner thighs, even the glistening water on her pubic hair from her shower, she was a vision. She reached up and undid the band in her dark brown hair. She tossed her head from side to side, letting her hair slowly fall down past her shoulders. As she walked over to the bed, she smiled ever so slightly, trying to be shy, yet frisky. Looking at the bed, she could see that what she was doing was having a positive effect. The bed looked like a pup tent.

"Are you ready for me?" asked Sylvia.

"Obviously!"

Bill tossed away the bedding and stood in front of Sylvia. Her eyes opened wide when she saw him fully erect. He pulled her to him and kissed her softly, causing her to quiver. He gazed into her eyes and kissed her again, more passionately, as if he were trying to devour her. Their hands were searching each other's bodies as they kissed; clenching each other so tightly that each breath they took was one.

Sylvia leaned her head back and Bob kissed her neck. Then he started kissing her lower and lower, exploring her body with his mouth and tongue. He licked her cleavage and worked his mouth to each side to kiss her breasts and erect nipples. He knelt and his mouth reached her midsection. She breathed in deeply as he slipped his tongue into her bellybutton. He slowly slid one hand down her leg to lift it over his shoulder. He could smell and feel the heat of her anticipation as he worked his way down her leg. Without hesitation, he grabbed her ass and plunged his tongue inside her, tasting her sweet nectar. She let out a deep moan, arching her back and gasping as he tugged at her with his teeth, trying to bury his mouth deeper inside her. Her legs were getting weaker as he drove his tongue in and out of her. She ran her fingers through his hair. He stopped for a second and looked up at her face. He saw a tear trickling out of the corner of her tightly closed eyes as she pulled at his hair to continue.

She let out a shriek as a wave of pleasure rushed over her, causing her entire body to shudder over and over again. He couldn't wait any longer; he had to have her! After he picked her up and threw her onto the bed, he looked down at her writhing body. Sylvia sat up and took all of him into her mouth. She dug her nails into his chest, pulling at the hair, while she savagely dragged her hands over his body. Bill moaned deeply as he closed his eyes, enjoying the sensations. She let go of him, gasping for air and commanded, "I want you. Now!" She spread her legs open wide, begging him to explore the depths of her desire.

Bill leaped on top of her. They were like two animals going for the kill. Their passion had reached its peak, and the two of them would erupt in climax together like a volcano. He grabbed the small of her back with one hand and finally positioned himself to thrust inside her for the first time. The sweat was glistening on their flesh and he…

"Cut!!" the director yelled. "Okay, everybody, we'll finish the scene tomorrow morning at six-thirty. Have a nice night. Come on, Sylvia, I'll give you a ride home."

The Bath

❧

The door closed and Becca fell against it in relief. It was two a.m. and she was exhausted from her date. Her legs were sore from dancing and walking on the waterfront before the rain started. Everything had gone so well that she didn't want to spoil it by jumping Mike's bones on their first date. Even though she'd felt his bone in the car — by accident of course.

Becca was a petite Asian woman, a little over five feet tall, with long black hair and tinted highlights. Her date with Mike had been a fluke thing set up by friends. He was a huge man. Six feet six inches tall, black hair, handsome and very funny.

Becca left a trail of clothes and shoes down the hall toward the bathroom. She started the water in her antique tub, making steam rise. She lit a few scented candles and poured herself a glass of brandy.

She looked in the full-length mirror at her small frame. While removing her black lace bra and leaning over to shimmy off her frilly underwear, she noticed her breasts were very perky and she had what was referred to as a teardrop-shaped ass. It was a nice body. The small patch of pubic hair was well manicured. Her red fingernails dragged along her skin, and she felt it tingle at their touch. Her eyes closed and she envisioned Mike touching her this way. Flustered, she turned the faucet off and stepped gingerly into the hot water, setting her glass of brandy by the tub.

The heat soothed her aching muscles but not her other ache. Becca drifted off a little, letting the warmth of the water and the brandy relax her.

The showerhead above her dripped slowly as she lay back. She rested her head on the pillow and sipped her brandy. She lifted her hand up and felt the water cascade between her fingers and down the back of her arm. She lay farther down in the tub. The trickle of the faucet became a slow pulsing against her lower abdomen as she raised her hips. She closed her eyes and moved up a little and the small splashes of water reached her pubis. Like a bass drum the thump slapped her tense skin. When Becca leaned her head back and pulled her hair out of the tub to let it hang, the water splashed between her legs and against her already aroused clit. The hot water seeped between her lips and soothed her. She took a long, slow drink from her brandy and set the glass on the floor.

She lifted her leg up, laid it over the edge of the tub and glided her hand between her legs. The water hit her hand as she moved it between the lips of her pussy. Her body rose in the bath as she spread her lips, letting the water clash with her heat. With each pound of the water she imagined it was Mike. The water licked her pink flesh and in her mind it was Mike licking her. Her head turned as the first wave seemed to rush through her body, a signal of arousal. Becca opened her eyes, looking at the flicker of the candle, and saw something in the mirror. She continued letting the water caress her and she saw Mike reflected in the mirror, looking at her through the window. His hair was damp from the rain. She saw his transfixed gaze and it made her heat inside to a burn.

Becca slid her finger inside and clenched her eyes tight as pure ecstasy pierced her flesh. Her other hand moved to her small, pert breasts and she pretended it was Mike who caressed them. Small twists of her nipples added the needed boost to the rhythmic probing from her fingers. In her mind she saw his massive hands groping her petite frame almost enveloping her with his size. The soap in the water made her skin slippery, and her hands slid along the slopes and curves. The candlelight shined on her skin and reflected the yellow flames. Not wanting him to know she saw him, Becca moved her head to the side again and sneaked a peek. He was breathing heavily and his hand was pressing against his crotch. Her mind wandered as she pictured Mike eating her out, his tongue probing deep inside her, taking her to the next plateau. She peaked as she spread two fingers apart inside her pussy and the firm rubbing of her clit made her buck and splash. Her eyes closed and a tear trickled out the corner as she felt a rush of emotions wash over her as she came. She melted back into the tub. The soothing warmth of the water wrapped her in a blanket of serenity.

She smiled and looked back at the mirror...and didn't see Mike anywhere. She thought to herself, *Oh my. I must have scared him.*

Becca slipped her robe on and looked out the windows as she walked around the house—to no avail. In the living room, she turned the lights off and saw a shadow standing on her patio. With a gentle turn the light was back on, and the shadow came to the door. It was Mike, dripping wet from the rain. Becca moved to the sliding door and opened it. A cold wind rushed against the opening of her robe and exposed her naked body. Mike looked down and whispered quietly, "I was so envious of the water in the bath caressing you. I want nothing more than to be with you."

As she stepped outside Becca whispered back, "I am yours tonight, and this is going to be a long night."

The cold wetness of his clothes made Mike shiver. Becca grabbed him by the belt and guided him back inside the living room. At the doorway, she stopped him and knelt down to take his shoes off and run her small hands along the inner seam of his pants up to the ridge of his erection. The hardness ended just above his knee and she bit her lip wondering where she'd put all this meat in her small oven. Her arm reached under him and her small hand grabbed his ass as she clenched his leg like a snake wrapping around its prey. Her mouth was inches from the swelling of his crotch, and the thought made her salivate. His clothes were cold and wet against her hot body. She looked up to see his eyes burning with want for her. Her fingers fumbled with the buttons on his shirt until she reached in between the buttons and ripped it open. His chest was muscular and hairy. The muscles flexed at the soft touch of her tiny fingers.

She wrapped her arms around him. Her head only came up to his chest. She whispered, "This can't be a raging moment of passion. This has to be a slow, deep, penetrating fuck." She giggled under her breath and Mike laughed.

She could smell his cologne mixing with the sweat on his large chest, and she kissed it gently. The hair tickled her nose as she moved her face to his nipples, bit one and pulled back slightly. As Mike leaned his head back, her petite hands stroked along the hardened rise in his pants.

Mike reached down to open her robe, then wrapped his arms around her and cupped her ass. When he picked her up, she slid her legs around his waist and her warm moisture mixed with the cool, rain-soaked heat of his skin. He kissed her mouth—gently at first, as if afraid to mess up the seductive mood of the dark night. Becca slipped her tongue through her red lips then licked along the edge of his mouth and kissed his now wet lips, meshing together in a passionate embrace.

His arms were like a vice pulling her against his huge frame. Mike carried her down the hall to the bedroom, laid her on the bed and took his shirt off. He threw it over her head and told her to close her eyes.

"I want to explore you," he whispered.

Becca swallowed. She felt scared and excited by his advances. His hand overwhelmed her breast as he molded it to his palm and kissed her tummy. His firm jaw rested above her inferno then slid along the crease as she clenched her eyes tight, trying not to moan. His hot mouth was her weakness, so she reached down, grabbed his hair and pulled at it, begging for his mouth to encompass her pussy.

Mike grabbed both her ankles in his hands, gently pulled them apart, and sighed at the sight of her. He kissed her ankle. With the shirt and darkness blinding her, this became a deeply erotic exploration. His mouth was hot as his breath caressed down her thighs. His tongue slid between her pussy lips and became engulfed in her juices as he devoured her like a wild beast. His large hands groped over her body touching and squeezing every inch of her.

Her arms spread like an angel and she arched her back, rising to his mouth. She looked up and saw the glimmer of light reflected from the rain on the dark ceiling above her. Becca's moans guided him as Mike probed gently inside her with his finger and searched for her perfect spot. Her silky insides tightened around him as he slid his fingers between her labia.

"I can't stand this," Mike whispered. "I want you so badly."

Mike stood up, furiously trying to undo his pants but Becca slapped his hands away. She slowly undid his pants as she laid her head against his groin and felt the rigid throb of his cock pulse inside the fabric. She looked up at him as she pulled his pants down his legs and saw his eyes fill with desire. She was surprised at the wet spot on his underwear from his desire for her. She slid her hand inside his underwear and grasped the shaft, a little scared by the size of it. He was truly gifted with more than a great body. Her petite hand grasped him and she licked the tip through the fabric. His hands grasped the back of her head and he motioned for her to continue.

As Becca pulled his cock from the confinement of his underwear, she giggled, wondering where the hell she'd put it. She licked her lips and smiled as she took the tip between them, tasting ever so slightly the hot essence of his loins. His moans deepened as she slid almost half of his shaft into her mouth. She almost gagged as his body jerked, trying to contain his urge to slam into her.

Shaking, he grabbed her firmly in his hands, picked her up and threw her onto the bed. This was becoming increasingly primal. She was scared but so aroused by the thoughts and feelings encompassing her body that the mere touch of him made her shudder with delight.

Mike was so big against her small frame. She wasn't sure if she could handle this. He kissed her mouth deeply and she wrapped her arms around his neck as he lifted her and positioned himself between her legs. Mike was shaking as he held her legs and tried to pierce the opening of her pussy. Becca reached down, guiding him to the entrance. As he slowly pushed, the tightness of her small inner sanctum stretched to accommodate him. Mike looked down watching his cock disappear into her pussy. The pain almost caused her to cry out. She dug her nails into his chest and strained to hold back. She screamed as he plunged fully into her.

Knowing he was hurting her, Mike asked, "Do you want me to stop?"

And she said, "No. Please don't stop. I want you. I want this. I need this!"

Mike leaned down to kiss her again and started stroking in and out slowly. At first Becca got lightheaded until she adjusted to his size and the pleasure she received from him. His chest was covered in a fine sheen of sweat and his heart pounded as he started driving deeply into Becca, stretching her and feeling the tightness of her pussy against the skin of his cock. He licked his finger and reached down to caress the top of her pubis and rub against her clit.

Becca reached up to push him away and told him to lie down. "I'm tired of this. If we're gonna do this right, let's just fuck."

She straddled him and he grasped her hips and watched as she lowered herself onto his large cock. She picked up her legs, letting him get into her as deeply as possible. Mike closed his eyes and moaned.

Her hands dragged against his chest as she rode him. "Oh damn. Fuck me, Mike. Let me feel you explode inside of me! I need it!" Her words empowered him and he furiously grabbed her hips and slammed into her without care. She flailed, trying to keep control as he forced himself deeply into her over and over. As the heat and friction of their sex heated up she seemed to float into a state of bliss. Her fingers dug into the muscles of his chest as her ass slapped against his flexing legs. Mike's hands couldn't grope her body enough as they grabbed and pulled at her with a desperate search for something to hold on to. Becca leaned forward and Mike grabbed the cheeks of her ass and pounded up into her.

Becca felt the speed quicken and saw how hard Mike was breathing so she put her finger in his mouth and felt him tense, shiver, and stop. She tightened her inner muscles hard and felt him explode with a cry. The force lifted her up as again and again she felt his spurts come out. Becca's eyes closed and she came, deeply, soothingly mixing the juices of their desires. He felt her flexing inside and her vaginal walls caress him as her orgasm flowed from within her. The slow glide had stopped and she felt both full of his essence and her own fulfillment as they cuddled together. She played with his chest hairs as she lay on top of him.

After a time, they got up because he needed to go. As Mike stood there fixing himself and combing his hair, he noticed some pictures on her nightstand. They were of a military man. On closer examination, he noticed a half-dozen pictures in the room of the same guy. Trying not to be alarmed Mike asked, "Who are these pictures of?"

"Oh, these are of my father. I haven't seen him in ages. He and my mom were married in Vietnam a long time ago and we haven't seen him for about fifteen years. We moved here about ten years ago. Why do you ask?"

"No reason," Mike said. "But these are pictures of my dad!"

The Infatuation

ဢ

It was an average night for Scott. He was standing there naked, except for his Bugs Bunny slippers, listening to Weird Al Yankovic's Greatest Hits while drinking a Dr. Pepper and eating peanut butter, jelly, and sardine sandwiches. He had a pair of binoculars focused on the other high-rise apartments across from his studio in New York.

As he scanned the buildings, he saw various windows with their lights on, some with the shades only partially drawn. Some people never think that some sick bastard would peek into their lives.

In one room he saw a man and a woman snuggling on a couch in front of the TV to watch a movie. It looked like *Sleepless in Seattle*. In another room a woman was making a banana split in the kitchen. She was dripping chocolate syrup onto three scoops of ice cream melting on a woman's crotch. But where was she going to put the banana? *Oh, it goes in there.* He'd have to come back to this one later. On the thirty-second floor there was Mr. Adbul having sex with his secretary—bent over a desk, going at it. Who'd have thought he was gay? Then there was the regular Thursday show in Mr. Johnson's room. He'd dress up like a farmer and have sex with a chicken.

He saw a light go on in an apartment. The curtains were open slightly and he zoomed in with his high-powered binoculars to see the figure of a woman. She turned on the light in her bedroom. She was gorgeous. Long dark brown hair pinned up in a bun that fell slowly down her shoulders as she undid the barrette in her hair. He reached over to get another bite of his sandwich and gazed through his binoculars to see her unbuttoning her blouse.

Thank you! he thought to himself as he turned on the vacuum cleaner with that furry attachment on the end. With every button she undid with her long, red fingernails, he got more and more excited. She let her blouse hang open, revealing her black lace brassiere and lifted her long muscular leg up onto her bed to unsnap her red garter belt. (Oh how Scott loved garter belts, especially red ones.) Then she slowly slinked off her black silk stockings. He had to see more. This was truly a great night. He took a big drink of Dr. Pepper, belched loudly then stared back into the binoculars.

Scott's eyes were transfixed. He was truly mesmerized by this woman. She turned around and tossed aside her blouse. Then she unzipped the side of her skirt and let it fall to the floor. Coldness crept through Scott's body because his dangling appendage had risen and was pressing against the ice-cold glass of his window. He had to meet this woman. Maybe he could find out her room number and send her a bouquet of flowers to thank her for the show. Her back was toward him as she unsnapped the front of her bra and set it on the end of her large brass bed. Every minute seemed like an eternity as his anticipation grew. When she pulled down her silky red panties and let them slide down her legs he grabbed his hardness, trying to control his urges.

When she turned toward the window Scott gasped, dropping his sandwich to the floor, which knocked his soda all over his slippers because standing in front of him was an extremely beautiful man. A rather well-endowed man at that.

The Afterglow

The night was hot, intensely hot. The soft rock station in the valley was playing Boyz II Men and a cool breeze blew in through the open hotel window. Sally and Eugene lay on the bed smoking cigarettes and drinking margaritas. He rolled over, scratched his balls, farted, and then slowly stroked her hair.

"That was intense!"

"It sure was."

They'd just had one of those sexual encounters that diaries and porno movies are made from. The whips and handcuffs were scattered across the floor with their clothes, some Jell-O molds, cooking oil, a double-sided dildo, rubber chickens and puppets.

"Wow, I've never had that much fun, honey. You are such an incredible woman."

"What are you talking about? You are the greatest lover a woman could ever want. You're a real man—big in every way, strong and handsome. You're such a stud that I never want to share you with another woman. I don't care how badly they want you or what they offer you. You're mine! No other man can satisfy me like you can. They're all amateurs compared to you!"

"Tell me more."

"Fuck you, stubby! This sweet-talking bullshit's gonna cost you extra. Now give me my three hundred dollars. I've gotta get back to my street corner before my pimp beats my ass!"

The Dance

🔊

The club was alive with the rhythms of the music and the pulsing bass. It was a hot Friday night and the place was packed and jumping. Vincent and Beth wound their way to the bar and ordered a couple drinks when Vincent spotted Sandra at the end of the bar with her friends.

Sandra was a stunning woman with the stature of a supermodel—tall, lean, but beautifully curved. Vincent was a rock—muscular, good-looking, confident and well endowed in many areas. He never let Sandra's beauty intimidate him like other men did, which is why she adored him. Their tumultuous, deeply sexual relationship had gone on for over a year until he finally gave in and moved in with her. It ended badly when she found her two friends trying to get him into a threesome, and she didn't believe that he'd refused.

She hadn't gotten over him and the past month had been tough. Her other men were so typical and she missed the way Vincent made her feel so alive. They'd seemed destined to be together.

Sandra asked him to dance and he agreed. There are some men who know how to arouse a woman while dancing and to his credit, Vincent knew how. As the music started, Sandra led Vincent to the floor for a dance, a slow dance. He'd brought Beth to the club but everyone knew he and Sandra had a past. The music was slow and the lights dim, perfect. At first they were cautious but soon they clutched each other tightly.

She pulled him close to her, wanting him to melt into her. A fire burned between them. Everyone was looking at them out of the corners of their eyes and Sandra didn't care. She wanted Vincent back and would do anything to get him, even embarrass herself by almost having sex on the dance floor.

It was difficult for Vincent to be calm when she smelled absolutely wonderful and her motions were arousing him, a lot. He nuzzled closer and she wrapped her hands around his strong neck pulling him even closer.

As the new Toni Braxton ballad started playing, their grind became more sexual. They used to make love to her music all the time. Vincent started humming the song as they danced and the deep vibration of his voice ran through her like a lightning bolt directly to her yearning heart. It also made a buzz between her thighs as he muffled his humming with her body.

Slowly, Sandra caressed the back of his neck and ran her fingers through his hair. Flowing with the music, he moved his hands down her back to her ass. Grasping the cheeks hard he pulled her body tight against him and moaned as her sweet smell and soft skin reminded him of the way they used to be. Her eyes started tearing and she closed them as his hands reached under her skirt and touched the soft flesh of her bottom. Vincent breathed her deeply into his lungs falling for her all over again. He pulled on the thong, just knowing it was the red one he'd bought her for their anniversary last year. His finger followed the line of her tense ass to the base of her moistening love canal.

His mouth watered remembering the sweetness of her taste. He had spent many a night between her legs, waking to the smell of their love only to make love again until exhausted. As the music set the mood, Sandra moved her legs so his grinding body rubbed directly against her pubis. Vincent knew how much this excited her. Trying to hide what was going on, they danced slowly and close in the corner of the dance floor next to the wall.

Sandra was wet and hot from the heat they generated from a simple dance. He grasped her ass in his strong hands, pulled her hard against him and moaned deeply, sending a vibration through her body. Her knees weakened and she didn't care what they looked like as she leaned back against the wall, making his forceful motions more intense.

The music changed to a dance song and she opened her eyes to the stares of couples looking at them. Vincent stepped back and looked over at Beth to see her glaring at him with a shocked look in her tearful eyes.

"Come on, let's go home" Sandra begged.

"Sandra, sex has never been a problem for us. You are a beautiful, sexy woman. There isn't a man alive who could resist you. But..." Vince paused. "We had our time and it's over. We're too different and I'm with Beth now."

When she started crying Vincent hung his head. "I'm sorry. She and I are alike and people won't stare at us like they did when you and I were together. It's not easy being a dwarf. I mean we can't even dance without people wondering why my face is buried between your legs."

You see, Sandra is six feet tall and Vincent is two feet ten inches — the perfect height for a dance partner.

The Dirty, Filthy, Cheating Bastard

ঞ

Lea is what everyone calls a good wife and great mother. In other words, she's married to a complete asshole of a man who treats her like crap, but she bears the pain because she still loves the schmuck—Steve the schmuck to be precise. Their seven-year marriage has been a roller coaster of ups and downs, filled with Steve's numerous extramarital affairs. Now, finally, they are seeking help from a hypnotist. I know what you're thinking, but it's their last hope because nothing else has kept Steve's pecker in his pants.

"Steve, you're getting sleepy, very sleepy, asleep," the female hypnotist calmly says. "Lea, wake up! You wanted to hear this."

"Steve, I'm going to ask you a couple of questions and I want you to answer them, okay?"

"Yes," Steve answers in a hypnotic state.

"Do you love your wife?"

"Who?"

"Your wife Lea."

"Oh, yes I love my wife. She is so special to me. She does everything I ask her to, but that bitch can't cook to save her life. Also, she snores and…"

"That's enough. Steve have you ever had extramarital affairs?"

"Duh, doesn't everyone?"

"How many?"

"Let's see…how much time do we have? There was the baby-sitter—nineteen years old and what a body. Now those were real breasts, none of that silicone stuff like my wife's friend Linda. Linda always made noises like a mouse. Squeak squeak. That drove me almost as crazy as her Aunt Vera's nasal whining in the garage during our anniversary party. I had to put a sock in her mouth to shut her up.

"Let me think. There were the two mothers from the daycare center in the break room. That stupid Disney music in the background is enough to make any parent loony.

"There was that time with the lady selling lingerie at the all-women party downstairs. She came upstairs and we tried out a couple of her toys. My favorite was the metal balls women put inside their pussy then slowly pull them out. She musta had a dozen in her and as she pulled them out I could feel them rub against my penis while we were having anal sex. Lea sold quite a bit at that party.

"Whenever her best friend Lisa had troubles with her husband she'd come over when Lea was at work. I'd come home for lunch to talk about things and get a nooner and a sandwich every other day. That lasted until she became pregnant and wasn't sure if the kid was her husband's or mine. The boy has my eyes.

"This is tough, there's been so many. Hmm. Oh yeah, when we went on that romantic cruise to the Caribbean, the maid came into our room to straighten up. I was in bed so she showed me how they do it in Spain, with a bullwhip and some tequila. And I showed her how we do it in France, ya know, tongue in between her cheeks. Damn that woman couldn't speak a word of English except 'more'.

"When her friend Kate came out from San Francisco, we went looking at houses. Lea and Kate's husband browsed through the two stories while we browsed through each other's clothes.

"I wouldn't count the time at the circus with the fat lady because, well, you know, that was more of a mercy lay. I wasn't sure if I was in the right roll of fat until I felt a wet one.

"I felt really bad that time we went out for Lea's birthday and I nailed her friend Geri in the ladies' bathroom stall at the movies. Geri was very athletic and limber. Then we went home and I passed out drunk on the couch.

"There were the twins on our Disneyland trip. Lea had to watch that damn Fantasia show so the twins and I went on that stupid Pirates of the Caribbean ride. We nearly fell out of the boat with both of them on top of me—one on my mouth, the other on my pole. I almost got seasick.

"One embarrassing time I got drunk and accidentally went into her mother's room. Good thing the light was out. I've got to say her mom is a very passionate woman for her age. She must not be getting it from her dad because she had about five orgasms and kept pulling on me to slam her harder. I knew it wasn't Lea when she went down on me and didn't spit it out.

"I remember when I went to that appointment with the sexy marriage counselor by myself. The counselor's husband and I made a jam sandwich out of her; one of us in each end and we jammed her in the middle.

"There were a few of those President Clinton-type affairs where I finished the job by hand. And the time when my buddies and me went on that fishing trip. We had the hookers in a cabin on the boat and whoever caught the first fish went first. I always ended up fifth or sixth.

"Of course I can't forget my bachelor party. That stripper is the finest looking woman I have ever seen and the things she did in that back bedroom of our apartment arouse me to this day. She had so much muscle control she could open a screw-top beer bottle. I should have washed the sheets for our honeymoon the next night but I was so sore and worn out that I barely made it to the wedding.

"Then…"

"Stop. That's quite enough." Both women were in a state of shock from Steve's revelations.

At first Lea felt sick to her stomach. It passed. Then she threw up.

"Well, there's only one way to remedy this," said the hypnotist. "Now listen, Steve. Picture your wife Lea in your mind. Blaze her image in your brain. Everything about her — her face, her body, her smell. Her image and her image alone is the only thing that turns you on. Only her. If you see another woman and have impure thoughts, flirt, stare lustfully or have any real sexual feelings for her, you will become ill. Not just queasy but violently sick. Also, if you can get past the sickness, you will be impotent with any woman other than your wife. No matter how much you play with your ding-dong, it won't even flinch — we're talking wet noodle. Now, the sight of your wife will arouse you beyond desire. You'll feel such a rush of lust that you'll want nothing more than to have her. You will obey her needs and dreams and become her sexual slave. Do you understand?"

"Yes, I want Lea to sit on my face right now!"

"On the count of three you will awaken. One...two...three!"

"Steve? How do you feel?"

"What were we talking about? Hey, babe. Wow, let's go home! I want to take a shower with you and play drop the soap. Sorry, doc, but for some reason I feel very horny."

All the way home Steve kept staring at Lea. He pawed at her dress, pulling it up and poking his fingers at her underwear. He drove quickly on the freeway and slipped his finger around the edge of the panties and into her wetness, thrusting in and out vigorously, causing her such pleasure. She leaned her seat back, slipped her panties down to her ankles and opened her legs to let him explore her with his rough fingers and hands. He rubbed and poked her opening all the while driving dangerously fast to get home.

She couldn't control herself any longer. It had been so long since they'd had a sexual experience like this. She sat up and leaned over to undo his pants then pulled them away from his large, hard penis. Even the fragrance of another woman's perfume on the front of his pants couldn't stop her lust. She scooted over on the bench seat and straddled him and buried his manhood inside her. He didn't even slow down on the freeway trying frantically to get home. It had been such a long time for them and it only made Lea more emotional. She cried as they made love. When they climaxed together and merged, as couples in love should, the accident happened.

It took three months of therapy and surgery but Lea was going home again. She hadn't seen Steve in a while because he couldn't bear to see her like that. She walked into the house with her cane and looked into the living room to see a picnic set up by the fire.

"Steve, I'm home!"

"I know. I've been expecting you. I've been cooking all day, making your favorite meals. I could smell you coming home and I can't wait to make up for the lost time and play 'bury the salami' all night. I have to stop talking like this. I've already got a hard-on."

Steve walked into the living room and stared at Lea. Their eyes met and he…dropped the tray and started throwing up. We're talking serious heaving.

"Who the hell are you?"

"It's me, Lea!!! They said the plastic surgery made me look different. I've lost thirty pounds and dyed my hair red. What's wrong?"

"I don't know! As soon as I saw you, I got all turned on and my stomach started hurting. And I can't stop feeling like I'm going to blow chunks. It's like the sight of you is making me sick!"

The Edge

℘

The darkness of the night left only the faint light from the passing cars and a flickering light on the wall at the end of the alley. The music in the bar pulsed through the walls as he pressed her against it and kissed her deeply. Their bodies were moist from sweating in the crowded bar and their clothes clung like another layer of skin, showing every detail.

Mick grabbed her waist and pulled her tightly against him. They swayed from side to side as he kissed her more deeply, grinding like the dance they'd done in the bar. Karen moaned as his knee rubbed between her legs. He pulled his knee higher and she rested her weight on it and rubbed. He pulled the top of her dress open just enough to see her nipples strain for his attention. He kissed her mouth again, exploring it with his tongue as he undid her shirt buttons. Mick smiled as he opened the front of her blouse, exposing her black bra. His intent was obvious and she stood still and shivered, wanting him so bad. Her eyes closed tight as he touched her softly and outlined her nipples with his finger through the fabric. Electric shocks of excitement shot through her body to her clit, making it throb.

As she looked down the alley, the blurry shadow of people walking by made her wonder if they could see them. In reality she didn't care.

Mick's hands caressed her back. And as he kissed her lips, his hands grasped both breasts and she moaned as he squeezed them. She bit his lip as he pulled away and reached down to cup his crotch. The tightness of his pants clearly demonstrated his desire. Karen held his gaze, her lips parted, as she undid the button and zipper on his pants, feeling the strain of his hardness force the zipper halfway down by itself.

She finished opening his pants and caressed his balls as she kissed his neck and shoulder. Mick's hands reached down, grabbed her ass and pulled her hard against him. He reached under her skirt and pulled her thong up, making her moan. Her juices seeped through the fabric. Her sweet smell was so distinct Mick could almost taste it.

"You know what I want," Karen moaned into his ear. She pushed his swollen manhood down, resting it in the notch between her legs, against the fabric of her thong. "Give it to me."

Breathing fast, heart racing, she stepped back against the wall under the light. The way the shadows lay on Karen's body made her look unreal. Her body glistened from a sheen of sweat and the open blouse accentuated her breasts. A few beads of sweat trickled between them. She lifted her leg and put her foot on a nearby bucket. And as the skirt rose, the black fabric of her thong became visible against her white skin, encasing the treasure he craved.

Mick was breathing deeply, in such a state of want he felt a little dizzy. He stepped up to her and kissed her, probing her mouth with his tongue. She grabbed the back of his head and forced it down between her breasts. She shrieked as she felt his mouth nibble on the nipple through the fabric. He reached into his pocket and straightened. Confused, she looked at his hand as he released the blade of his knife. His eyes were crazy and his chest heaved with each breath. Slowly, he traced the edge her bra with the blade and gradually moved it toward her nipples. Then he placed the blade between her breasts and under the front of her bra. As he pulled up on the knife, she felt the tip hard against her skin, Karen's knees went weak as if she had been stabbed and her breasts popped loose as the bra fell open. The cold edge of the knife outlined her full naked breasts. He kissed the small spot of blood between her breasts, left from the knife tip cutting her soft flesh. He licked the nipples and bit gently on them, the fear and danger were making her crazy. The way he held the edge of the knife against her flesh was terrifying and exhilarating. A wave of heat flushed across her chest. His fingers found the spot she wanted to be touched. He moved the slick fabric aside and dipped a finger into her wetness. Her mouth opened as if she couldn't breath from the excitement and a moan of desire rose from her. Her juice ran down his finger as he slid it in and out of her.

"Oh please, don't stop, Mick. Please...give me...fuck me, Mick!" her body desperate for his. Her pleas only excited him more.

Again, she grabbed his hard penis and pulled it toward her wetness. The tip glistened from desire. The way she shook from the knife empowered him and made him even more aroused. He looked down as she leaned back and he moved the blade along her thigh. The wetness soaked her underwear and between her thighs. She was so desperate she had almost come from the sheer fear and enthralling aspect of the experience. He ran the blade though her juice, and then brought it back to his mouth. He breathed in the scent then licked it with the tip of his tongue. It was warm, sweet, and tasted of her burning desire. He moved it back between her legs, making her spread them. And she watched as he slid the blade under the fabric. The blade moved through the light patch of pubic hair to her center. The tip of the blade rested against her clitoris. And she came as he twisted the knife, cutting her underwear loose. Her lust flowed down her leg and gleamed as she released the passion inside.

She felt weak and she slid down to her knees, grabbing the front of his pants to pull him to her. The front was wet from expectation and she yanked his pants down to his knees as she looked up at him. Mick looked down and saw her slowly take him into her mouth, inching deeper into her throat. She would almost release him then plunge him in again. Remembering the thrill of the knife, she pulled back almost to the tip and bit gently with just enough pressure that he put his hand on her head and reached toward the wall to hold himself up. Karen reached behind him, grabbed his ass and dug her nails in deep as she dragged her teeth along the base of his shaft. He wobbled, trying to stay standing. She had control now. She let him loose and he breathed in deeply. She looked up to him and whispered, "Let's finish this right." She stood up.

He grabbed Karen's shoulders and forced her around. She put both hands on the wall as she bent over and the tip of his penis pierced her pussy. The wetness nearly burned him she was so hot. She stifled her scream as he plunged mercilessly into her. Her body shook as he hammered deeper and deeper. Karen's legs weakened as she tried to keep them apart and bent at the perfect angle. Mick grabbed a handful of her long hair and pulled her head back, driving her harder. Karen wept as the pain from her scalp combined with the sheer pleasure of him thrusting into her, overwhelming her. She reached between her legs to finger her clit as he buried himself inside her again. As she pulled up at the top part of her labia, the opening of her pussy tightened against Mick's stiffness. The pressure against her clit was so direct she went up on her toes and her pussy flexed hard around Mick's stiffness. She never wanted it to end.

He let her hair go and she could feel him pulse inside her, trying to sustain the glory of the sex. As his breathing became shorter and his thrusts more rapid, she reached between her legs and dragged her nails against the veins on the bottom of his penis. Mick moaned loudly and thrust harder. She did it again. He stopped, buried fully inside of Karen, his hands straining on her shoulders and exploded inside of her as the wetness of her labia grasped the fullness of his manhood, pulling and milking him in orgasm. Her voice shrieked by the pain of his hands squeezing her shoulders and the sheer pleasure of his fluids flooding her. Over and over she felt the wet heat engulfing within her vaginal walls.

They grinned at each other as they both collected themselves. Their bodies ached but it was worth it.

Suddenly the door burst open and a man glared at them. "Your frickin' break was over ten minutes ago. We need the dishes washed, Mick. And, Karen, the other waitresses need their breaks too. Let's get back to work."

The Exotic Vacation

&

Freddie woke up when the plane landed in Jamaica. He had a tequila hangover that wouldn't quit. All he could think about was lying down in his hotel room and sleeping through his vacation. It had been a bad week.

First he took his last week of vacation, which couldn't be rescheduled, and then his girlfriend decided she didn't want to go to Jamaica. In fact, she decided she didn't want anything to do with him or men in general. She hooked up with his sister and blamed his lack of manliness for making her go lesbian. Talk about getting screwed over and not enjoying it. The topper was that after he'd decided to go without her—his flight was delayed, he was mugged in the airport bathroom, and he got airsick on the flight and spewed all over the stewardess and the lady next to him during dinner.

After about eighteen hours of sleep, a bottle of Advil, and a couple Bloody Marys, Freddie was feeling a little better. Lying by the pool felt really nice and he could forget about his miserable existence in this cruel world.

He was moving his folding chair into the shade when he spilled his drink and fell backwards into the hot tub. He climbed out and sprawled on the patio. Then he looked over and saw this incredible vision resting quietly on a lounge chair in the sun.

She glanced over at him, lowered her sunglasses and started laughing.

"Can't you go anywhere without making a mess?" she giggled.

"Do I know you?" Freddie replied.

"Blaaaahhhhrrrrrfffff!!!!"

"Oh crap, you're the lady I puked on," he said shamefaced as he shook his head. "Are you staying here too?"

"No, I always hang out at pools in Jamaica for kicks."

She was utterly stunning in her yellow bikini with the sun shimmering on her ebony skin. Picture Toni Braxton and Halle Berry combined. That's how fine this woman was. Her hair cascaded across her shoulders, waving in the breeze as she sat up to put on tanning lotion.

Don't just stand there staring, you asshole, say something.

"Do you need any help with your back?" Freddie asked nervously—his voice even cracked.

"Can I trust you not to break something, or spill anything on or around me?"

"Scout's honor." *Thank you, God.*

She rolled over onto her toned stomach, exposing her back and backside to his wandering eyes. As he spread the oil on her skin, his hand stopped shaking and the nervousness drifted away. She untied the back of her bikini top then closed her eyes.

She was like an exquisite piece of art. His hands were the brushes and her flesh was the canvas. Every curve of her body looked like it was sculpted. Her ass was teardrop shaped. Her legs were toned and everything was firm. And I do mean everything. *This has got to be a dream,* he thought to himself. *How can a woman so fine even talk to me let alone allow me to stroke her soft skin with my hands?*

"Uh, excuse me? You're drooling on my back."

"Sorry." His mind was a blur as he tried to think of a way to hook up with this marvel of womanhood. "You've got to let me take you out to dinner to make up for getting sick all over you."

"Well, I don't think you owe me anything, but it would be nice to have a quiet meal out on the balcony and watch a glorious sunset," she said. "Sure, why not?"

The sunrise wasn't the only thing Freddie imagined going down tonight. When she stood up to leave, Freddie stood up and so did his penis. He rummaged for a towel and pulled one from the chair next to him so he wouldn't embarrass himself further.

"Until later then. I'll meet you in the lobby at seven o'clock." She kissed his cheek and whispered in his ear, "I love it when a man is standing at attention. It gives me something to look forward to later."

As he watched her leave, he felt a tap on his shoulder. He turned around to see an incredibly massive man with tomato juice in his hair pointing at his towel and motioning to the drink Freddie spilled on him and his girlfriend.

Hopefully the ice will keep the swelling down. If everything goes well tonight it will be well worth it.

The closer the clock ticked towards seven, the more eager Freddie got. Every second seemed an eternity. He couldn't wait any longer — he was going to go early so he wouldn't miss her. I mean it was already four-thirty. *What if she doesn't show up? What if I'm a pawn in a cruel game she's playing? What is her name anyway?*

After sitting at the bar for over two hours, he had quite a buzz going. The four double Jack Daniels with beer chasers had helped too. *Why do these peanuts taste so damn good?* When he looked up from his drink, he saw her come into the bar. As he stared at her uncontrollably, everything seemed to move in slow motion. Every move was like a symphony playing a perfect note, powerful and awe inspiring at the same time. The white satin dress clung tightly against her beautiful skin. He was jealous of the dress because he wanted nothing more than to be hugging her gorgeous body.

"Well, Freddie, you look very nice. And from your eyes I can see you've been here a while." She looked at him and lifted her hand to close his mouth since it was dropping to the floor. "I'll have to catch up. I'll take a double Black Velvet with a lemon twist."

After talking for a while, they decided to dance. Jazz music played softly and she pulled Freddie tightly against her. The beat from the bass line pulsed in time with their hearts as they gazed into each other's eyes. They kissed softly then more deeply and passionately. The longer they danced the more their bodies melted together until they ended up in his room.

Firelight lit the room faintly and champagne chilled by the bed. They continued dancing. Their hands stroked each other's bodies, careful not to miss anything in the exploration. Freddie's nervousness was gone. She held out her hand and led him to the bed. Then she sat him down and stood in front of him. Her scent was as exquisite as her beauty. She untied the top of her dress, and it slid along the lines of her body and fell to the ground, exposing her beautiful body. Her sensuality alone made Freddie burst in his pants. I mean he actually burst in his pants. Luckily she didn't notice because her eyes were shut and she was swaying slowly, slipping out of her lace panties. She picked them up with her toes and placed them on Freddie's face. As he breathed deeply to get the full scent of her womanly fragrance, she leaned over and brushed her breasts against his face.

"I'm going to step into the bathroom to put on something sexy and take care of protection. You just get naked and in bed."

As soon as she closed the door, Freddie jumped out of his pants, peeled his sticky boxers off, and threw them against the wall where they stuck. He sat in the bed and tried to relax. *Baseball, I've got to think baseball. Singles, doubles, triples, homers. I'm going to score a grand slam!*

The door opened and she stepped out wearing nothing but a smile.

"Is this too much clothing or just enough?"

The sight of her almost made him jump out of his skin. She was indescribably sexy. We're talking wet dream sexy. When she slipped into the bed, Freddie was already hard as an iron girder. She ran her fingers along his body and he could see the perspiration on her skin. Freddie placed his hand over her bush and when he slid a finger between her lips, the wetness almost ran down his hand. Wasting no time, she climbed on top and slid right down, stopping only momentarily to adjust the angle of his penetration. His eyes rolled back and he grabbed the sides of the bed, holding on for a truly unforgettable ride as she clenched him tightly inside of her.

Her mouth opened as she rose upward and her eyes closed tight. She dug her nails deeply into his muscular shoulders and drew him back inside, as if daring him to try to escape her grip. Her hands and fingers brushed ever so lightly against his sides then slid slowly to the inside of her thighs and grabbed the base of his manhood while driving in and out of her love tunnel. She pulled back until she could feel only the tip spreading her opening wide, teasing him. Then she sank him all the way to the depths of her constricting cave. Her hands moved upward along the sensuous lines and curves of her body and she twitched and shook as the impending fury approached. Freddie could see the glazed look in her eyes as she pushed her breasts together and grasped the tips between her fingers. She shuddered when he arched his back and drove his swollen member deeper inside, making her legs spread wider. He wanted to grope her body with his hands, but she was doing everything herself, spoiling him with passion and undying pleasure.

She leaned over, grabbed the bottle of chilled champagne, and popped the cork. "Let's drink a toast." She took a drink then filled her mouth with more champagne. She leaned forward and when their mouths met she shared his drink with a kiss. She moved his hands to the top of the bed so he could grasp the bedposts. With Freddie inside her, she leaned back all the way and rested her head against his legs. Then she rotated her pelvis in slow rhythmic circles, stretching the muscles and then tightening them, causing him to pull hard on the posts. The bed was creaking loudly and Freddie reached up and grabbed on to her stomach.

"Don't touch me or I'll stop!" she gasped.

"Don't stop, don't stop. I can't take this anymore. I'm about to explode!"

She rose up and took another drink of champagne. She let it run down the sides of her mouth, trickling to her breasts. The farther she sat up, the more champagne she dripped on her chest. A small pool filled her bellybutton and then trickled to her pubis. The coldness spread to their joined bodies, and she slowly started rising up and sliding down, never stopping the flow of the cold champagne. Freddie frantically wanted to let go, but he didn't want this incredible sexual experience to end. With her other hand she reached back and stroked the inside of his thighs and pulled teasingly on the hair on his testicles. It was so incredibly stimulating that he thought he'd have a stroke.

She filled her hand with cold champagne and splashed it on his balls. He yelled loudly, grabbing on to her and pulling on her hips to drive faster as her muscles tightened around him with orgasmic spasms. He let out a grunt then exploded like a stick of dynamite. Over and over he felt the pulses of his juices flowing into her. They both collapsed, exhausted and flinching slightly from the muscle spasms. On a scale of one to ten this was definitely an eleven.

After the initial glow faded, she stood up and walked to the window. She opened the drapes to expose a wonderful view of the ocean. When she opened the sliding window and stepped onto the patio, a cool breeze rushed through the room and the smell of the ocean permeated the air. It was beautiful to see an absolutely elegant woman standing naked against a starlit sky. The moonlight accentuated her silhouette. The curve of her perky breasts, the way her ass rounded at the top of her long legs. She was absolutely hypnotizing. Freddie walked over to her. He brought a blanket from the bed and stood behind her to wrap it around both of them. The faint sound of the band downstairs filtered up to the balcony, and she started swaying rubbing her ass casually against his hardness. The more she swayed the more excited he became.

"Let's go back inside," Freddie whispered into her ear. He kissed the back of her neck and moved her hair to continue along it. She reached her arm up and cupped the back of his neck. He stroked the soft skin under her arm and on the side of her breast.

"Why go inside? Isn't it just glorious out here?"

She placed both hands on the railing and leaned over to look down at the beach. He reached under her and caressed her supple breasts, squeezing them firmly in his hands. Freddie ran his fingers along her spine and grasped her hips. As she rose onto her tiptoes, he slid into her, stroking back and forth. She moaned deeply while biting her bottom lip. Freddie glanced out at the ocean waves crashing against the beach and felt the salt air gusting and it made him think about how incredibly erotic all this was. Steadily he increased his pace. Her contracting muscles pushed him to the threshold of another mind-boggling climax.

She stood up, releasing him from her pussy. In one movement she turned and leaned against the railing. Then she wrapped her legs around his waist and her arm around his neck. She grasped his manhood with her other hand and rubbed it along the labial lips letting it slip just inside to the tip. She looked into his deep brown eyes and smiled nastily, holding on to it, teasing it. First she kissed his Adam's apple then licked his ear, while continuing to stroke her opening with his penis. She bit his nipple and lifted up to plunge him back inside. Freddie groaned with pleasure.

"Whatever you do, don't sit down. Stand up and I'll do the work."

He grabbed her ass and she wrapped herself around Freddie, tilting her pelvis and making his penetration deeper than before. His legs began to buckle when he felt her wetness convulse with her orgasm. He couldn't stand the pressure and slammed into her and shook from the intensity of his orgasm.

She squeezed tightly around him, milking his throbbing penis. They collapsed on the balcony and wrapped up with the blanket—both feeling content and weary.

After they rested, a warm tropical rain began to fall. She stood, letting the rain cascade down her body. And Freddie laughed while she twirled around, playing like a schoolgirl in the rain. They went in to take a real shower and clean off. It was one of those large Roman showers that fit two or more people easily. Freddie stared while she soaped up and rinsed off. When he closed his eyes to rinse out the shampoo, he felt warmth engulfing his penis. He gazed down to see her on her knees in front of him. She grabbed his rear end and sucked him quickly. The water ran down her face and red lips but she never slowed down. In and out, faster and faster, it was like she couldn't get enough. She licked him like a lollipop and then reached under him to massage his balls. His eyes closed tight and he clutched the showerhead to keep his balance. She reached up with her long fingernails to dig into his chest and abdomen and made his skin bleed while she deep-throated him. He collapsed onto the floor and she finished him off. Then she washed him clean, helped him into bed and kissed him softly on the forehead.

"I'm going to go get something other than you to eat from room service. I'll order something for you too."

His head still spinning, he rolled over and fell fast asleep. The loud banging on the door woke him and he staggered to the door, holding on to his sore family jewels.

"Room service!" The guy brought Freddie a nice omelet breakfast and a note. The waiter handed him the bill, and Freddie gave him five bucks and slammed the door behind him. He sat down still holding his sore balls and opened the note.

"Thanks for a great evening and a great Jamaican vacation. Freddie, you were wonderful." It was signed "V."

He sat there bewildered. He'd finally met someone he connected with mentally and physically and now she'd vanished. *Damn, this really sucks.*

The next morning while Freddie was checking out, he looked around the lobby, hoping in vain to see her again. He didn't even know her name. *Why doesn't anything ever go right for me?* Well, at least he had a grand night to remember and he'd forgotten his problems for a while.

"Uh, sir, your credit card company won't cover your bill," the clerk said.

"What? That's a gold card with a ten-thousand-dollar limit. Let me see my bill. What the fuck is this? Two rooms, room service for both rooms, a three-hundred-dollar bill for a dress, a two-hundred-dollar bar tab, three thousand dollars for special privileges and airfare to Boston? These aren't mine!"

"Sir, your wife had your credit card, passport and your ID so we assumed…"

"But I'm not married!"

"Well she was with you in the bar the other night and at the pool when you checked in. She was a lovely woman and a great tipper."

"What else could go wrong?" Freddie was crestfallen.

"How will you be paying, sir?"

"Uh, I'm not sure."

"Can I see your passport?"

"Uh oh."

The Urge

ഔ

They laughed as they walked up the stairs after their romantic dinner. Leanne was a little tense. She wasn't very experienced at bringing men home and the thought of being clumsy or looking frigid made her nervous.

Dinner had been extraordinary. They'd gone to a Mexican restaurant and had her favorite, chili verde and refried beans. She'd also had a few margaritas and flour tortillas that she'd playfully rolled up and slid in and out of her mouth, teasing Will. Leanne was a pretty woman. She was a little tall for most men at five feet ten inches but most of it was long legs, and she often wore skirts to accentuate them. Will had no problem with her height since he was over six feet tall. He had a medium build and was handsome.

After she opened the door, she leaned back against the frame and touched his face with her hand. She pulled him toward her and they kissed softly. He sighed. He kept kissing her slowly, moving his hand up her side to just below her breast. She backed into the house, leading him with her hands grasping his neck. The door swung shut and the dim light from the kitchen was enough for him to see. He knelt down, wrapped his arms around her bottom and lifted her up. Will buried his face in her cleavage and her perfume filled his lungs. The soft skin of her breasts made his mouth drool. He could see that she wore silk undergarments with a lace ruffle, his favorite. He carried her and followed her directions to the bedroom, clutching her tightly and licking her breasts. Her long hair hung down her back as she threw her head back, feeling wanton and scared at the same time.

It had been a long time for Leanne and she did not want to be obvious. She tried hard to keep herself in control and mute her heavy breathing. When Will set her down she grabbed the matches she'd left on the bureau and walked around the room lighting candles. As she lit the last few, Will came up behind her, picked her up and laid her on the table. She moaned softly; it was as if the beast in her wanted to be set free. She'd needed to be wanted like this. Although they'd only had two other dates, she wanted Will. She was already moistening her underwear and the fires in her heart made the nectar sweeter.

"I want you so badly that I can taste it." Will whispered as they kissed on the table. His weight crushed against her and she loved how he felt against her. She felt him harden as he pressed his groin against hers, making love to her through their clothes.

Leanne had been holding the feelings in since after dinner. She wanted to set them free. Her passion increased the need to let herself go, but she held it in. She couldn't lose control yet. She wanted to so badly but was afraid of what Will would think of her. She knew she looked very proper and probably seemed a little stuck up. But Will kept kissing her and moved his hands to her supple breasts, massaging them softly, molding them to his hands. She enjoyed the attention he gave to details and knew where he was heading.

He glided his hands up her long legs as he kissed her midsection. His fingers found the wet lace and could feel how nervous she was by the twitching of her stomach as he kissed it. She was so soft, so sweet, so sexy. Her anticipation was apparent to him. The way she moaned and leaned her head back as he pulled her soaked panties down her luscious legs were his cue to what he should do. Will kissed her ankle, moving his hand down the back of her leg, opening her legs wide for him. She was nervous because she'd never had a man go down on her the right way. Her other boyfriends had never taken the time to appreciate how much pleasure a woman derives from oral sex.

The sight of the succulent lips between her legs made his pants feel like a cage to a beast. The way the folds opened as his finger touched them made him gasp. She was Venus. The tight opening tensed around his finger, but he felt wetness build as he slid his finger in all the way to his palm. He grasped her muff in his hand using his thumb to massage around her clit. Her arms fell over the side and she almost succumbed to the feeling to let go of the swelling desire to burst.

Will's mouth was hot against her soft inner thigh. She was losing control and her mind wondered at the forceful way he was moving her toward heavenly fire. His tongue dripped saliva on her pubis as if he were an animal getting ready to eat his prey. He kissed her patch of pubic hair and smelled the perfume she'd put there just in case. Then he licked the length of her opening, making her moan loud. She couldn't hold it any more when he pressed hard on her abdomen and buried his mouth against her.

In some cultures it is a compliment, in others an insult. But after a great meal and the tension of the moment, she let it go. With his mouth firmly pressed against her pussy she ripped loose a Richter scale fart that echoed across the room and made the table tremble. It must have lasted fifteen seconds and was wet, loud and, most of all, stinky. You could hear a pin drop afterwards. So she ripped a smaller one that ended with a hiss.

Will looked up and saw the fire on the candles flicker and glow brighter. As he pulled his mouth away, the rumbling sound of a motorboat was heard from her anus and she giggled hysterically.

"Oh my goodness!" she said and she started to cry. "I am so sorry. I've been holding that all night and I did that at the worst time. I'm so embarrassed."

"It's okay. Are you done?" Will asked inquisitively.

"I'm not sure," she said. A slow hiss eased out as she sat up.

Will walked over to the table and kissed her mouth. It was a kiss that showed her how much he really wanted her. He wasn't going to let a little—or a lot—of gas spoil their night even though it stank really bad.

She leaned back down as they kissed. Their tongues entangled in her mouth and she tasted her own juices. With her head resting on the table, she reached over and undid his pants and pulled them down. She moaned as she saw the protrusion of his excitement trying to free itself from his Fruit of the Looms. The smell of cologne was on his midriff and she stroked his swelling through the fabric with her fingers, making him smile. She lowered his underwear and he popped out right in front of her face. Will reached forward and caressed her breasts. The skin of her chest was like flower petals. The small bumps around her nipples were still soft even though her nipples had risen to his touch. Her beauty was undiminished as the smell dissipated. She had a perfect body, dying to be worshiped. While he moved his hands across her breasts, she lowered her head and slid him into her mouth and wrapped her tongue around him. Will was almost beyond pleasure. He slowly withdrew himself, then eased back in, as if making love to her wet, warm mouth. He looked down to see her red lips purse as he pulled out.

Will had seen this in movies and the feelings were so erotic he was almost insane with desire. With every deep stroke he grasped her breasts tight in his hands. His hand moved and found the sweet spot between her legs. A river of juices flowed; she was as aroused as he was. Leanne opened her legs wider to let Will slide his fingers between the lips of her pussy. The more he played between her legs, the harder she sucked his cock. He suddenly stopped and felt his stomach tighten then he erupted.

Now men do this all the time. Mostly as a way of showing off but, like Leanne, he'd been holding it in for a while. Now if hers was an eight on a scale of ten, his was definitely a nine. (A ten makes you puke so it wasn't a ten.) Anyway, with him still inside Leanne's warm mouth, she mumbled for him to get out because she couldn't breathe. A bead of saliva dripped off Will as he pulled his throbbing member free and stood with his pants around his ankles and a hard-on.

They were both surprised for a moment. They tried not to laugh. But then it overcame them and they could hardly contain themselves. With each belly laugh they would cut loose another fart, making the moments even more hilarious. The smell was atrocious and Leanne sprayed perfume on her muff and in the crease of her ass to cover the aroma. Will put some on himself to help with the smell too.

Will told her about how in college the guys would light their farts when they were drinking. Leanne laughed and asked Will to show her. So in the tradition of his fraternity, he did. The first attempt was rather lame. A little gasser that only made the candle glow brighter. The next one was pretty good. Leanne felt braver and they decided to do one together as a joke. Now it was a great idea, but sometimes the best-laid plans aren't always smart.

When Will held the candle between their legs he'd forgotten about the perfume on her pubis. As she hissed out a little silent but deadly fart, she stopped and breathed in and her pubic hair caught fire. When she screamed, she forced out a burst of gas and blew the flames onto Will's perfume-soaked pubic hair, which ignited.

In the hospital, the talk of the floor was the couple in room 203. Leanne had third-degree burns on her labia, and her pubic hair had burned clean off, which made her itch constantly. Plus the ointment burned when she put it on. The skin grafts on Will's nuts would make everything like new but the doctor said the hair might not grow back. At least they got to room together.

The Affair

೪౧

Her eyes teared as she restrained herself from crying out from the sheer passion of the moment. Love's purest form of expression was causing her both emotional pain and extreme physical pleasure, confusing her feelings. As she kissed his forehead, a cry of deep ecstasy left her, and the sweltering heat inside her was filled with the pulsing fluid of their sex. This was her darkest desire.

They'd met a few months ago on the Internet, having what her friends called a cyber relationship. The chat rooms became their sanctuary — a place to share not only their hidden selves, but also dreams, desires and fantasies. They'd spent hours chatting after their first discussion. They had common likes and dislikes and it seemed to open them up to each other like kindred spirits.

This was their first real meeting. They kissed deeply and long. Her hair fell forward as he leaned back. The strands brushed against him as she kissed his chest. She released him from her shaved, wet pussy and lowered her head to his tightening stomach. Her long, auburn hair almost covered his chest and her tongue became a pen, drawing along every muscle indentation on his flexing abdomen. She deliberately licked along the sides of his manhood, watching it grow. Her mouth took in the tip and she sucked it, tasting his cum. Her own wetness was still glistening on it and the taste of her pussy lingering on his skin made her even hornier.

Everything about him made her hot, but it was his words that had first attracted her to him. He was different, more real and honest, but mainly more erotic to her. She slowly gave him the pleasure of her mouth, caressing the length of his shaft, sliding it in deeply. She heard him moan and felt him move his hands over his head, enjoying the feeling of her mouth and tongue wrapped around his cock. And she remembered their first Internet meeting in the chat rooms.

* * * * *

She was becoming accustomed to the barrage of men wanting private, dirty chats and giving rude instructions about wanting her to suck cock or fuck. She didn't like how blunt the men were but she experimented, talking to them as if she were a phone-sex girl. She never really got anything out of it except the knowledge that her words alone got them off. She couldn't bring herself to the point of masturbating to someone else's words. It seemed too intimate.

One lonely Friday night, she was about to log off when she noticed an unfamiliar nickname in the room, Guest492. He was new and didn't have a clue about what was going on so she helped him. She taught him the essentials like word shortcuts and how to pick a nickname. The one he picked instantly intrigued her—SlowJam. To some it was no big deal, but she loved music and slow R&B always made her relax and feel sensual. Her own was a perfect fit—Nightfire. She was a night owl.

As time passed, they continued to chat and became friends. They never talked about each other's significant others because they both felt that this was their special, secret Garden of Eden. They had discussed meeting each other sometime or maybe having lunch or whatever. But they were afraid to take it to the next level since they were both married. Until one dark, rainy night, she was sitting at her computer watching people chat and flirt and jabber incoherently and her mind wandered. She found herself caressing her breasts. She had masturbated before to ease her heartache since she hadn't seen her husband in quite a few days. Her husband was a computer software salesman and traveled a lot. He took care of her well money-wise, but she needed physical attention and being alone so much made her doubt her own attractiveness.

Her body wasn't perfect, but it was attractive. People complimented her on it but not the man who needed to tell her. She'd been feeling a little down lately, but for some reason she felt different tonight. Her body seemed more alive, more sensitive, and it made her uncomfortable. She had a deep itch that needed to be scratched. She had small firm breasts and tonight they were very aroused. Her nipples were taut and tented the fabric. And she squirmed in her chair with arousal, which made them rub against the silk.

Her heart jumped when she saw his name enter the chat room.

After they'd both exchanged the usual gibberish about the weather, their day, and other inconsequential things, he asked her if she was alone. Her heart beat hard and her thighs tensed. She told him she was alone and described her dark purple sleep shirt and frilly white underwear. His deafening silence made her wonder what he was thinking. She was becoming increasingly aroused by her own thoughts.

"Do you want to play?" he asked.

They'd never explored this possibility before, but her loneliness and arousal prompted her to answer, "Yes." This was new and she was torn, feeling she was cheating on her husband by doing this. She told him.

He said it was just pleasuring herself with the aid of another's words. She wasn't sleeping with another person or having someone else touch her. She was using her fantasies and imagination to get herself off. That did not make her feel better, but his answer made her realize how badly she wanted to share this with him.

She pulled her leg up against her chest as she sat in the desk chair. The tightening of her underwear outlined the creases of her labia and pressed against her pussy, moistening it even more.

"Touch your breasts," he said.

Reluctantly she did, sending a breathless rush through her body as she cupped her breasts in her palms and her erect nipples tightened. The tingling feeling in her body made her melt into the chair. She stopped to type, "OK."

"Now touch your nipples," he commanded.

As she gently twisted the tips, a throaty moan murmured from within and her hands shook as the tension caused her to shiver. She typed again that she'd obeyed and there was a short pause.

"This isn't the way it should be," he typed. He told her it wouldn't be this way if they met in person. His words were direct and made her wonder what it would be like if he were there with her.

"Then tell me what you'd do if you were here," she answered.

"Don't type," he said. "Just do what I ask."

His words seemed more relaxed and she complied. He asked her to open her nightshirt and take her underwear off. Every word made her feel so sensual, so overtly erotic. She sat there, surprised. Her hands glided across her breasts and up the sides as she read his words, as if it were his hands touching her. An image of him was in her head, gently stroking the skin around her nipples. Her reflection in the wall mirror glowed from the monitor and she saw her body in a totally different way. Her fingers trembled as she tried to free her emotional boundaries enough to touch her pubis as if it were him. The wetness and heat between her labia were intense. An abundance of tormenting feelings filled her as she did as he asked. She slid her finger between the lips but not inside. The slick, smooth flesh reacted like butter melting as she pictured his mouth licking her sweltering pussy. She blinked a few times trying to clear her sight as he asked her to put her leg on her desk and open herself to the screen so he could virtually see her womanly mound as they explored. This increased her stimulation.

As if he knew her thoughts, he asked if she had a toy. She'd already opened the bottom desk drawer and the box she used to hide the vibrator from her husband. The shimmer of the vibrator's shaft and the way she caressed it was the same way she appreciated the shaft of her husband's dick. That and her liking of giving oral sex was beginning to make her hunger for the taste of him. He told her to turn it on and massage her nipples with it. As she did, the slow humming vibrations sent signals down her torso to her already exposed clit. He'd taken over her mind and freed her, making this crazy situation seem real.

Her body was so alive and so in tune with him. The rhythms of her soul were like an instrument and he was playing it perfectly. She opened her legs wide and slid the vibrating shaft inside herself. A lingering tightness was still there, caused by her fear of being this open with someone. The mystery of his face and the journey into the unknown world of cybersex made everything new. She was a virgin experiencing everything again. Hopefully it would be better than her first sexual experience, which had lasted all of fifteen seconds when Billy shot his load all over her prom dress, making it stick to her hip all night.

Her hand jerked as the tip of her toy pressed her cervix. The slow hum sped up as she withdrew it and slowed as the length plunged inside her tightening cavern. The slow pulsing throb of her need made the vibrator almost seem alive. She glanced at the screen, straining to keep her eyes open despite the intense pleasure she felt. His words guided her. She left the toy buried within and moved her hands along her abdomen and up to her breasts. The shimmer of her sweat made the smooth skin seem like silk. Her nightgown was open all the way and her hands were touching her sides as she imagined him there with her. She reached for the humming toy inside her pussy and began the slow motions of lovemaking, picturing his cock pushing deeper and deeper inside the inferno burning between her legs. She couldn't even watch everything he typed because the moment of passion swept her up and took her. She glanced at the screen and read him telling her to picture him slamming hard into her. This was a fantasy melding with reality as she grasped her breast and pushed it up, licking the tip of her nipple, thrusting the vibrator faster and in a circling motion so it would rub her engorged clitoris. She threw her head back as he begged her to fuck him. The experience took a whole new meaning as she envisioned him holding her hands down and slamming into her deep and hard.

Her mind spun as she threw her head back, squeezed her nipple and felt her pussy squeeze the toy as her orgasm flooded her with a tidal wave of release. Sweating, she came again and the pulsing of the muscles made her feel spent and desperately relaxed. The humming had stopped when she set the toy on her computer table and stared at it. The glisten of her juices made it shimmer.

That was the beginning. It all led her to this moment—a sordid meeting in a downtown hotel—the dim room with the flashing, flickering light from the neon "vacant" sign.

She knew the way she used her tongue to follow the line of the hot vein along the underside of his cock made him crazy. Their cyber experiences would never be enough again after having him in the flesh. From the depths of her heart and body she would ache for more of this burning desire and a lust for his sex.

As the slight taste of his juice seeped from the tip, she almost devoured him whole, taking the entire length down her throat. The scent of his cologne intertwined with the scent of his sweat from the heat of their experience. His hand rested on the back of her head and his fingers combed the strands of her hair as her lips pulled the skin back slowly, sucking the essence from his body. She gasped and he pulled at her hair almost begging her to finish him and free him from this building pressure. She gasped and again thrust him deep into her mouth, furiously tugging at the base with her hand as if milking the fluid from within his loins. She knew he was close.

His stomach flexed and the tension in his legs made his toes curl as he moaned and erupted in her mouth. Again and again he freed the fluids from deep within his testicles and her mouth took all but a small trickle down the side of his shaft as she slowly pulled her mouth away. She kissed the side of his cock and watched the fluids still dripping as he throbbed.

This was ecstasy—this was pleasure. She had finally crossed the line. She'd become the woman she thought was lost. Arriving at the hotel, she knew she couldn't betray her husband like that. She knew how much they loved each other and that he would never do anything like this either. Until she went into the hotel bar to meet him, and she saw her husband sitting in the designated booth. After the initial shock and disbelief, they sat there for what seemed like forever and talked about how things had reached this junction. Why were they even thinking about meeting someone else? He used to make her feel wonderful, loved, but life had taken its toll on them. Kids, work, time, until life's basic needs took over their own.

* * * * *

Her head lay on his chest and his hand slowly caressed her skin. The long strands of hair whisked across her face as the wind blew in from the window. Was she wrong to need this closeness and the feeling of completeness?

Tears fell as she climbed on top of him and kissed his lips gently. She fell in love again. It had been a long time since she'd held him like this. In that instant she was eighteen again. She'd met her husband and their lives were just beginning. Their passion was unparalleled and the way they made love was almost unearthly. Every time was the first time. After all the years and all the changes, it took a meeting on the Internet to find that spark again. What she told that stranger about, and the feelings she had were being told to the man of her dreams. The man she had married ten years ago. He too had felt lost in this life they had made. As time had passed, they'd forgotten how magical their love was. And talking, as if to a stranger, had made them open up.

The First Date (Peter and Susan Part 2)

∽

Peter finally decided hiding his relationship with Susan was impossible and wrong. Their chemistry was so obvious it was uncanny. Besides, she drove him absolutely crazy with her intense sensuality.

They had decided to enjoy a nice dinner and a movie so they could really get to know each other. So far their relationship had been almost totally based on sex...well okay...entirely based on sex. For this date they set some ground rules so that it would be more like a regular date, just like they'd never met.

After much complaining and begging on Peter's part, the rules agreed on were these:

1. No sex.

2. The object of this date is to get to know each other so it is important to follow rule number 1.

3. Topics discussed can be about the past and other relationships, but try to keep it clean. (See rule 1.)

Peter went to Susan's beachfront apartment to pick her up. There was a wonderful view of the ocean and the breeze brought the smell of the sea rushing in. She strolled out from the bedroom wearing a thin sundress that hugged her body like another layer of skin. The light behind her showed through her dress and he could see she wasn't wearing anything underneath it.

Baseball, think baseball, he kept saying to himself, trying to remember the rules.

Susan stepped onto the balcony and gazed out over the beach. "What do you think of the view?" she asked. Peter adjusted his pants as he looked at her. The wind was blowing her dress against her and the cold air made her nipples rise under the fabric. *Baseball, think baseball,* Peter kept repeating in his head as he walked out to Susan and leaned on the railing and gazed at her. There was a gleam and radiance in her eyes as she smiled and looked back at him.

Susan hooked her arm in Peter's and rested her head on his shoulder. They stood on the balcony and watched the sunset. It looked as if the sun melted into the ocean water and the darkened blue sky took over, making it night. "We better get going, dear," Peter said not wanting to leave this beautiful moment.

In the car Peter had a romantic compact disc playing to set the mood. Throughout the ride to the restaurant they made small talk about former jobs, relationships and life in general. Neither one of them would remember it tomorrow — their minds were elsewhere.

At a quiet corner table they ordered their dinner and drinks — Bacardi 151 and Coke for Peter and a margarita for Susan. After the third drink they both started relaxing.

As Peter leaned forward to take the last bite of his lobster, he felt something press against the swelling between his legs.

Cough cough. "Uhhhhhhhhh, how's your lobster?" Peter asked.

Susan grinned back mischievously, "It's okay but I'm actually in the mood for something a little more filling. You know, some really mouthwatering beef."

"Check please!" yelled Peter.

Peter excused himself to go to the restroom. Susan sat there for a minute then she smiled slowly and got up from the table.

In the men's room all the urinals were taken so Peter stepped into the stall next to the wall. Not really paying attention, he pushed the stall door closed and it swung back open. Susan had slipped into the stall with Peter and closed the door behind her. She brought her finger up to his lips and said, "Shhhhhhh, I'm still hungry."

As she undid his belt and unzipped his pants, her petite hand reached in and grasped his penis. Using his dick as a handle, she turned him around and put the toilet seat down and sat on the lid, which put her face-to-crotch with him. She grabbed at his clothing and tried pulling his pants down as Peter wiggled them loose.

"But the rules were no sex," he whispered.

"I know, but we're not having sex," his pants hit his ankles. "Yet."

He reached for the top of the stall walls with both hands and closed his eyes as she ran her fingers down the length of his swelling shaft. She watched it grow with a knowing grin, aware that he was anticipating the feel of her smooth red lips wrapping around it. Peter moaned softly to himself as she traced the veins of his manhood with her tongue.

His ecstasy built as she looked up at him. Gazing into his eyes, she took the tip into her mouth and let her tongue draw against the sensitive fold of skin on the head. He pulled on the walls of the stall, making them creak, as she slowly inched her way down the length of his pulsing shaft.

The other men in the restroom weren't sure what to make of the soft moaning in the last stall. A few peered under the stall walls but all they saw was a pair of feet facing the toilet with his trousers around his ankles. Susan was sitting cross-legged on the toilet seat.

Peter looked down. He could see down her dress, view her naked skin, her glorious breasts.

She reached around his torso, grabbed his butt cheeks in her hands, and pulled him forward in a slow rhythmic motion. Each time she sucked him deeper into her mouth. His penis twitched as she paused for breath and licked the underside. She made soft, moaning sounds while pleasuring him. At the end of each pull she would suck on the tip with her lips, catch her breath and start again. His breathing was quickening and she could taste how close he was. She stopped for a second, gasped for breath, and then started a more aggressive and vigorous attack on his throbbing manhood. He pulled hard on the walls, shuddering as she drew him all the way into her mouth. Susan tilted her head to the side and pulled him against her until the tip of his penis hit the back of her throat.

He was not sure if it was the fact that what she was doing felt absolutely glorious or that they were in a public place, but he was losing control. Susan wrapped her fingers around the back of his legs and slid them along the crease of his thigh and butt. She dug her nails in his tightened scrotum, her mouth a wet cavern for his shaft.

Peter completely lost control. He threw his head back and moaned loudly as his knees nearly buckled. He shook as he flooded her mouth with his essence. Over and over he gushed and she did not slow until he was spent. She took a tissue and wiped the sides of her mouth.

Susan stood up and unlocked the door. As she stepped out, she pinched Peter's ass and kissed him on the cheek. She walked up to the mirror and the men stepped closer to the urinals. While Susan reapplied her deep red lipstick with the slow strokes across her moist lips, each man fantasized about what Peter had just gotten. They imagined themselves in his place as Susan recapped her lipstick and strolled out the door.

Peter staggered out of the stall, washed his hands and rinsed the sweat off his face. Once he was able, he walked out to the table where Susan was sitting. She smiled and winked at him as he sat down.

The waiter stepped up and asked how dinner was.

"Everything was good," Peter said.

"Would either of you like some dessert?"

"No, I've already had mine." Susan replied as she licked her lips and put her foot back into Peter's lap. "Besides, we have a movie to catch."

The Long Distance Love Affair

&)

As she sat on the plane for her rendezvous with destiny, Kate wondered to herself, *Am I crazy or what?*

Here she was, twenty-eight, petite, cute as a button with long, curly, light-brown hair, and still insecure about men.

It all began as harmless fun online. Nobody ever met Mr. Right on the net. There might be an occasional lucky person, but generally it was a washout. Now here she was, flying three thousand miles to meet a guy she didn't really know. He'd generously paid for her trip and a hotel room. They'd chatted for hours at a time, talked on the phone and even exchanged pictures, but they'd never actually met.

The closer her plane got to its final destination, the more Kate's nerves started to take over. Obviously, she needed a little buffer to help her relax. Vodka sounded like a good buffer—screwdrivers always helped her relax. After the fifth one, she was definitely feeling a little mellower, and a little number. Airline peanuts and screwdrivers, the true breakfast of champions.

As the plane taxied into the terminal, Kate had one final shot and a last look at the picture of Bill through slightly blurred vision. Bill was a tall man with salt and pepper hair, above-average looks and a nice physique. Not bad for an older man.

Now, as the drinks and her anxiety started taking over, she stepped out of the plane and looked around the terminal. She wandered around aimlessly looking for Bill. The picture in her tightly clenched fist was her only guide. She turned and saw a man standing by the luggage racks. He turned to look around and she knew it was him. A chill swept her body. *Wow,* she thought to herself, *I've never felt that before.* (Actually, the air conditioner had just kicked on, and she was standing under the vent.)

She was overwhelmed by excitement. In a rush, she dropped her bags, leapt into his arms, wrapped her legs around him and planted a long, wet, exploratory kiss on him. As he staggered to keep his balance, he smiled and asked, "Miss me?"

They both laughed and he set her down.

"You look much better than your picture!" Kate exclaimed. She kept holding him in her arms, not wanting to let him go. The initial rush of excitement hadn't faded yet and they were both in a state of shock and befuddlement. This was definitely lust at first sight. Bill stared into Kate's beautiful blue eyes and winked at her. They were past the first test—they liked what they saw. Now it was time for a test drive.

Kate felt like a schoolgirl on prom night. She had butterflies in her stomach and wetness between her legs. Bill, on the other hand, was relatively calm, except for the bulge in his pants. That would teach him to wear tight slacks when picking up a woman. They looked around and saw a storeroom door for maintenance. Enough said.

They went into the small, closet-size room and Bill locked the door. Before he could turn to face her, Kate came up behind him. She slid her hands around his waist and up his chest, ripping his shirt open. Then she pulled the shirtsleeves down, but not off, binding his arms behind him. She kissed his back and shoulders, using her hands to explore his hairy chest and midsection. All Bill could do was moan with pleasure as she undid his pants and slid her hand down the front, grasping his swollen manhood. She pushed him hard against the door and kept stroking him with her hand. Then she ran her long fingernails down the middle of his back and dug them into the soft skin at the small of his back.

For the first time in a long while, she had control of a sexual situation. There was nothing she couldn't do. *She* had the power and that really turned her on. Bill begged to use his hands. She pulled on his nipple and whispered, "No, let me have this moment." As she teased and tugged his hardness, euphoria pulsed through her. Her long fingernails raked against the soft skin on his inner thighs. She slowly unbuttoned her blouse with her free hand. Then she pressed her soft breasts against his back and licked his shoulders as her erect nipples dragged against his back. She longed for his touch as she pressed her nubile body against his large frame, squeezing his throbbing member rhythmically in her hand. Bill pulled his hands free from his shirt. He reached around and grasped her ass in his hands and pulled her hard against him.

She couldn't help but melt in his hands. The drinks, the passion, the desire were more than Kate could handle. When Bill turned around, his pants dropped to the ground, revealing Scooby Doo boxers and his dog sticking out the front flap. She was overcome and slowly fell into his arms. Their lips met and he explored her mouth with his tongue. She succumbed totally and lost control. And she didn't care. She lay down on the small table and he slipped her out of her wet white panties. As Bill pressed his mouth against her seething hot pussy and moved his tongue in against her clit, she came almost instantly. She was in total abandonment to her senses. If heaven is a place on earth, then she was there at that moment.

Bill kissed down her leg to her ankle. When he stood, her leg draped over his shoulder, and slowly pressed his hardness against her wet velvet vise, she leaned back against the wall to support them. At first he just wedged himself at the opening, teasing her with his swollen manhood. Then as Kate looked up at him, he slowly drove himself into her. Bill's eyes rolled back as her tight sheath squeezed him. Good thing she worked out. Kate pulled her arms back and pushed herself up to brace against his driving force. He pushed against her, slowly at first, then faster. He pulled himself all the way out and she reached down with her hand and pulled him back into her. The incredible pleasure was almost too much. He took long, slow strokes as he slid in and out of her fiery box. She could tell by Bill's breathing that he was close too, very close.

Kate reached down and started stroking her clit as he quickened his pace. She reached up her wet fingers to feel the side of his face and trace his lips. Slipping her finger into his mouth, he sucked hard on it and bit the tip, sending electric shocks straight to her sweltering hot box. His fingers pulled her nipples and rubbed his thumbs across them as he pressed against her. Bill's body started shaking and she could feel him swell inside her. She flung her head back when Bill grabbed her upright leg and turned his head to kiss her ankle while he slid in and out of her. His eyes closed as the passion kept building. He reached down and held Kate's ass tightly in his hand. Then he leaned forward, slid his hand down and grabbed her other leg, lifting it over his other shoulder. He held her spread legs wide so he could pound more deeply. She couldn't muffle the moans she felt escaping. Her mouth opened and she gasped for air as Bill grabbed her lower torso and slammed harder into her. She shuddered from the tightness and the friction this caused. It was too much for them and they climaxed uncontrollably together.

A few of her fingernails broke when she dug them into the table as she tried unsuccessfully to keep herself up. As her hair hung off the edge of the table Bill kissed her chest softly, licking beads of sweat from between her breasts, caressing her soft, silky skin. She closed her eyes and fell into a special space between reality and heaven. She giggled as he withdrew from her and the juice from their love trickled out. She lay there, totally spent. *This is what sex is supposed to feel like.*

They slowly got dressed and walked back into the main part of the airport. Bill kissed her cheek and said he needed to pick up his Lexus at the lot. While she stood there, in a dreamlike state of fulfillment and dripping a little, she glanced up and saw a man with a sign. It read "Welcome to Florida, Kate!"

The man was small, balding, and looked like Homer Simpson.

"Oh, Kate, you look even better than your pictures."

"Who me?" she asked, staring at the stranger.

"It's me, Bill. You know, cyber-man," he said smiling and bragging.

"Ummmm, you don't look anything like your picture. I didn't know it was you." Kate stared out the door looking at the Lexus pulling up at the front gate. "I'm a little flustered about all this, um, silly me."

"I'm sorry. I wanted you to like me as a person first. You said looks weren't important and, well, I'll tell you about it in my mom's car on the way to the hotel. I want to do some of those kinky things we talked about doing online!" Snort, snort. "Hey where were you? Your plane landed about thirty minutes ago. I was beginning to worry about you, hot mama. The Volkswagen is out in the parking lot. Let's go, baby. "

The wind blew through Kate's hair. She smiled and put her legs up on the dash, letting the air sweep under her sundress and against her body. She finally leaned back into the lap of her cyber-man—well, after giving Bill two thousand dollars for the trip and telling him "Sorry, I have a rash." At least she met the man of her dreams. And the ride in the Lexus convertible wasn't bad either.

Who says you can't meet Mr. Right on the Internet?

The Phone Call

ꙅ

The phone rang loudly at precisely five-thirty p.m. just like every other evening. Janet had been busy lately and the calls to Richard at work were usually necessary information about their upcoming wedding instead of the regular "kissy, kissy, love you" talk you'd expect. So Richard trudged over to the phone and picked it up indifferently.

"Hello?"

"Hi, babe. You'll never guess what I'm wearing right now."

"Flannel?" he replied.

"Actually, it's a silk thong and a matching lacy brassiere that really doesn't cover much."

"Uh, Janet, is that you?"

"Well if it isn't me than you really shouldn't be talking on the phone with a woman this horny. One who's waiting in bed for a real man with a bowl of strawberries and whipped cream to feed you while I sit on top of you and slowly ride up and down, while leaning back so I can rub that certain spot you said could only be rubbed while you grow inside my hot bush."

"What's all this about?"

"Did I tell you that I just finished painting my fingernails ruby red, and I can't wait to dig them so deep into your back that I leave marks when you climb on top of me and drive your manhood inside of me so deep that it pushes against my cervix, and I explode in waves like the ocean crashing on the beach?"

"Okay, what did you buy and how much did it cost?"

"You're going to think I'm crazy, but I can't even go grocery shopping without thinking about sex with you. I went to Lucky's and could barely control myself. First, grabbing the bananas. I had to have one. So I peeled one and pushed the whole thing in my mouth until it was touching my tonsils because I thought that if I could do this I might be able to handle all of you. But a banana is no comparison, so I bought a cucumber. I had to find just the right one. The other women asked me what I was doing when I kept moaning whenever I grabbed a firm, smooth, thick cucumber. So I told them I needed to feel my Richard or have something close to his size in my hands to stroke. They all wanted your phone number when I finally showed them the cucumber that was just your size. The scale nearly broke. In the car I was so wet that I just laid it between my legs so I could imagine you there, every bump in the road rubbed me against it and almost made me climax."

"Babe, are you taking those herbal vitamins Marilyn was selling or something?"

"You know just talking to you and saying your name, Dick, is making me so hot that I'm going to slip out of these damn confining panties. Ooohhh. These things are like a straightjacket for my passion. Wow. They're so wet just from thinking about what we're going to do when you finally get home. Mmmmm, god, I can just imagine you caressing my body with your big strong hands. Whoops! I just slipped my finger into my mouth and bit the tip, but I know you don't like me to bite. But I don't mind you biting a little on the tips of my nipples. Oooohhhh, or on my lips when we kiss. Or my other lips when you're spending what feels like an eternity between my thighs with your tongue darting in and out of me while you lap up the flowing juices that only you can release."

"I don't care what you've done or how much it costs, having you tonight will be worth it!"

"Ooooohhhhhh! I am on fire. Dear me, I can't wait much longer. This is torture. Like a building wave before it breaks and sprays its wetness across the beach until it builds again, and again. This is so unfair. Can you get off sooner so you can get me off? You don't know how badly I need to let go. Mmmmmmmm, I can fit three fingers inside of me. Please come home. Now. Please hurry! I can't wait another second. Get your ass over here! Oh please, come to me. Now, now come to me."

Fuck this! "Scott, I need to get home right now. I know you can't pay me for this, but it's an emergency!"

"Yo, dude, you're out of here. Just fill out your timesheet and you're gone," Scott said.

As Richard furiously rummaged through the paperwork to get his timecard, Scott walked up to him.

"Hey Rich?"

"WHAT, MAN? I'M IN A HURRY!"

"Your fiancée just called and said to tell you not to rush home. She said that the cucumber she bought at the store was perfect and the ocean waves have subsided, and she's exhausted. Whatever that means."

The Piercing

∞

Music blasted loudly through the house. The party was at its peak. People were buzzed and a thick layer of smoke floated above the crowd. It was Rachell's first party since starting college.

She was a Goth and so she'd always been a little different from everyone else in high school. She wore black and had jet-black, shoulder-length hair and a few piercings. She was tall with a medium build and a great set of…umm… We'll say she filled out a shirt well and loved wearing leather pants. Other than that, she was quiet and quite smart. She'd received a nice scholarship to Cal Berkeley and wanted to start anew. This was a chance at a new beginning. She was nineteen and all the horrors of high school were over.

Lars walked into the party with his friends and scoped out the scene. Dressed like he was, he demanded attention. His leather jacket had chains on it. His Mohawk was snot-green. And his ear, nose, eyebrow, and nipple piercings were proudly displayed. His eyes locked instantly on a vision. He stared at Rachell, like a deer into headlights.

Damn, he thought to himself, *She's hella fine!*

The hair on the back of her neck stood up and Rachell knew someone was looking at her. Nonchalantly, she looked around the room. When her eyes met Lars, it was mystical. The room became quiet and her vision was filled only with him. Of course the drinks could have had some effect on that too.

Damn, she thought to herself, *He's hella fine!*

He awkwardly walked up and started talking gibberish to her, which she couldn't hear because the music was so loud. She smiled and acted amused, oblivious to the room, and just watched him. She tried to read his lips while he talked, but her mind was envisioning kissing his lips. She thought about exploring his mouth with her tongue. She imagined his mouth caressing her body. The twinkle of silver in his mouth showed he had a piercing. Because she had one too, she knew what someone who was talented with a piercing could do during sex.

They yelled back and forth and they laughed as the party got louder and more furious. They had a chemistry between them. Six screwdrivers for her and five rum and Cokes, two beers and a shot of Jose Cuervo made a lot of chemistry. He had another shot of tequila and kissed Rachell. The sour tang of the drink mixed with the sweet taste of her lips. Lars kissed her again and she ran her fingers along the tips of his spiked Mohawk hair. Their tongue piercings clinked in their mouths, making them both laugh.

Rachell felt loose and relaxed and very horny. She leaned over, resting her hand against Lars' groin, and whispered softly in his ear, "Let's go upstairs."

"What?" Lars yelled, not able to hear her.

"Let's go upstairs," she said again a little louder.

"I'm sorry, babe. I can't hear you," Lars yelled.

As the music paused, she screamed, "I WANT TO TAKE YOU UPSTAIRS SO WE CAN FUCK!" In the quiet room, people looked around at Rachell, grinning and giggling.

They went upstairs. And, room by room, they opened each door to see beds occupied by college coeds and even college team mascots—the mule was a bit kinky—having sex. When they opened the bathroom door, Lars smiled and yanked her in. Then he locked the door. She didn't even know this guy but he made her feel great about herself since he was a little different too. As they mashed their bodies together against the bathroom wall, his hands groped and fondled her flesh. Her own hands kept a steady grip on his growing cock.

Their lips parted and she shoved Lars away and stepped back against the bathroom sink. Rachell leaned over and pulled her shirt down over her shoulders to expose her sheer bra and the nipple hoops piercing her and pressing through the fabric. Lars bent down and kissed the nipples through the fabric, flicking the hoops. The wetness of his mouth moistened the fabric and Rachell pulled the straps aside, letting them fall. Lars pulled the bra down and stared at her breasts.

She had perfectly round breasts and two small loop nipple piercings. The nipples stood out strongly. He licked his lips as they swayed while she took her shirt off. Rachell lifted her ass up onto the countertop and Lars pushed her backwards to lie on the porcelain. He kissed her tummy and moved up to her breasts, holding them firmly in his hands. He grinned and licked her nipples and the tink, tink of his tongue piercing against her loops made her shiver and squirm. Wetness gathered between her lips, both sets of lips. His mouth encompassed her nipple and pulled up on the loop causing her to cry out in bliss. Her hair fell back as she leaned back to expose her neck and chest to his wandering eyes. She was so fresh, so sensual. No man had ever used her nipple piercings correctly, but Lars had her climbing the walls wanting him.

All the while, her legs were parted and Lars' chest rubbed against her inner thighs, making the inferno of desire deepen. Lars' hand found her pants and grasped her crotch through the fabric, feeling the heat and wetness through her spandex. She sighed and grabbed his face to kiss him hard. She bit his lip as he pulled back. She wanted him badly and wasn't going to be denied satisfaction. She was so aroused there was actually a wet spot on the fabric. Rachell lay across the bathroom countertop like a dinner tray and Lars planned to eat the entire buffet.

Lars' hand searched inside her pants and, when he discovered she wasn't wearing any underwear, he moaned. He licked her tummy and bellybutton piercing. As he peeled the spandex down and his mouth followed it. He kissed her black pubic hair, which glistened distinctly with her desire as he continued to pull her pants down over her thighs then her calves and finally off. Lars moved down to her feet to spread her legs apart and saw the luscious, wet labia. A paradise where a man can lose his mind and free the beast, wanting to play forever. Her mouth watered and she closed her eyes as Lars found her clit piercing with his tongue. He showed her no mercy as he vigorously sucked and licked her clit. Rachell wiggled and moaned, her pussy awash in his saliva. He thrust his tongue in and out of her, flicking her clit piercing with his own tongue piercing.

The bathroom counter became slippery and wet. As she wiggled and thrashed, closing in on an orgasm, Lars spun her around. He moved her so that her legs hung over the side and her back pressed against the mirror. Her bottom rested right on the edge. He knelt in front of her and pushed both of her legs up. Rachell grabbed her thighs and Lars sucked on her clit, pulling the piercing with his teeth. As he slid his index finger deep inside her, making her groan, he squeezed a handful of her ass in his other hand, molding it like clay. He rubbed the opening with his thumb while his finger kept probing her and his mouth assaulted her clitoris.

Her orgasm was hard and intense. Her neck ached from pushing her head against the mirror. The spasms of ecstasy made her jerk and wiggle. A gleam of sweat covered her stomach and she felt moist and relaxed. She giggled as Lars kept licking her. After one last, deep suck, Lars stood up and kissed her tummy and each breast softly, then he kissed her mouth passionately so she could taste her own juices.

Rachell sat up, proudly arching her chest forward. She looked up into Lars' eyes devilishly as she twisted her nipple loop. She touched his cheek and ran her black fingernails down his chin to his chest. She pushed him back against the wall as she stood up and ripped open his shirt. Then she grabbed his leather-covered crotch. She licked his neck and bit hard on his ear and whispered, "Hold on, this may get a little rough."

Instantly he was at attention, in all areas. The sweat on her breasts made a slippery mix on his pounding chest. She still grasped him through his pants. She looked down and smiled when she pulled the pants away from his stomach and saw the glistening tip of his cock. She focused on the toy she wanted to play with. She bit his nipple piercing and rubbed her breasts against his abdomen. He yelled out as she released the piercing. She wrapped her legs around his calf and rubbed her hot wetness up and down the fabric. She fumbled with the buttons on his pants then pulled them open and rested her head against the swollen front of his underwear. Her cheek felt the wetness of his desire through the fabric. Her teeth tugged at the waistband of his boxers as she slid his pants to his knees. He fell back against the wall. She reached up the leg of his boxers to fondle his balls. Then she pulled his underwear down and saw her prize. Like a kid with a box of Crackerjacks this one had a toy inside. He had a Prince Albert piercing on his penis.

She giggled and looked up at Lars, his eyes straining to stay open as he watched her mold her breasts around his cock. He held on to the wall to keep his balance as he watched himself disappear into her mouth. Her fingernails dragged against the vein along the base of his hardened member. He was average size, but the piercing drove her crazy as her tongue played with it.

Lars moaned loudly as she pulled hard on him. Again, she yanked on him as if trying to pull his cock off. She moaned loudly, but Lars seemed oblivious because of the attention he was getting. Rachell reached up and pinched his balls hard.

"Ouch! What the hell did you do that for?" Lars yelled.

"Mime Maught" she mumbled.

"Huh?"

Rachell pulled back and he moved with her. It seemed that in the vigor of passion, she got her tongue piercing caught in his Prince Albert and all the jerking made it worse. She tried tugging again but there was a sharp twinge from her piercing poking him. "Ahhhh! Quit that! It's hurting."

"Mell mhat mam mi mupposed mo mdo?"

Suddenly, there was a banging at the door. Seems the police had been called about the noise and kids vandalizing the neighbors' homes. When they broke the lock and opened the door they stopped, stunned and bewildered. Rachell knelt there naked with her tongue out, Lars' penis partially in her mouth. And Lars sat on the toilet with a pair of tweezers and a flashlight he'd found in the drawer, trying to unhook them.

Doctors finally got them separated at the hospital.

Rachell got the notoriety she'd always wanted. She was now known as Dental Dawn at school. And in fact, a well-established porn studio bought the movie rights and she paid for her first semester with the royalties.

Lars finished school and never went out with Rachell again. He had his piercings removed and is now happily married to an Amish woman in Massachusetts.

The Quickie

ဢ

Dale: "Hi."

Pamela: "Hi."

Dale: "Alone?"

Pamela: "Yes."

Dale: "Thirsty?"

Pamela: "Horny!"

Dale: "Cooool!"

Pamela: "Hot!"

Dale: "When?"

Pamela: "Now!"

Dale: "Men's?"

Pamela: "Ladies'."

Dale: "Nervous?"

Pamela: zzzzzziiiipppppp

Dale: "WOW!"

Pamela: "You?"

Dale: zzzziiiippppp

Pamela: "Impressive."

Dale: grunt

Pamela: moan

Dale: grunt

Pamela: moan

Dale: grunt

Pamela: moan

Dale: "Ahhhhhhhhh."
Pamela: "Mmmmmmm."
Dale: zip
Pamela: zzzziiiippppp
Dale: "Thanks."
Pamela: "Bye."

The Blind Date

ဢ

The moon was glowing brightly in the starry sky and they danced slowly on the balcony with the sound of crashing waves echoing down the beach and soft music from the stereo setting the mood. The chilled bottle of wine was almost gone, and the room service dinner had gotten cold as they just talked and nibbled, not wanting to miss anything. If there was such a thing as love at first sight, this might be it.

Stan was an average kind of guy. He worked in the computer industry and was reasonably well off financially. But to be blunt, he was average height, had an average build and average looks. Kelly was a little taller than Stan, with dark hair and long features that made her look slender. This meeting was a blind date. Some friends of Stan's from work had met Kelly at a company function and hit it off.

The warmth from the wine made her feel relaxed and loose, almost uninhibited. The ocean breeze smelled wonderful and she breathed it in deeply. As it swept over her, the coolness made her nipples sensitive and perky and she moaned softly. She leaned back in her chair and closed her eyes, oblivious to everything around her but Stan. Her long fingernails dragged up and down her legs, moving her skirt up her thighs. She parted her legs a little so she could feel the breeze rush against every part of her body.

She knew Stan was watching and it made her feel more alive and more aroused than usual. Kelly moved down a little and raised a leg up over the arm of the lounge chair and moved her skirt higher. She slipped a long finger into her mouth, wetting it, then moved it between her legs and rubbed the red silk fabric of her underwear. Stan sat a little dumbfounded but extremely aroused by what he was seeing. His bulging pants made it apparent the effect she had on him.

The wine had also relaxed him. He sat in front of her and watched intently as Kelly moved her underwear to the side and he could see the dark pubic hair shimmering with wetness. Her fingers moved slowly but knowingly along her hips and back between her legs. The red nail polish accentuated the vision as he saw her finger disappear between her labia and peek back out at the base of her pussy. She moaned as she slid a finger all the way into herself and pulled it back out. She sucked on it then putting it back inside as if to taste the wine from the bounty between her thighs.

Her other hand moved up and cupped her breast, pushing it upwards, holding it tightly. Kelly's thumb rubbed her erect nipple as she deepened the probing of her pussy with her finger.

"Mmmmmmmm. Do you like this, Stan?"

"More than you know," he replied, keeping his hand from pressing down on his bulge.

Kelly moved both hands between her legs spreading them apart and opened her lips wide showing Stan her beauty. The shimmering light made her wetness glisten and the pink inside looked pure and tasty, making Stan almost drool to look at her. The fragrance in the air was like a drug, making him crave more. She massaged her protruding clit, driving herself nuts, but knowing exactly what she was doing. She slid another finger inside her opening and continued to massage her clitoris with the other one. Stan was transfixed and wanted to help her.

"Stan, can you come over here?" Kelly whispered.

He stood up, adjusted his pants, and went to kneel in front of her.

"Did you like watching me play with my pussy?" she asked.

"Oh yeah. It's beautiful." Stan gulped.

"Would you like to eat my pussy?" She smiled, asking another question. All the while she stroked her clit deeper and faster feeling the swell of her desires growing as each moment passed. Stan reached up to unbutton her blouse and nuzzled her chest. He kissed the cleavage between her breasts and moved his hands in between her thighs. Kelly moved her hands behind her head and moaned, "Make me come, Stan. Help me come."

Stan slid his finger into her soft, hot wetness feeling the lubricants flowing. The heat was scorching but her moist, soft inner walls felt made Stan want to explore deeper. Pulling his finger upwards, he felt a small, smooth spot deep within her. As he rubbed it, he sucked her nipples hard through her bra and moaned, aroused. She reacted to his probing as if he'd pushed the gas pedal on a car, making the motor race. Kelly gasped for air. He moved to grasp her ass in his hands and slid his thumbs into her pussy. He opened the lips wide, exposing her clit, and nuzzled into her pubic hair, groaning, "this is the most beautiful thing I have ever seen."

He moved his tongue along the inside of her pussy. Kelly moaned deeply and wantonly as he focused his attentions on her clit. Here she was on a balcony, in a lounge chair with a man eating her out, no hiding. And her moans were getting louder and more powerful as he bit down gently on her clit and hummed, sending vibrations through her body.

"God, I want to fuck you so bad!" he growled as she squirmed in the chair. The words cut through her like a knife. Over and over he pulled down on his thumb stretching her pussy and nuzzled on her clit. Kelly caressed her nipples and pulled them, not wanting to be left unfulfilled. Her head fell back and her eyes closed tight as he buried his thumb into her slippery opening and sucked hard on her clit. She felt as if she were falling when the release of her orgasm swept her away. She gasped for air and grabbed his head, pressing it harder into her, not wanting the feeling to fade inside her. Her juices flowed heavily and she was so fully spent Stan could have knocked her over with a feather.

Her mouth opened wide and she shivered, the small jerks were leftovers from the release of tension. "Damn, I needed that!" she said smiling.

She reached out to touch his stomach and undo his pants. She sighed from the feelings were growing in her once again. Stan was embarrassed about the small wet spot on his underwear from the excitement he felt. Kelly moved him in front of her and stopped her playing to pull his underwear down his muscular legs. She moved her hands back up to grasp his butt in her hands and rested her cheek against his hardness. She moved closer, removed her blouse and undid her front snap on her bra, releasing her full breasts. She moved her arms together and pressed his hardness between her breasts like a tunnel. As she rubbed his cock up and down with her breasts, she would lick the tip of his penis whenever it peeked out. His penis pulsed in time to his heartbeat.

"You want me to suck your dick?" she whispered nastily.

"More than anything!" he groaned, watching her take all of him into her mouth pausing only to suck the head a little. She kept taking him in and out, letting her tongue drag against the vein on the bottom. She could taste the growing pressure at the tip as she let him out for a minute to catch her breath.

"Oh, my, this is sooooooooooo, uhhhh, fuckin' incredible." As he spoke she sucked in until his penis touched the back of her throat. Stan's eyelids fluttered and he closed them.

"Mmmmmm, you taste good! I'm not sure I want to let you go."

She moaned again and the vibrations went through his penis and made his legs weaken.

Kelly stood up and walked in front of him, grasping his penis in her hand like a handle. He hobbled behind her with his pants around his ankles, trying not to trip.

"Lie down. I want to be on top. This is something I've dreamt about and I want you to make my dream come true." Kelly knew exactly what she wanted. She wanted control. She reached down, bending over in front of him, sliding her soaked underwear off and grabbed his pants. She pulled the belt out of the loops and grinned wickedly. "Uh oh, what's that for?" Stan asked.

"Relax," Kelly whispered as she wrapped the belt around his wrists and through the top of the brass headboard. She lowered her head, caressing his skin with her hair. She moved her breasts to his mouth and he nibbled on her nipples, straining to free his hands. This was her wish, to have total control. "Do you want me?" she whispered in his ear as she licked his earlobe.

"I can't handle any more. I'm about to explode. Please, please."

Smiling, she sat up and straddled him. "I want you to see this," she said as she held his penis in her hand. Teasingly she moved it along her wet opening letting only the tip slip in.

"Oh, this is incredible. Please, let me feel you." As Stan watched, Kelly lowered herself down. He watched his hardness slowly inch into her, saw the skin pull tight as he penetrated deeper and deeper. She threw her head back and screamed, "This feels fuckin' great!" Her labia rested moistly against him, and she rocked back and forth as if stretching the tight muscles wrapped around him.

She leaned forward and kissed his mouth, darting her tongue in rhythm with her strokes on him, in and out. Everything about her was overwhelming. His eyes teared as she dug her nails into his chest and hurriedly fucked him. The belt around his wrists burned and bruised the skin as he fought the desire to touch her. It was slow torture as she kissed and licked his neck and ears, biting his lip. Her wet pussy caressed him and the moist heat trickled down between his legs along his tightening testicles. Her legs raised and lowered her body and her muscles tightened inexorably as she rode him. She licked her fingertips and rhythmically rubbed the hood of her clitoris, causing spasms to vibrate through her pussy and her wetness to melt like butter. Deep inside she felt the head of his penis swelling and his breath become labored and fast.

The bed creaked and his wrists were pulling on the belt, wanting to hold her. "Oh, damn, I'm gonna come!" he yelled. Stan's body shook and his legs straightened out stiff as he thrust his pelvis up. Kelly leaned back and tightened her vaginal walls around him and pulled up, dragging his length against her clit. They came almost simultaneously. He gushed out all the hot fluids burning deep within him. Her second orgasm was more relaxing. She lay there on top of him, feeling his heart finally slow to a normal state. The slippery warmth between them, a reminder of this dream come true.

"I better take you home. I wouldn't want you to get in trouble," Stan said.

They held each other tight and then got dressed and ready to go. As they walked, she held tightly onto his strong arm, allowing him to guide her up the steps to her apartment. It was strange to think she had this handicap, and you would never know except for her dark glasses and cane. When they'd said blind date, they weren't kidding.

The Awakening

ဢ

Floyd came into the house, late as usual and shivering from the night air. After getting a drink of water and warming up, he walked into the bedroom. On the bed was Ana. He stared longingly at her as she slept so quietly.

She was a vision. The light from the full moon cast a glow across her body. The satin sheets and moonlight made her look like she was sculpted out of stone. She was perfectly still and her attributes were visible through the clinging bedding. She lay on her side with her hand above her head. The curve of her back and the way she had her leg pulled up only accentuated her round, firm ass.

He felt playful. He crawled to the side of the bed, pulled the covers a little and slipped underneath them from the bottom. As the bed bobbled, Ana rolled onto her back, exposing even more of her ample breasts and cold-stiffened nipples. Floyd's legs were still on the floor and he moved up a little more, positioning himself between her legs.

Floyd took in a deep breath, smelling the perfume from her bath and her natural womanly scent. He softly rubbed his face against her leg. As if it were a signal to his sleeping beauty, Ana parted her legs slightly and sighed. Of course Floyd thought this was an open invitation to continue. She had told him she loved being awoken like this. As he snuggled up closer to her legs, she parted them even wider but was still deeply sleep.

Floyd moved up between her legs to his favorite spot where it was always warm and smelled heavenly. In one movement Ana picked her leg up and swung the blankets away from her body, totally exposing the glory of her nudity.

One leg was propped up and the other lying flat, dangling off the side of the bed. Her breasts were pert and the nipples were small and tight.

Floyd repositioned himself and kept moving his nose closer to his destination. He peeked up to see if she was still asleep. Ana giggled as his face brushed against her thighs. His hair tickled her soft skin. Floyd couldn't wait any more. He took one long lick of the outer lips of her vagina and growled like an animal in heat. Ana moaned as Floyd did it again.

Suddenly Ana's eyes opened up as Floyd put his cold nose into her hot box.

In shock, she looked down between her legs and screamed, "Floyd! You get the hell out of my bed you dumb frickin' mutt!!"

With his tail between his legs, Floyd jumped off the bed and ran for his doggy door. I guess dogs aren't always man's, or woman's, best friend.

The Homecoming (Peter and Susan Part 3)

80

Peter and Susan finished their dinner date. The movie was a little dull but Tom Hanks can't always make a perfect movie. The restroom had been a moving experience for Peter, but they still had agreed not to have sex. Oral sex didn't count according to Susan.

As they pulled up to her apartment, nervousness and hope swelled in Peter's heart, as did the erection in his pants.

"Now we agreed to become better friends and not let sex rule our relationship," Susan said.

"I know," Peter grumbled. "But it would be nice to get a kiss goodnight."

The car motor was rumbling as she leaned over and softly kissed his lips. The sweetness of her kiss was like tasting the finest wine. The softness of her lips moistened his thirsty mouth. He was absurdly aroused and dumbfounded by what he should do. Even though his mind knew Susan's rules, his dick had its own thoughts about the matter.

As they kissed in the car, he started feeling like a schoolboy on a date with a cheerleader. She was on a pedestal, a woman all men desired, although few were graced with her presence. Their kiss became a little more passionate and he reached his hand up to touch her breast through the fabric. Her moans were subdued, but it was apparent that she didn't mind his touch. Her tongue licked along the line of his lips, and then she slid it into his mouth. The sweet taste of her was like a strawberry, succulent and always pleasing.

Susan was warming and wetting to his caress. She leaned forward and took his face in her hand, longingly pulling him to her. As she leaned, her breast pushed more fully into his hand. Susan turned her head, resting it on Peter's shoulder, and he kissed her neck. Her hand found its way to his crotch and slid up and down along the front of it. She unzipped his pants and slipped her hand inside, grasping his cock. She kissed him again, opening her mouth as she felt him throb in her hand. Peter was growing extremely aroused and wanted to disregard the rules. He wanted her badly.

"We can't, Peter. We just can't," Susan said sadly.

"If we are going to become more than lovers, we can't base everything on sex." She hung her head and continued, "I want you so much but we better not."

Peter mumbled under his breath, disappointed but understanding. As they straightened themselves in the car, Peter noticed she hadn't let go of him yet and his penis still throbbed in her hand. "Oh sorry," she said, releasing him and zipping his tight pants back up carefully.

"Can I at least walk you to the door?"

"Of course," she said.

As he opened the door for her, he held his jacket in front of himself so his erection wasn't so apparent. The moonlight and streetlamps dimly lit the street and the stars filled the sky. The smell in the air was crisp and fresh and clean. His mind was on the smell of her perfumed body, and his eyes studied her body through her clothes. She walked slowly with him, holding his waist and resting her head on his shoulder again. At the door she rustled through her purse for her keys and fumbled about until they fell to the ground. Susan bent over, picking them up, and her ass pressed against his hard dick. The flinch and deep sigh from Peter showed her how badly he desired her.

As she stood up and faced the door, Peter stood behind her and took her shaking hand in his. He kissed the back of her neck, causing her to shiver, and guided the key to the lock while pressing his erection firmly against her. It was a perfect fit along the crease of her ass. Peter reached his hand around

S.L. Carpenter

and pressed against her abdomen and then moved it down between her legs. Susan moaned and reached her hand up and around his neck as he rubbed between her legs vigorously.

They stood there in her doorway. She was being felt up by a man who made her feel so free and uninhibited that the difference between right and wrong didn't matter anymore. This was pure, unbridled lust.

She managed to open the door and Peter followed close behind. She tossed her purse and keys onto the floor and turned around. She kissed Peter again, delving her tongue into his mouth, and grabbed his hands as he dropped his jacket. She licked down his chin to his Adam's apple. She took his hands and placed them on her shoulders. Frantically, she pulled his shirt open and pulled his undershirt up. Then she seductively undid the buttons on her blouse. The fabric of the bra was smooth against Peter's chest and abdomen as she slowly edged her underwear down her legs and slipped them off. She rose up and put the panties in his smiling mouth. Then she lowered herself back down, spreading her legs as she squatted.

The taste and fragrance in his mouth were a temptation and her soft skin caressing his body made him thirst for her. She released the front clasp of her bra and dragged her nipples against his abdomen and down the front of his pants. With her fingers she unhooked and unzipped his pants and they fell to his ankles. She playfully licked him through the fabric of his underwear. Peter kept his hands on her shoulders, knowing it was what she wanted. Susan molded her breasts around his extremely aroused cock and moved up and down kissing his flexing stomach. Peter felt her wetness as she rubbed her pussy up and down against his leg.

Susan suddenly stood up and walked into the dining room. She leaned against the table with her head hung low.

"I can't, Peter. Is this all we are? Just sex partners?" Susan asked, desperate for an answer.

Peter waddled over to her, pants at his ankles. "I don't know what we are. All I know is there is something very strong between us. And we can either let it flow or let our damned pride and thoughts about what we should do get in the way of what we feel."

Peter held her tight against his chest, not wanting to let her go. "All I know is I want you more than I've ever wanted any woman and that scares me. I think about you all the time and just the thought of you gets me hard." Susan looked down and saw his point.

"Well show me then," she whispered as he stepped back. She leaned back and pulled her skirt up showing him what she wanted.

Peter adjusted the front of his underwear and pulled off his shoes and pants from his legs. The fragrance from her pussy was that of an inferno of built-up passions. He knelt in front of the table and looked into her pink, wet flesh and got even harder. His mouth melted as he kissed her lower lips. Susan sat up, wanting to see him eat her out. She saw his tongue lick up the flowing juices. As he inserted a finger to feel her around him, her eyes closed. She moaned as his finger glided in and out and his tongue flicked her swollen clit. Her arms were weakening but she still wanted to see it. She threw her head back and groaned, then smiled and giggled when he teased the opening with little kisses. Peter looked up to see her face glowing but she grabbed his head forcing it back down.

"Oh god. I'm going to come, Peter!" she screamed. "Please, let me feel you inside of me."

Peter stood up tugging frantically at his underwear and bent his hardened cock down to the opening of her pussy and watched it disappear into her. The tightening muscles snuggly embraced him as his body met hers. The slow smooth rhythm of his strokes weren't enough. She wanted what was building inside them to erupt like a volcano.

"Take me, Peter. *Make* me feel you deep inside of me."

Peter grabbed her, pulling her from the table, and turned her body around to bend her over it. He held her hips and slammed deeply into her. Susan moaned and whimpered at the sheer force of his thrusts. Her body was on fire as he pressed her breasts against the cold tabletop. As her hair flowed over the edge, she could see her breath fog against the surface. The contrast from the heat burning inside her and the cool surface sent a rush of tingles up her body. With every moan, her breathing increased until she was for gasping for air as her excitement mounted. She pressed her body up off the table, arching her back and pushing her ass against his body as he moaned loudly. Feeling the pressure begin to peak, the tips of her fingers turned white as she pushed them hard against the tabletop desperately trying to hold herself up. He reached his massive hands under her breasts and clenched them tight while her nipples protruded from between two fingers. As he buried himself deep into her, his hands tightened and squeezed the nipples. Each stroke was a mixture of unbridled lust and a desire so profound it only made sense for it to happen.

He grabbed hard on to Susan's hips and jerked against her. Her inner walls were wet and the way she caressed the skin of his cock was soothing and arousing.

She raised her leg, setting it up on the table. Peter touched her ass as he kept grinding into her. Reaching under her leg, Susan rubbed her clit gently as Peter's thrusts massaged her from inside. She held the edge of the table, trying to keep her balance. Susan wept and the convulsing ripples of her pussy made Peter understand the orgasm of a woman in a whole new way. Hearing the short bursts of her breath and feeling the shaking of her body, he felt the tidal wave coming. He splashed his hot wave through her over and over again then he collapsed on top of her.

His body was warm and his breaths more controlled. His once hard cock was spent and semi-erect between her legs, still wet from their sexual encounter.

"Damn, you make me feel so alive," Peter whispered in her ear as he started to stand up.

"And you make me feel so...so, *jeez* you made me a mess!" Susan said smiling.

They slowly got themselves straightened out and dressed. Peter was hesitant about asking to stay the night. They kept gazing at each other wondering where their relationship was heading. As they walked into the entryway Susan looked at Peter then looked up the stairs.

"Susan, I respect you and think we should take our time like you wanted. We don't know where or how much this will grow, but let's enjoy what we have. I'm going to be a gentleman and go now, out of respect and because I feel that's what you want." Peter smiled feeling proud of his restraint. He knew they would continue seeing each other because this was more than a few chance encounters. They were meant to be together.

At the doorway she kissed him softly and stood looking at him and said, "You know, I appreciate what you said." Peter smiled. "But what I really wanted was to have you stay here tonight so we could fuck all night. Goodnight."

As the door closed, Peter stood in the dim light, wondering how a man could be so damn stupid.

The Island Paradise

છ

After all those hard days and tireless nights of working, Bianca was finally enjoying the ultimate vacation on a little-known Caribbean island.

Bianca was a tall brunette with dark brown hair falling to the middle of her back. She had a nice figure, not too big, not too small. Even though she was an attractive woman, she didn't have a boyfriend at the moment and hadn't for quite a while. She'd tried, but every time she liked someone the lies and deceptions destroyed any possible relationship. And her fear of catching something kept her from one-night stands, making it even harder. So she concentrated on her career. Being the president of a dot-com business kept her traveling and she had enough money to do whatever she wanted.

Currently she was rather bored by the lack of direction from the guide so Bianca decided to venture off the trail a little on a nature walk.

Through the brush she found an absolutely gorgeous spot with a small waterfall and pool of water just big enough for swimming. She didn't see anyone around so she stripped down to her swimsuit, leaving the T-shirt and wrap beside the pool, and dived into the cool water. It was breathtaking. After swimming around the water for a while, she ended up by the waterfall. She climbed up onto the small sandy ledge below it and let the water splash against her body.

The water cascaded down her body as if it were another layer of skin. She leaned her head back and let the cold water rinse her hair. Laughing slightly for feeling like a shampoo commercial, she flung her wet hair around. For some unknown reason her body seemed more alive and sensitive than usual. Her nipples were always a focal point for her sexual pleasure so she pulled at them through her bathing suit. Shock waves raced through her body to the point between her thighs. Warmth crept through her and she leaned back; the cool water caressed her passion-heated flesh, cooling the fire burning within. Forgetting where she was, Bianca slipped her hand into her bikini bottoms and rolled her fingers against the lips between her legs. The urge to probe herself took over as she pulled upwards on the opening of her vagina, exposing the top of her clitoris and letting the water strike it directly. It sent tingles through her body.

She looked up and saw a figure racing across the small beach. Stunned, she stopped and saw a local tribesman kneeling on the side of the beach, bowing to her. Bianca laughed as he bowed one last time then dived in and started swimming toward her. He rose from the water then knelt again and took her hands in his. She couldn't understand what he was saying but his motions and mannerisms seemed to imply he worshiped her.

He motioned to his chest saying, "Gores. Gores." He seemed to be telling her his name. She felt no fear of him as he stood up. He was a little taller than she was, muscular, with dark skin, and somewhat handsome features. And she was so aroused and so overwhelmed by his constant admiration that she took his hand and slipped it beneath her bikini top and onto her breast, moaning softly as he grasped it in his large hand. He knew exactly what to do as he knelt in front of her and kissed her nipples through the material then pulled it off her. Her nipples, already sensitive, stuck out as he sucked them. Gores switched from one to the other. And he slowly slid her bottoms down her thighs, caressing her legs as he inched the clothing downward. Then moved his hands up the back of her legs to her ass. He pressed his face against her tummy and licked her bellybutton. Without care she lifted her leg up and pressed her flaming bush against his face. His hot tongue darted inside her.

Bianca ran her fingers through his hair tugging on it each time he slid his tongue against her pulsating clit. He abruptly stood up and kissed her on the mouth. She was like butter melting to his hot touch. She reached down and grasped the pulsing hardness trapped in his loincloth. She loosened the tie in the front and it fell to the ground. Gores moaned as she stroked it in her hand, rubbing it against her own sweltering opening, almost daring him to enter her. They kept kissing and he moaned at her touch.

The excitement and arousal were almost unbearable. She felt a tingling racing through her veins as she lifted up on her tiptoes, bit his neck and wrapped her leg around him. Guiding his stiffness along the lips of the moist opening between her legs was too much for him. He lifted Bianca up and moved her into the small cavern behind the waterfall.

There was a small patch of sand between the rocks, big enough for two people to be hidden from view. Like an animal he laid her face down and reached under her tummy, lifting her ass up. Gores moved behind her, spreading her legs apart as he lifted her higher. Bianca didn't care; she was in such a state of need she just wanted to feel him inside her. He entered her wetness and she shuddered, never having had a man of his thickness penetrate her before. Her arms weakened against the sand as she felt him fill her to the hilt, his abdomen pressed against her ass. He pulled his thick hardness from her and she shook and came. The intense spasms of her vaginal walls contracted around his manhood. She could almost feel the veins throb with his pounding heart from the tightness of her pussy contractions. The constant friction against her clitoris with every stroke he pulsed into her forced her orgasm to go on and on.

When Bianca recovered from her near-unconscious state, she leaned farther down till her breasts pressed against the ground and she could feel him penetrate deeper into her, almost pressing against her cervix with every thrust. The melting feeling was warm and comforting but he still kept driving into her. The mist from the waterfall filled the tiny cavern they were in, and the heat they generated should have made it steam as the droplets hit their bodies. Bianca was in another world as the pleasure from him driving into her deeper and harder made her climb to ecstasy again. He grasped her shoulder and put his other hand on her hip as he pushed longer and harder strokes into her. Their sex was becoming primal. Gores started groaning and she shrieked sharply from the pain and pleasure as her knees started to hurt from the intensity of his thrusts.

Bianca knew what she wanted and reached back to push him away. She threw him onto his back and took over. She dragged her nails over his nipples and hairy chest. With her hand she ran her fingers up his thighs to his testicles and licked her lips, and then she licked the tip of his gleaming penis. As she lowered her mouth over it, the thickness swelled. Tasting her own juices on him excited her as she sucked all the way up to the tip, causing a popping sound as she released him. She looked into his eyes; they begged for release. And the slowly gathering droplets on the tip of his throbbing manhood were a signal that he was close to erupting.

Acting more like a cat than a woman, she clawed at his chest and flicked her tongue on his penis. Then she bit his tightening stomach and climbed on top of him. Again she shuddered as she lowered herself onto the incredibly hard thickness. She lifted her legs up, balancing on Gores, making sure he was as deep as possible. He moaned. Bianca looked into his eyes and saw them roll back in his head. She controlled the pace of their lust and she wanted it fast. She leaned back, moving up and down, and made him thrust from below. She felt her vaginal walls stretching and convulsing. She started shaking as she orgasmed. Without warning he exploded inside her with such force it lifted her up and she screamed, "Oh god yes!" and came again. Over and over she felt his essence burst from his loins. Their fluids trickled from her as they stopped and she collapsed on his chest. Feeling

* * * * *

The next day at work a faxed memo arrived for Bianca's CEO.

Dear Sir,

It has come to my attention that an extensive and difficult problem has popped up in the islands that needs my personal attention. I alone must find the strength to diligently work through each and every person's needs in this matter, dedicating as much time as it may take to get the job done. Please forward my mail, as I am not sure how long I will be here. There seem to be at least a hundred individual issues that I must attend to.

Thank you and I'll keep in touch with my progress.

Bianca

NAKED LUST

ஐ

Dedication

&

I want to thank everyone who encourages me to write my strange views on things.

This book was my release and one woman was a real inspiration to me.

Shelly, this one's for you.

Trademarks Acknowledgement

&

The author acknowledges the trademarked status and trademark owners of the following wordmarks mentioned in this work of fiction:

Chia Pet: Joseph Enterprises, Inc.

Popsicle: Unilever Supply Chain, Inc.

Scooby Doo: Hanna–Barbera Productions, Inc.

The Visit

∞

Anna heard the door close and the walls of the trailer trembled.

"Just a second. I'm in the restroom," she called out.

She stared into the small mirror and wiped the little smears of her eyeliner from the corners of her deep green eyes. Anna primped her hair a bit and flattened the wrinkles in her dress. She wanted to look her best for her man.

As she walked out of the bathroom, she took one last peek at herself. *Why was she going through this again?* she thought.

She saw him push his shoes off with his feet and climb up on the bed, resting his head on the thin pillow. On the bed he lay waiting. His body tanned from the hot summer sun. Muscles flexed across his chest and abdomen with a hint of hair peeking from the waistband of his already unbuttoned pants. The tattoos on his arms were a sign of the bad-boy image so many women found attractive.

It was sad that they had to meet in a place like this. Nobody saw them. This was their special trashy rendezvous.

Anna's thin, flowered dress hung on her loosely. She wore nothing underneath except a red thong. The floor was even hot as she walked barefoot across it. The blistering heat made her body sweat but inside she burned hotter. Lust filled her soul and she became wet with want.

In a dance of sinful release, Anna crept forward, swaying back and forth, untying the thin strings on the front of her dress. It excited her to strip for a man. She controlled what was happening and that excitement turned her on. She watched as her man rubbed his hand over the front of his jeans where an obvious bulge had risen. Her seduction was working.

"Damn, baby, you are so fucking hot." His deep voice echoed in her head as she continued her dance.

She finally reached the bed and stood before him. The nervous tingles of excitement made her skin electrify. She was now in desperate need of what she came there for. She wanted her man to take her.

She shrugged her shoulders and tugged down on her dress. It fell along her naked flesh, revealing her tight, erect nipples. The scent of her desire filled the room. She knelt down and picked up the dress to lay it at the foot of the bed then locked eyes with him again.

He now sat admiring her supple body. She could see the hunger in his eyes as he swallowed hard and rested his rough hand on her hip as he moved her closer and between his legs hanging off the bed.

He gazed into Anna's eyes while he pulled the last remaining piece of clothing from her body. The red fabric of her thong was wet and clung to her swollen pussy as he gently pulled it down her thighs. It finally fell to her feet and she stepped out of it. She felt a hot rush of exhilaration as he pushed his face to her abdomen and took in a deep breath and moaned.

"I miss the smell of you." His tongue licked just below her abdomen and across the sensitive flesh of her pubic bone. "Damn, you feel and taste good."

Anna swallowed as her eyes fluttered. She wanted this. She was a neglected woman and this tryst would satisfy a need suppressed within her for too long.

Stepping back, she took a deep breath and pushed against his shoulder. "Lie down," she commanded.

He lay back on the small bed as she wanted and put his hands behind his head. The muscles on his chest and abdomen glistened as they flexed. Anna knelt down and tugged on his pant legs, pulling them off. His cock was hard and rested against his body.

Anna bit her lip. An evil hunger crept through her as she spread his legs apart and laid her bare flesh to his. Her face rested against his chest and she felt his heartbeat. His rigid cock pressed against her and she slowly began descending his torso with kisses. When his cock split the space between her perky breasts, she moaned and moved her body side to side, letting the rigid hardness brush against her sensitive nipples. His moans accentuated her own arousal.

She reached her hands to each side of her breast and pushed them together, making a narrow passage between. In a rhythmic motion, she went back and forth, letting her breasts feel the sensations of being fucked.

He lowered his hand to the back of Anna's head and ran his fingers through her hair. She could tell he was enjoying this as much as she was. She looked up then slid her body lower to let her lips rest against the head of his rock-hard cock.

She could taste the small trickle of anticipation as her tongue wet the swollen head. His soft moans guided her tongue and lips while she teased him.

Anna sucked his cock and her pussy began to ache with want. Her lips were being pried apart by his cock and her pussy wanted to feel him too. She hadn't been fucked properly in a long time and this may be her only chance for another span of time so she wanted to savor it.

She reached up and grabbed the shaft of his cock tight. She quickly began to suck and stroke, making it swell even more.

With a pop she let him free. "You wanna fuck now? You wanna fuck me, baby? Come on. I want you now."

He sat up and grabbed Anna. His movements were rough and forceful. She smiled as she let him take over since she was going to get what she needed so bad. He groped at her body, as if he hadn't felt the softness of a woman's flesh before. His hungry mouth suckled on her nipple as Anna ran her fingers through his coarse, black hair. She hung her head, letting the locks of auburn fall around her face. She closed her eyes and let him take over.

He grabbed her hips and lowered her to the bed, rolling her onto her stomach. His hands caressed and massaged her back. He stroked her spine down to her round ass. With a playful smack, he spanked her. Anna giggled then wiggled from the sting.

His hand found its way between the split of her cheeks and he slowly rubbed around her anus. She didn't like anal play but her pussy was so electrified, any kind of play made her cream with want.

He lowered his finger and found the wetness and heat of a woman on fire. With a moan, Anna instinctively spread her legs a bit wider and arched her ass upward. With her pussy more exposed, he began making circular movements with his fingers and slipped them into her slick pussy. Each time he'd brush against her clit, she'd shudder and tense.

God, she wanted him to stop and just fuck her.

He stopped and Anna opened her eyes to see him holding his cock, staring at her naked body.

"Fuck, baby, I'm about to pop seeing you like this. I can't take it anymore."

"Fuck me. Fuck me good, dammit. I want you now." Anna turned away and pushed her torso up off the bed. She looked between her dangling breasts and between her legs and saw him standing behind her, pushing down on his cock.

As he entered her tight pussy, she felt the muscles stretching to accommodate the thick head of his cock. It was a mixture of pain and pleasure. There was no mercy as he sank into her from behind until his body pressed against her ass. He breathed out a deep sigh. She lowered her face down to the pillow, letting him go deeper into her scorching-hot body.

With hard, driving thrusts, he began to pound into her welcoming pussy. Her fingers clawed at the cheap sheets on the battered, creaky bed. She closed her eyes, letting this beast of a man have his way with her.

How she got to this point, she didn't know. Lying facedown on a dusty bed in a rusty trailer and feeling like a twenty-dollar whore was a low point. The trickle of juice between her hot thighs soothed the burn of the man's rigid cock as he plunged in and out of her. He moaned loudly then paused, taking a deep breath before he began to hammer into her again.

Sex for Anna had become a distant dream. She was married but never saw her husband. Her love life was like her period, happening once a month. Things were so chaotic that her life was sucked into a pit of despair. She longed to be properly fucked by a man again. Her vibrator took the edge off but it wasn't real. It didn't hold her, it couldn't cuddle after she came for the fourth time.

She missed the simple pleasures like holding hands, cuddling by a fire, having a man eat and lick her pussy until she screamed. Like an addict, she needed her cock fix and substituted sucking her man off with lollipops and Popsicles. Her mouth ached to suck a cock and feel the essence of her lover coating her throat. And yes, she did swallow.

But instead she was treated like this. Like a cheap, streetwalking fuck. Traveling for three hours to a secluded desert area to let her man fuck her. This was the price she needed to pay to be with him. It all seemed so desperate, so downright nasty. She had to act like a whore to give her some sense of life. A way to feel partially alive until things returned to normal.

"Oh fuck, Anna, I'm gonna come, I'm..."

Anna pushed back against him as he ground his cock into her pussy. She wasn't going to get off this time, but he was. The hot spurts of his seed endlessly spraying within her. His body shuddered and he strained to keep inside her as his body relaxed.

Anna fell to the bed, sore and sticky. He lay across her, their skin wet from perspiration.

"Goddamn, I missed you."

"I missed you too, Ben." Anna began to cry. This all seemed so wrong.

"Don't cry, baby. It's okay." Ben stroked her hair from her cheek.

Bang, bang, bang.

"All right, Watson. Time's up. Get a move on, the next guy needs the trailer."

Anna rolled over and grabbed her clothes from the end of the bed. "I can't stand this shit anymore, Ben. You're my husband and I have five more years of just these conjugal visits. Fuck you!"

The Best Men — Part One

The mirror didn't lie. Shelly stared at herself after splashing water over her blushed cheeks. She drew in a deep breath and tried to compose herself. This was almost impossible to do. It was hard to regain a cool attitude after having a man — well, having him — do what he had done to her.

She was already late for her weekly morning gathering at the coffee shop with the girls. She'd be given the third degree as to what kept her. Shelly was never late. Even her monthly periods were on time. She even had the little red dots on her calendar done six months in advance and she hit each one. In a way that was kind of sick.

At a little over five feet tall, she was a petite woman. Her hair was straight, brown and swayed lightly over her shoulders. Over the past few months her life had been utter chaos. Except for her love life. She had been freed and the inner slut awoken with a welcome jolt of excitement. Basically she had been getting properly fucked and satisfied. But she had kept everything low profile. She may be having a sexual awakening but she couldn't tell Gabe, the man she loved, because hearing about everything would break his heart.

Shelly wasn't a bad person. She just needed to keep these little affairs a secret. Sex like this wasn't a necessity, but it damn well felt like one.

Her relationship with Gabe was a good one. They shared a lot of the same likes and dislikes and lived pretty close to each other so they could see each other frequently. They had talked about moving in together but decided to wait until they someday were married.

She had a steady job and enjoyed the freedom she had. She wasn't ready to settle down quite yet. She loved Gabe but a few new men had entered the picture.

A quick shake and fluffing of her hair and she was ready to meet the girls. She strutted into the café with a bounce in her step and a glow to her smile. Shelly was a satisfied woman. Her aching pussy was proof of it.

* * * * *

"I can't believe Shelly's late," Robin said when she looked at her watch. "I thought I was anal, she's always bitching at us when we're late. We only meet once a week to catch up on gossip and things and she ends up fifteen minutes late."

Jaymi spoke up. "Speaking of anal. Did you girls see that show on cable last night about the *Hookers of Hollywood*? Almost all their clients wanted anal sex because their spouses wouldn't do it."

"Anal? Marv talked to me about it one time. I told him that if he wanted to try it that bad to get arrested and try it in county jail. Anal sex is a pain in the ass." Robin paused, noticing what she had just said.

The ladies all giggled as Shelly walked up to them.

"And where exactly were you?" Robin asked.

"I'm so sorry. I was detained." Shelly could barely contain the need to giggle and scream. *If they only knew*, she said to herself. The glares and raised eyebrows from the girls told their feelings at her delay.

Jaymi tapped on Shelly's shoulder and whispered in her ear.

Opening her eyes wide, Shelly reached around and pulled the back of her skirt from her thong. She had tucked it through her panties by accident in her haste. After last night, she was lucky she still had underwear at all.

There are small signs people see that give away hidden things. Shelly sat down and when her rear hit the chair, she gave her friends a sign.

"Oh shit, that hurts! Damn, my ass is still sore." Before she caught herself, two of the women had spewed coffee and the other had the eyes of an owl.

"Pardon? Your what?" Jenny wiped the coffee off her chin. "Weren't we just talking about butts and anal stuff?"

"Uhhh…"

"All right, spill it. Who have you been seeing now?" Robin wasn't too shy to ask the obvious question.

Shelly wasn't the type to talk about her sex life but things had changed so much the last few months. "Wes came over."

Robin looked at the other girls and said, "Wes, not sure we've ever met Wes."

"He's kinda quiet. He just shows up at my place when he wants sex—er—or dinner, well, you know."

"So he's a sort of fuck buddy?" Robin wasn't one to politely mix words. She was more to the point.

With a smile Shelly replied, "I guess that's a good way to say it." She motioned to the waitress after turning her coffee cup over. A little caffeine pick-me-up would hit the spot.

"So what happened? Come on, Shelly, we girls don't get to go out and have different men. Our sex lives are more like a nudge and a slam-bang-suck-my-wang kind of sex. We're married and most of our excitement happens when we get a new erotic book by S.L. Carpenter."

"What? You want me to tell you about my sex life?" Shelly grinned as she mixed cream and sugar into her coffee.

"Fucking duh, well, yes. What happened?"

Shelly took a sip from her cup and added two more packs of cream and another sugar. "All right, I'll tell you but you can't say anything. Gabe can't find out about this. Woman's vow of secrecy, right?"

The ladies all nodded in agreement and huddled around Shelly.

Shelly took a deep breath and remembered back to last night as she once again adjusted her sore ass on the vinyl seat. She hoped her description of the all-night carnal journey would cause a stir for her friends. As she started telling her story, she felt a wetness creep between her legs, and like a movie, it played out before her again...

Shelly paused when she came to the door. She slipped her key into the lock but she could hear noises coming from inside. After the door opened, she grabbed her keys with the jagged edges sticking out. A trick her Aunt Marie taught her.

"You're late, Sheryl." The man's voice was deep in tone and had a raspy echo.

She slowly opened the door and saw the dull, flickering light from the television blinking in the living room. She looked then sighed in relief.

It was Wes. He always called her Sheryl, everyone else called her Shelly but he had to be different. He also knew it pissed her off so he took delight in using it. She hadn't seen him in a month or so but he had a key to her apartment.

"Had a long day at work?" Wes mumbled, asking her the obvious.

She replied, "Yes, very long day. I need to get up early for work and then meet the girls in the morning for coffee. Our weekly ritual of bitching and chatting about life, that kinda stuff."

Wes sat stoic in his chair. Shelly waited for a response but he just continued sitting there staring at the television. She looked to see his hair messy and dark. He wore his standard black T-shirt and ragged jeans.

"You haven't been around for a while. You okay?" she asked while tossing her coat over the small dining room chair. She tossed her keys into the gold bowl on the table. It was used to hold extra change and her keys so she always knew where they were.

"Yeah, but I'm pretty horny. Been sitting here thinking about your tight little pussy for hours."

She swallowed and took a deep breath. Wes was the typical bad boy all women wanted. Crass and he tended to sound rude, but his words were direct. He was darkly handsome with an aura of confidence surrounding him.

They met a while back at a party. He had been drinking then suddenly came over to her and stared directly at her chest. After licking his lips, he looked at her and spoke. "You want to stay here at this boring party or go to my car and fuck?"

First impressions are important to Shelly and Wes impressed her. She had also been drinking and even with her inhibitions slightly exposed, she wasn't going to turn her "slut" attitude on. She was attracted to him but she wasn't that easy. So she waited a few hours *then* fucked him in the car.

Fucking on the first date wasn't her usual style, but something triggered her libido and it was intense. The darkness, the moon roof open and riding his thick cock. The cool night air didn't keep their heat from fogging the windows. Everything was so incredibly primal with this basic fucking until she triggered the car alarm and the lights flashed off and on in the car just when she came. Her parents haven't asked her over since.

Wes now only showed up sporadically and it was usually when he wanted to fuck. She never worried about commitment or anything along those lines.

But tonight she was tired. Exhausted was a better word for how she felt. Maybe he'd understand and let her just rest and watch television. She grabbed a beer from the fridge and a glass of ice water. Walking around his chair, she handed him the beer and sat on the floor in front of him. She wiggled her shoulders to move his legs apart, leaning against them.

"What are you watching?"

He twisted the cap off his beer and flipped it onto the table beside him. "Some stupid movie on cable. You know, fake tits and bad acting."

Shelly shook her head. "Oh, those type of movies."

"Well, you don't keep any good porn around and I had to improvise so I rented one through the cable company."

She just knew this conversation was going to lead to something so Shelly decided to cut it off. "I had a bad day. I'm tired and just need to go to bed."

"So do I," he quickly responded.

"Noo, not like that. You know, sleep, rest. I have to get up early tomorrow and I think I caught a cold. My throat is sore."

"I know something that would coat your throat, Sheryl." He tugged at his crotch in typical male fashion.

Ignoring his obvious hints, she sipped her ice water. The movie was worse than expected. The women were all big-breasted blonde bimbos who leaned toward lesbian sex. Even though it wasn't her cup of tea, the constant moaning was getting to her.

Watching the women tangled up in a sixty-nine position and licking at the shiny folds of each other's pussies caused Shelly's to twitch with want. Maybe a little envy had crept into her mind. She may be tired but she might be able to muster the strength to let Wes eat her pussy for who knows, two hours?

She took another drink of water. The cold crept through her, soothing her burn. Shelly adjusted the way she was sitting. Her arousal beginning to make her uncomfortable.

Wes was transfixed and sporting a hard-on in his jeans that she peeked at when he took the last swig from his beer. He enjoyed porn and dirty stuff. Sexually, he had Shelly explore things she never could around someone like Gabe. She knew he couldn't see in front of her so she let her hand slide up her thigh.

The movie was getting more graphic in its content. There was one woman pouring lubricant oil over a glass dildo. The other woman lay spread wide, begging the first to fuck her with the toy. Shelly had memories of a glass rod she had bought a long time ago. There was something about when she chilled the dildo in the fridge. The cold would excite and make her so aroused that she came after only a few minutes of play.

Her pussy remembered it too, she could tell by the sudden moistening of her panties. Creeping her hand along her thighs, she moved her skirt up. When her fingers touched the space between her legs, she brushed against the wet fabric.

Shelly turned her body slightly and looked back to Wes. Her gaze moved down to his crotch. She could see the stretching of his pants. A sexual ache was making itself noticed. Again she looked up to Wes, this time she wanted something.

He shifted his gaze from the television to Shelly. "You want to suck my cock?"

His words caused her to almost squirm out of her clothes. His bluntness always got to her. She pressed her finger against her panties, daring herself to pull the thin, wet fabric aside and fondle her clit.

Wes tugged at the buttons of his jeans.

Shelly moved away and let him lift up, pulling his pants and underwear down his legs. She grabbed the back of his shoes and pulled them and his socks off. She then tugged his pants off and tossed them aside. His cock was hard, showing his excitement. With a thump he sat back down and scooted down in the chair. She grabbed both of his knees and spread his legs apart.

Looking back at the television, the two women were now being joined by a man. She knew Wes would like this part of the movie most.

"Why don't you warm up your pussy with your fingers like you were doing a few minutes ago."

Shelly didn't really care that he saw her playing. She wasn't normally an exhibitionist, but having him know what was happening was a big turn-on. She usually pleasured herself in the tub or on those late nights alone in her bed.

Moving closer, she leaned and flicked her tongue over the head of Wes' cock. "Don't worry about my hands, just feel what my mouth is doing."

She wanted to have his complete attention, therefore she wasn't just going to blow him, she was going to make his eyes roll.

His deep groan followed her descent on his cock. Her mouth was a vacuum, sucking as she rose back up. Shelly closed her eyes and listened to Wes' breathing. He'd breathe in and hold it as she filled her mouth with him. Each time he'd gently touch the back of her throat, almost making her gag.

"Fuck, you give good head, Sheryl. Fuck, fuck..." His words faded as he spoke.

Arousal flowed through her like blood. His comment made her give in. She began to stroke the outside of her underwear, which squeezed against her puffy pussy lips. She kept crossing and tightening her toes, trying to keep her own needs at bay. Her legs were flexing. The juices from her pussy trickled as she fought to keep from piercing the opening with a lone finger just to ease the pressure building inside.

With a pop, she let his cock free. With a gasp, she wanted to catch her breath.

Her head was spinning then became filled with the moans of passion echoing behind her.

She turned to look at the television. The women were on the bed with the guy. One was below on her back and the other doggy style above her. The man was fucking the girl on top and would pull out and let the woman below suck his shiny cock then he'd go back to fucking the top one.

Shelly couldn't take it anymore. She stood and unfastened the button on the side of her skirt. It fell along her legs to the floor. She turned around, facing away from Wes, and began to peel away her underwear. It stuck to her skin from the wetness of her pussy. She was bent over and a wave of heat rolled through her body.

Wes' hands grasped hard on her ass, squeezing and spreading the cheeks apart. He kissed the soft flesh of her bottom, teasing her. His tongue began at the sensitive base of her cunt and worked upward along the split of her cheeks. He tickled her anus with the tip of his tongue, sending jolts of excitement through her body.

"Oh shit, Wes. What are you doing?"

"Mmmm, I love this ass. Can't wait to fuck you, Sheryl."

She reached forward and held her balance on the television as Wes continued to fondle and lick her ass. She wasn't much for ass play but had dabbled in college. However it was nothing like this. Nothing this erotic. Her eyes looked at the movie before her. The guy was slamming hard into the woman bent over. He was sweating and the look in his eyes showed he was close. The woman moaned as she was being fucked and the other girl licked her pussy as the guy pulled back.

Shelly could only imagine the amount of pleasure the woman felt.

Heat shot through her body as Wes poked his finger into her pussy. Her knuckles whitened as she bent her back down, forcing her ass out. Like a fresh peach, she felt her juices begin to flow out.

"Damn, your cunt is so fucking wet."

Shelly threw her head back when Wes made a slurping sound as he tried to suck the juice from inside her cavern. A moan kept deep within a woman's body rose from Shelly. Wes was licking her pussy and up to her ass. The growls vibrated up her spine like a wave.

"Fuck, Wes, I don't know what you're doing, just don't fucking stop." Shelly's eyes closed and even though her legs were sore from bending over, the aches disappeared as he licked her.

"Mmm, Sheryl, you have my cock so hard I could cut glass with it."

The harshness and no-bullshit way Wes talked always stirred her. He was a bad boy that brought out the bad girl in her. She shook as Wes slid his finger into her pussy again. He pulled it out and she relaxed. Then a chill swept over her as he slid his slippery finger into her anus. His mouth kissed her rounded ass as he slowly breathed against her.

The sensations electrified her body. It wasn't painful but the pressure was different than anything she felt before. Her only foray into anal sex had been in college with her boyfriend, who had gotten her drunk and wanted to try something different. This wasn't awkward or disturbing. This actually felt good.

Wes kept kissing her ass as he moved his finger around in her anus and rolled his thumb between the fleshy folds of her pussy.

"I can't take this, Wes." Shelly was on the verge of letting go. Her mind a blur. "Fuck me, baby, fuck me now. I want to come."

Pulling loose, Wes stood and swept the few knickknacks off the top of the console television and pushed Shelly over it. The TV hummed beneath her and Wes rubbed his cock between her legs until he found the slick opening of her pussy. With a satisfying groan, he sank into her wet cunt.

Grunting, he ground his stomach against her ass. "Fuck, you are so damn hot."

Like a jackhammer, he pounded into her. The only problem was his knee kept hitting the volume button and the porn movie played louder and louder with each thrust.

Everything had built up and was now releasing in a rumbling of pleasure through Shelly's body. "I'm coming, Wes, oh fuck, I'm coming." Right as her orgasm rushed through her, the girl on the TV screamed, "Fuck me in the ass, you big-cocked bastard."

Wes thought it was Shelly and pulled his juice-soaked cock free and slowly pushed it into Shelly's ass.

Her head began to throb from the pounding of her heart. This was a dark desire she had wanted to experience but could never ask for. A taboo that had been hidden from past men in her life. Wes tapped into her darker side and he was tapping into it over and over.

With a shriek of pain, she shook and then began to come. Her body was so sensitive from everything that the feeling of Wes entering her ass became even more arousing. The tightness eased each time he pushed into her. She held the sides of the TV as Wes started fucking her more aggressively.

"Your ass is so fucking tight, baby. Oh yes, I have wanted to do this for a long time." His tone was filled with happiness and almost tearful.

Shelly began to feel the pleasurable jolts of pain shooting through her body. The slapping of their flesh was drowned over by the blaring sound of the porno and the people moaning below her. With a jarring push, Wes stopped.

The pressure was too much as he arched back, moaning, "Fuck, fuck, I'm gonna come, I'm gonna..." He stopped, fully buried in her ass. Hot spurts of seed shot deep within Shelly. She could feel the burn within her as he came over and over. Wes' body shook as he pulled out and continued to seep the seed from his loins down her thigh.

Wes rested his chest against Shelly for a moment, catching his breath. "Damn, Sheryl, you are such a fine woman. I think I'm going to stay here and fuck you all night."

As she lay on top of the TV, still blaring the sound of bad porno music, Shelly thought to herself, *This was incredible but it's not what I want.*

* * * * *

The girls all sat staring, faces flushed and mouths watering. She had just had the kind of sexual experience most of them dreamed about. Some had lived out such carnal carnival rides when younger but most were a bit taken aback by what their friend had done.

Jaymi cleared her throat and asked, "Um, Shelly — er — do you happen to have this Wes guy's number handy?"

After turning multiple shades of red, Shelly smiled and patted Jaymi on the back. "Sorry, I don't know when he'll show up or how to contact him. He just comes around when he wants sex, you know. And he comes over and over again."

The Date

&

The party was over and Will was going through all those anxious moments at the end of a date. He called it a date because after the company picnic he asked her to go out for dinner. So technically it was a date because he asked — and he ended up paying for dinner.

Alicia always seemed so shy and quiet. Will had seen her a few times at company functions but working among over a thousand people, he didn't get to see her very often. But tonight a few of their friends thought it would be nice to have them meet and set them up with each other.

Will's buddies knew he had been single for way too long after his bitchy girlfriend left him. Being pals and mainly being guys, they knew their friend was in need of getting laid. It's a male credo to try to get single buddies some pussy. The married guys knew *they* weren't getting it so they lived vicariously through their single friends.

The girls in Alicia's customer service department had also gone along with the plan to hook her up. They were tired of hearing her constant bitching and moaning about never finding the perfect guy. If they had to listen to her anymore, they were going to hire someone to kill her and hide the body in a shallow grave in the desert. A date with a guy in another department would be easier and they wouldn't have to dispose of the corpse. A good fucking would clean out the cobwebs in her head and between her legs.

Which brought them to tonight, in the car, in front of her condo.

Will leaned in for the move. He sensed it was time. Their idle chatter was becoming boring and he saw a look of longing in her eyes, making them shine. That...or her allergies were acting up.

Their lips met in a soft kiss. Alicia kissed him back so Will knew the attraction wasn't just one-sided. She brushed the wet tip of her tongue along his lips. Whispering between their mouths she said, "Would you like to come inside?"

Will wanted to come any way he could. The place didn't matter.

As the door swung open, Will saw a very clean and stylish condo. She took pride in her place, which he could tell because there were no empty pizza boxes, porno magazines or beer-can pyramids in the living room like he had at his apartment.

There was a leather couch in front of a nice gas fireplace that she lit while they talked. "Would you like a drink? I have some wine."

"Sure, that would be nice."

He watched as the silken green dress she wore clung to her curves. She pulled a couple of wineglasses and a bottle of wine from the small bar she had in the corner of the main room. Sitting on the couch, she set the glasses on the small glass table. Their conversation turned to worthless babble about everything from the weather to fax machines. This was definitely a night for romance and yes—sex.

Will leaned over to kiss her and a loud sound echoed from his ass. He jumped. "I swear it wasn't me, it's the leather."

Alicia raised her eyebrow and started to laugh. She knew.

They both laughed while they rolled around on the couch and made constant farting sounds that echoed 'round the room. Will lay back with his leg dangling down and felt a strange wetness around his ankle. He didn't want to look because Alicia had her tongue in his mouth and her hand was slowly creeping down his abdomen. His cock was standing straight and begging for her touch.

Will felt something tugging on his shoe and after a few moments he just had to look down. A little orange Pekinese dog was growling and gnawing on his seventy-five-dollar dress shoes. The wetness was a spreading stain on his suit pants where the dog had pissed. *Fucking mutt.*

Alicia had just brushed her palm against the head of his cock but sat up as he moved.

Don't stop!

"Aww, you met Puffy. He's my little buddy. Isn't he cute?"

Cute wasn't the word that came to Will's mind. "Yeah. But it looks like he had an accident on my pants."

"Oh no. I'm sorry. Bad Puffy, *bad* dog. He's a little protective sometimes." She reached to the end table and grabbed a few tissues, brushing them against the wet spot. "That's not going to help much."

She picked up the dog, holding it close to her face and scolding it. "Bad Puffy. You be nice to Will, all right?"

Will smiled. She looked so cute with her dog. His smile faded as he watched Alicia getting her lips and face licked by this mongrel. The critter was licking off her lip gloss with a lot of tongue and slobber. She set the dog back down and leaned back over to Will, kissing him again.

Now when it comes to getting some pussy, men will tolerate a lot of things they otherwise wouldn't. As Alicia's lips were bathing his mouth, still moist with dog spit, he looked over and saw Puffy licking his balls. A little doggy pink-headed warrior poked out.

Will suddenly felt a bit ill.

"Well, we'd better get you out of those pants so I can wash them."

The feeling of nausea vanished quickly as Will's own pink-headed warrior awoke once more at Alicia's words.

They walked into the bedroom and stood on opposite sides of the large white-covered bed that featured an assortment of pillows and other fluffy stuff.

"What's that?" Will pointed to a little carpet-covered step.

"Oh, that's so Puffy can get up onto the bed at night." She paused. "But tonight he's gonna stay down because I'm having you instead."

The lights were dim and sexy. The mood was perfect and romance filled the air.

They were both ready for the suggestive dance of seduction as they stripped, facing each other.

Will undid the buttons on his shirt slowly as he watched Alicia do the same. Tossing his shirt to the floor, he watched as Alicia let the silken fabric slither along her torso and accentuate the curves of her skin. He tugged the white tank top over his head and waited for his first prize. It was actually a set of prizes. Alicia reached behind her and unfastened her bra. Wiggling her arms, the bra loosened and two small silicone spheres fell out before she dropped her bra to the floor.

"Oh my God, I'm so embarrassed. I haven't had a man in so long that I padded my bra. I forgot." She looked ashamed but Will didn't mind. To him she was beautiful.

"No, baby, I don't mind at all. I hear women with smaller breasts are more responsive to having them sucked by their lover. I'm going to spend hours kissing and sucking on those." Will knew what to say. He'd read it in the *Idiot's Guide to Getting Laid*.

Will unfastened his pants. The slacks were loose and his boner was obvious as it protruded through his fly. He was ready for action.

Staring at Alicia, he realized how much he loved looking at sexy women undressing. His computer had bookmarks of multiple websites where he could watch women undressing and doing things with kitchen and bathroom appliances along with handheld devices. There was even one site with midget women, but that was for special occasions like his birthday or those Fridays when he was drunk and had eaten shellfish.

Anyway, he stood there, full of anticipation. He tugged down his tighty-whities and they fell to his ankles. Alicia raised an eyebrow and bit her bottom lip excitedly. She approved.

Coool. All those growth pills must have paid off.

It was now her turn to reveal the treasure. He watched as Alicia pulled down her skirt and underwear. In seconds she was naked before him and one thought immediately crossed Will's mind as his gaze fixed on her body.

I may need a weed-whacker.

He didn't think anything was wrong with a little patch of hair over the goodies. Some women go bare, others like some fur over the taco, but Alicia was more like a real healthy Chia Pet.

Will swallowed. He gazed back up to Alicia's face. She looked a little apprehensive and maybe embarrassed. This was the moment Will knew he needed to seal the deal. "God, you are *beautiful*, Alicia."

The perfect two-point shot was up — and *good.*

With a smile and a sigh, she peeled back the comforter and sheet and slid into the bed. Lying sexily on her hip, she patted the mattress beside her, beckoning Will to join her.

Will leapt at the chance to get into bed with a naked woman. The problem was he'd forgotten he still had his shoes, pants and underwear around his ankles. When he stepped forward, he tripped, falling face first onto the bed and slamming his knees on the wooden frame. His cock ended up stuck between the mattress and the box spring.

This must be how it feels to make love to an elephant.

The pain from his knees and a rapidly growing headache made him silently scream a few choice cusswords and several unrepeatable phrases. More than a few of which were physically impossible.

Finally kicking off his shoes, pants and underwear, Will hobbled to his feet and made it into the bed.

"Aww, you poor thing." Alicia rubbed his skin with her soft hands. "Let me check and make sure everything's okay."

Will lay flat on his back in a certain amount of pain. However, it quickly disappeared when Alicia lowered her warm mouth around his sore cock. This must be the bad medicine people talk about. Something bad feeling so good. Will lay there in a blissful state, finally getting some desperately needed attention to his cock. Her soft mouth was quickly sucking up and down his erection, giving him such pleasure he wanted to melt. The swollen head spread her lips apart and then she paused, letting the tip of her tongue wipe across the sensitive end. All the time, her hand stroked and squeezed his length.

Will was going out of his mind. "Oh no, Alicia, you have to stop." Will didn't want her to stop of course because his toes were curled, his balls tight and the urge to release the pent-up frustration filled his loins.

"Mmm, why?" she mumbled as she continued sucking his cock.

"I-I-I can't take much more. It's been a long time for me and I'm about to burst." Will tried to hold himself back by thinking of his grandmother naked, the church, how his team kept fucking up in the playoffs...anything to prolong this pleasure.

"Let me help. My mom taught me this trick." Alicia took Will's cock and wrapped her mouth around the head. Will felt her taking a deep breath then she bit down and blew hard on his cock.

He swore his eyes bulged out and he had horrible visions of his balls ending up like balloons, swelling and finally exploding. When she stopped blowing, she wrapped her fingers around his cock and squeezed. It's hard to be a grown man and cry, but tears welled in Will's eyes. What had started as a great blowjob suddenly turned into a *blow-up* nightmare.

After Alicia apologized for trying to turn Will's cock into a party favor, they continued their cuddling. Will, as promised, caressed and kissed on her tight, perky breasts. He loved the feel of soft skin covering the breast. How any gentle caress can cause a woman to purr with excitement. The skin would become hot and turn pink from arousal.

After a long, wet, luscious kiss, Will began to slide down Alicia's body. He was going downtown.

Will wasn't an expert but he enjoyed going down and giving a woman pleasure. The way his tongue and fingers made a woman squirm and moan really turned him on. The fragrance of passion was his ultimate aphrodisiac and he also knew that if he could take a woman to the brink orally, then when they fucked, the sex was that much more intense.

Creeping down Alicia's body, Will let his hands slide along the slopes and curves of her form. His tongue left a trail of glistening saliva as it followed the path traced by his fingers. He loved doing this.

Alicia moaned loudly when Will rested his palm against her pubis and then he gently parted her legs and settled between her thighs. He blinked a few times and had to squint closely to find the opening of her pussy through the forest of hair she had fertilized between her legs.

Taking a deep breath, he dove in. His mouth found her pussy and he let his tongue part the folds of flesh. Will kept his eyes closed—he had to because her hair kept poking at his eyelids while he licked at her clit. Alicia's moaning guided his journey. She wiggled and tightened her legs while Will ate her out.

He paused now and again to cough up a few renegade pubic hairs that found their way down his throat. He suddenly understood how cats got hairballs.

S.L. Carpenter

Before he could regain his breath, Alicia grabbed his head, yanking it back between her legs and grinding her pelvis against his face. Will kept his tongue out and licked frantically as Alicia guided him with sharp tugs on his hair.

"Oh my God, Will, I'm coming, I'm coming, oooh God, I'm…" Her voice tapered off.

Or at least it seemed to because she wrapped her thighs around Will's head, effectively shutting down his hearing. But she kept tugging his hair to bury his face against her pussy as she came.

When her spasms subsided, Will pulled back, gasping for air. His face felt as if it had been scrubbed with a scouring pad and he burned with what was probably a reddish rash on his cheeks and upper lip.

"Oh, Will, I want you to fuck me, baby. Fuck me now…" Alicia lay back on the bed, a thin sheen of sweat covering her chest. Will caught his breath and slid his fingertips over her abdomen to the nipples that were straining for his touch.

Knowing he needed protection, he climbed over her and reached for his pants where there was an emergency condom tucked into his wallet. It had been in there so long there was a visible imprint of the ring on the leather. He knelt and ripped open the package with his teeth. Five-year-old lubricant has a distinctive taste he discovered he really didn't want in his mouth. Squeezing the package as he ripped it open didn't help. Alicia rolled onto her side to watch him put the condom on.

Will almost cried as the rubber broke when he tried to sheathe himself. He was definitely having one of *those* days.

"Let me get one of mine. I've got some right here in the drawer." Alicia rolled onto her stomach and fussed in her beside table.

Looking at her nice, round ass, Will quickly forgot all his troubles. He noticed there was a small tattoo on her lower back and he leaned in for a closer look.

It read *Insert cock here* with an arrow pointing downward to her ass. Will grinned to himself.

Cool. A woman who comes with instructions.

"Here." She saw Will staring at her ass, holding his cock. She smiled as he took the condom. "I know what you want. You're a naughty boy, Will." Alicia pushed her body up and looked back as Will put the condom on.

Finally. With rising excitement, he positioned himself behind her.

Will grabbed her hips and pulled her small frame back onto his hard, thick cock. They had both waited for this all night. As he entered her, Alicia moaned and lowered her head to the pillow, closing her eyes. Will watched as he sank in and out of her pussy with ease. It was amazing—incredible. Better than any hand cream or blow-up doll.

His thrusts quickened as he became more aroused by her moans of pleasure.

"Oh shit, you feel so fucking good." Will leaned his head back and groaned.

"Oh, baby, you wanna fuck me in the ass? You want to? You know you want to." Alicia wiggled as Will sank into her pussy once more.

Pulling out, he felt a little lightheaded. He was so turned on he thought all the blood from his brain must have drained into his cock. He held the slippery tip and pushed it slowly into Alicia's anus. The tightness was so arousing he thought he would erupt then and there. He squeezed his eyes shut and only stopped when his body touched her ass.

His fantasies were becoming realities as the night unfolded.

"Oh, Will, this is so fucking *hot*, I'm almost there again. Fuck me harder!" Alicia started to squeal and moan, adding intensity to what was happening between them.

Will groaned in ecstasy, knowing he was about to explode. He leaned back and felt a sudden blinding pain shoot through his body all the way to his mind, sending waves of agonizing darkness across his brain.

He screamed.

Will came to, opening his eyes to see a dimly lit hospital room. Alicia was dozing in the chair beside the bed. It was confusing and scary.

"Oh, you finally woke up. Thank goodness. I was *sooo* worried." Alicia reached out and took his hand.

"What happened? What the fuck am I doing in a hospital?" Will managed to croak the words from a throat that was sore as if he'd been screaming for hours.

Alicia stroked his fingers soothingly. "Well, somehow Puffy got into the bedroom when he heard me crying from the orgasm I was having. He thought you were attacking me and he...well...he defended me."

She paused and squeezed his hand. "He saw your balls swinging and hitting my ass and bit them. It was rather difficult for them to stop the bleeding and it took quite a while. Eventually we found one of them—but the other...well, we think he..."

Will quickly pulled his hand away from Alicia's and grabbed for his family jewels. There was a bulky bandage, almost like a diaper, covering his package. He painfully reached into the diaper to find to his horror his cock was missing its two travel buddies.

"I-I he—" Words failed him as he stared helplessly at Alicia.

"I know, baby. I was terribly upset too." Then she smiled reassuringly. "But don't worry. Puffy's going to be just fine."

The Bitter Divorce

෨

Sela sat in her red cloth-covered recliner. Her robe kept her in a cocoon of warmth and pink bunny slippers kept her toes from falling off because of frostbite. The steam from the tea filled her nose as she breathed in the lemon aroma. A fire burned in the large brick fireplace, heating the room. This was her sanctuary.

Life had dealt her a great hand until recently. She finished graduate school in her home country of England. She made her way to America after school and married well. She didn't need to work because financially she was very smart with her investments. Also, she decided it would be better to be home for her children instead of sending them off to be raised in after-school care.

Her husband worked long hours and took many trips out of town. It didn't bother her except she needed to buy rechargeable batteries to keep up with her unfulfilled sexual needs. Still, she had the life she dreamed of apart from her darling husband being around all the time.

In her mind, things were peachy until the fateful Tuesday she heard a knock at the door. She went to answer it and a young man had her sign the legal document acknowledging she was being served papers. They were divorce papers ending her long marriage. Her heart was broken and her perfect world shattered.

The countless days of sitting with lawyers trying to dicker over everything was a ridiculous war of pettiness. Tom was suddenly ruthless and mean. His reason for leaving was a woman half his age. She was a tall blonde bitch named

Vanessa who had a firm grasp on his balls and squeezed to get her every whim attended to.

Sela warned Tom that this temptress in the red dress was the devil's bride and would take everything from him.

She still remembered the final day in his lawyer's office. They were going over a detailed list of all the things they wanted divided…

"Hey, I just want things split fifty-fifty." Tom motioned as if cutting something in half.

"All I asked you for was to let me keep my collection of art. You never liked or understood it anyway." Sela was back at the war of words over little, insignificant things. The art was worth thousands and she had accumulated the collection.

"Whatever. I'm tired of arguing. All I need is my electric toothbrush, a new razor and some clothes and essentials. I'm never home anyways so I'll go stay at Nessa's until you figure out all this bullshit with my lawyer. Split it up and fuck the rest. I just want this mess over. Now you know why I left."

"You worthless prick. You left because I didn't want anal sex and that step up from a whore lets you fuck her every which way you want, which makes you think you're worth more than your wallet. Mark my words, you crotch stain, she has you wrapped around her middle finger because she is going to fuck you out of everything." Sela couldn't believe she'd said all that in one breath.

"I hate you," Tom yelled.

"I hate you more, you worthless bastard." Sela's eyes swelled with tears.

Tom went to speak and an awful scent filled his nose. He looked down and saw Sela's Pekinese dog pissing on his Italian shoes. "Fuck! I hate that damn dog."

Sela smirked as Chelsea scampered to her legs, nipping at Tom as he kicked toward her. "Good, Chelsea, good dog."

* * * * *

For a woman who had been through so much, Sela sat calmly in her chair. She sipped her tea and flipped through a small bundle of photos she'd just picked up from the photo-mart.

She smiled as she looked through the pictures. Pulling a pen from the small drawer beside the chair, she addressed an envelope. It was to Tom. His new address was hard for her to write after all the years at their home as a supposed happily married couple.

Chelsea barked, wanting to get up on the chair with Sela.

She reached down and picked up her little dog. With an evil grin, Sela glanced at two pictures that she set aside from the rest. Showing them to Chelsea, she laughed.

"You remember me taking these pictures, Chelsea?"

One was of the dog getting her teeth brushed with Tom's electric toothbrush. The other photo was of the toothbrush being used to clean fresh little runny piles of doggy poo-poo off the newly installed shag carpet.

"I should have gotten these developed sooner. This just made my day."

The Best Men — Part Two

∞

Shelly's neck was sore from answering the phone all day. The men at her job expected her to do all the secretarial work and basically took her for granted.

On her break, she sat down and listened to the only other female she got along with who worked with her at the Doctors' Hospital Mental Institute. Melinda was a lovely woman. Tall, statuesque and had the most perfect chocolate-colored complexion imaginable. She was every man's fantasy. But all good things have a drawback.

Melinda was the talkative type. Not just about her life and such, this woman made an auctioneer jealous with a nightmare attitude to match. It was common knowledge to the men at the institute that one did not fuck with Melinda.

Three months after she was hired, a recently divorced doctor decided to threaten her. He told her, "I hired you for two reasons. One, you type faster then any person I have ever met. Secondly, and this is where your job security lies, I have always wanted to know what it was like to fuck a black beauty queen."

It was good that they worked in a doctor's office because she managed to get the doctor to drop his pants then turned evil. She grabbed one of his very expensive inkwell pens and rammed it up his ass. As he cried out in pain, she tore his new silk tie from around his neck and wrapped it around his balls then tightened until circulation was cut off and he passed out. After she stuck his cock in the cigar cutter, security busted the door in. The blade only cut halfway through his cock and when the guards grabbed Melinda, she ripped the dangling end off with her acrylic nails.

Out of the ordeal, the doctor was fired for sexual harassment and Melinda received a promotion to executive secretary of billing. They figured if anyone didn't pay their bills, she might be able to convince them. Besides, she threatened to put everyone out of business for sexual and racial harassment.

So Shelly liked Melinda and for some reason they connected.

Melinda was currently on one of her rants about gossip and the workplace.

"Randy bet Dave that he couldn't screw Chris' girlfriend JoAnn. Dave won that bet because JoAnn screwed him in the stockroom, which is why all the Walker case files were all stuck together. JoAnn then decided that she loved Dave. But Dave's ex-girlfriend flew into town so Dave dumped JoAnn after she gave him head in the VP bathroom following their lunch with Dr. Shlooker. After Dave dumped JoAnn, his ex-girlfriend dumped him again. Which was too good for that little fucker if you ask me. Meanwhile, Chris didn't want JoAnn back so Randy offered to take JoAnn off Dave's hands. After Randy and JoAnn had a one-night stand, JoAnn decided she'd rather be a lesbian instead of dealing with all the bullshit baggage the men she had in her life kept giving her. Besides, Randy gave her a nasty case of crabs. Then Randy's ex-girlfriend Gina was going to get married and Randy told her that he'd kick his present girlfriend out of the house if she'd come back to him. So the bastard kicked Cindi out to make room for Gina, who used to be a third of the Randy, Gina, Cindi ménage that was going on. You following me so far?"

Melinda took a deep breath and continued. "Anyway now enters Jennifer, the ex-striper we just hired in accounts. Nice girl but she has too many tattoos if you ask me. She has this one on the small of her back of an arrow pointing down that looks like a traffic sign and reads *Enter at Your Own Risk*. Just Randy's type only she's married with kids. Weeellllll, she's dumped her husband, who is a three-hundred-and-fifty-pound biker in prison for fucking a cow while on meth then assaulting a SWAT team, so she can date Randy, which is cool with Randy because he's decided to share her with Dave. Meanwhile Keith has decided he's gay, but is unsure if he should completely come out of the closet. One night he tried to hit on his best friend, who's totally not gay and got a black eye for his effort even after he blew his friend behind the bar. Andrew thinks this is all really funny but is willing to take JoAnn off anyone who doesn't want her because he hasn't gotten laid since high school and he's thirty-two, at least he was until JoAnn said she had some kind of VD and isn't sure who she got it from. So all the guys are in a panic. I'm sure there's more but…" Melinda paused and looked at Shelly. "Are you okay?"

Shelly had the lights on in her head but nobody was home. "I'm just tired, Melinda, just tired. It sounds like your whole department is fucking crazy."

They both looked at each other then started laughing.

"That's an understatement since we work in a mental hospital." Melinda got up from her chair. "Lunch is over, Shelly, time to get back. Talk to you later."

* * * * *

The phone rang and Shelly picked it up as usual because nobody else bothered to do their job.

"Doctors' Hospital, may I—"

"It's you. I was hoping you'd answer this time." The man's voice was soft and Shelly had had her share of crank calls. But this one was different. It seemed more personal.

"Um, sir, this is Doctors' Hospital, who are you trying to reach?"

"You. I wanted to talk to you."

Shelly swallowed and moved her finger to hang up.

"Don't hang up. I know we haven't met but I have seen you. I sometimes watch you."

"Really, like some kind of pervert? Do you watch me undress or something?"

"Nooo, even though I've thought about it. Each time I picture you naked, I grow hard. I bet you are getting a bit aroused wondering who I am."

Shelly couldn't lie to herself. The warmth between her legs made it obvious he was making her curious about a few things. Namely, what kind of face and body went with his sexy voice? "I'm with somebody. I'm not, um, well, I can't go out and, well…"

"You're curious, aren't you? I bet I know what you like. You seem the type of woman who likes it when a man takes charge. Likes it when a man just wants to take you. Just sitting here thinking about you has me wondering what it would be like to lick the tender skin behind your knees then move up between your thighs to your…"

Shelly pulled the phone from her ear. She felt such a rush of arousal that her panties became damp. He was mind-fucking her. But she wasn't going to be played.

She lifted the phone back to her ear and heard him breathing. "Go fuck yourself, buddy. I'm no tramp. You can just have phone sex with yourself while you jack off. Fuck you!"

"Suit yourself. I'm going to go hang out at Jonah's Bar in a bit. You can stop by for a drink. You'll know who I am." He fell silent on the end of the phone.

Shelly quickly hung up and squirmed in her chair. Now what should she do? She couldn't go. It just wasn't right But this guy got to her. He knew she wouldn't hang up. How he knew about the soft skin behind her knee shocked her. The particular place that made her cream must get to a lot of women and not just her.

She looked up to the clock — it was almost six.

"Fuck it," she said. "I'll just go play with this guy's head a bit.

"Yeah, go fuck with him then leave right when he thinks he's gonna get some pussy.

"That's mean but it'll be fun."

She was talking aloud and keeping a conversation going with herself. Grabbing her purse, she shook her head as she walked out the door. "This fucking place is getting to me."

* * * * *

Shelly enjoyed toying and teasing men now and then. It was harmless fun. It did have an effect on her though. She'd get that little tingle of excitement between her thighs. She'd think about taking one of the men at the bar for a little harmless sex. She knew bars weren't a place to go unless a person was looking for sex. Jonah's Bar was exactly as she'd expected.

Men outnumbered women three to one. It was small and crowded but not so much to be a cluster-fuck of loud music and bodies smashed into the room like sardines. It was a typical downtown atmosphere with the smell of beer and cigarette smoke filling the air. She was relaxed and quite comfortable in the surroundings. Gabe would never come to a place like this.

She wasn't the one-night-stand type but every now and then that desperate itch of forbidden sex stirred within her. The taboo of sex with a stranger lingered in her mind. Most of these men would be more than happy to oblige her with a quick suck and fuck. How would she know who the voice was? What type of man would he be? What if he were ugly with a wart on his nose and a hump on his back?

Tossing her hair back a bit, she caught the eye of a tall, dark man. He stood in the shadows of the bar behind a few other men. The other guys smiled with false veneer teeth and perfectly coifed hair. This guy was different. He stepped into the light and she saw what he looked like. She instinctively smiled.

His hair was dark and pulled back. There was a silent confidence and aura to him. He stared at her with lustful eyes. The type of look that made a woman's panties melt off. She turned back to the bar and sighed. Her nipples began to harden with excitement. Like a burning ember, her fire was set to blaze but she was waiting. *Fucking A, I hope that's him*, she thought. She played it calm and waited for *him* to make the first move.

A group of men all sat in the corner and did their best stud impressions. In typical male hunting fashion, they scanned the landscape to find a new, unsuspecting prey.

"Damn, that bitch looks like she's about to come over here and jump me," one short guy commented. "She was looking right at me and smiled."

"Dude, she wants me. I can tell. But I bet she's just a cock-tease and frosty between the sheets," a blond guy piped in.

"No way. Look at her sitting there." The short guy straightened his crotch and puffed his chest out. "She's perfect. Alone…hot…horny. Fifty bucks says I can get her to let me sit over there with her."

"I'll take that bet."

The guy turned around and was doing his best to be a badass. "Oh shit, it's some new guy. Who are you?"

"Derek, my name is Derek. That woman over there is on fire."

"Yeah, I know. Get ready to lose your money, Derek. Steve is making his move." The other guys watched as Steve strolled slowly over toward the bar.

A man cleared his throat and smiled as he leaned onto the bar beside Shelly. "May I sit down?"

"Sure, the seat is open." Shelly was polite even if not interested.

"You look very nice tonight. I couldn't help but notice you."

She could tell he wasn't very adept at pick-up lines. "Well, thank you."

"Steve, my name is Steve." He held his hand out to Shelly. She smirked and turned.

"Steve?" She paused. "I'm Shelly, nice to meet you. How much did you bet your buddies over there that I'd let you sit over here with me?"

"Um, I don't do things like that." His smile was now gone and his voice cracked.

Shelly turned and pulled a ten-dollar bill from her little purse and set it on the bar in front of Steve. "Go buy another drink, Steve. Tell your friends I'm not interested tonight. Thanks for the effort, but not tonight."

Steve pushed the ten back to her and shrugged his shoulders. "Thanks, but it never hurts to try."

Steve walked back to his pack of male wolves in their corner.

"Shot down in flames, huh, Steve?" the blond guy teased.

Steve held his hands up to the side, giving up. "Her name is Shelly. She said she was on her period and had major PMS. She did offer to buy me a drink though. I told her no thanks."

"I told you. Ice between those legs," the blond guy cracked.

Derek smiled as he kept his stare on Shelly. He was focused on her and when she turned and looked back at him, the slow burn of desire rose in his body.

It wasn't that Shelly wasn't thinking about sex. Just not with Steve. She sipped her drink and kept having the feeling she was being looked at. The small hair on her neck was bristling like in a spooky movie. As unnerving as it was, it excited the shit out of her because she knew it was *that guy*.

She couldn't help but look up from her drink and turn to find him. That stare. The way it crept into her body and flowed through her like blood. It rushed to the center of her sexual soul. This man made her passion boil and urges come to the forefront. He had to be the guy who called. This was going to be her one-night stand.

"Guys, I can't help but go over to that woman." Derek wanted her. Ironically, a slow jam of pounding R&B pulsed through the bar. The music wasn't loud. It was just soothing.

"You? Maybe you should watch and learn," the blond man said.

"Man's gotta do what he's gotta do." Derek started to leave.

Steve pulled a twenty from his pocket. "Twenty bucks says you get turned away."

With a shrug, Derek smiled and started to walk toward Shelly and stopped. He leaned over to the bartender and handed him a twenty-dollar bill.

Shelly was frozen. Except for the one part of her anatomy that was boiling. She was going to leave before crossing the line. She got up and walked along the bar to get out.

"You can't leave yet, I just ordered you another drink." She looked up to see those eyes.

He grinned and handed her a glass. "Hello, Shelly. My name is Derek"

"Hello, Derek, I'm just leaving."

"You don't want to go, Shelly. Not yet."

"And why don't I want to go?" she asked stupidly.

"Because the night just started and I plan to end it in bed with you." His smile widened across his mouth.

Instead of reaching out and slapping him, Shelly just pursed her lips and held back a smile.

"You're pretty confident, aren't you?"

"Well, when I see something I want, I'm not the type to let it go. Tonight I want you."

"So you expect me to just let you have me? Why you and not one of these other guys?"

"Because you don't want them. You want me. I'm good-looking, above average in the sexual equipment department, I have an insatiable appetite for eating pussy and want nothing more than to take you out back and fuck you."

Every nerve in Shelly's body was electrified. His harshness cut through the outer façade of all the dating and useless bullshit. He wanted her for nothing more than sex and she felt the same way. No ties, except maybe handcuffs. Just physical pleasures unleashed.

"Well, let me see how full of shit you are." Shelly took the drink in her hand and downed it in one gulp. Derek followed suit.

She pressed up against him and pulled her hand up his thigh, grasping his crotch in her palm. Her eyes never left his. A swirl of passion tickled her pussy as she found he wasn't bragging but rather was telling the truth.

He leaned forward, setting his glass on the bar. "I'm happy you showed. I was afraid I might have scared you when I called like that. Let's get the fuck out of here."

Shelly's knees buckled as she turned and set her finished drink on the bar.

* * * * *

The women's bathroom of a bar wasn't the most romantic of places but she was so fucking horny, she was oblivious to

152

the surroundings. Her mouth sucked on Derek's nipple while he tugged his shirt open. They were cramped in the handicapped stall but at least there was enough room to move around. Derek grabbed her hips and turned her away from him. His hands reached up and groped her swelling breasts.

A moan escaped her. The heat of the moment overwhelmed her body. Her breasts were swollen and sensitive. He pulled her shirt up over her bra and breathed heavily into her ear. "Damn, you are so hot."

Derek's hands slipped under her bra and cupped the soft mounds of flesh. Shelly closed her eyes, moaning again as he flicked his fingertip against her nipple. She bent down a bit, rubbing her ass against Derek's crotch. She could feel the hardness and was aching to feel him fuck her.

"You want me to fuck you like this, don't you?" Derek squeezed her breasts as he spoke.

"Nooo…this is wrong…but…" She gasped when Derek's hand slid down her stomach and grasped her slippery pussy. "Oh yes. God, yes. I just don't want to start something we can't fin…"

"…ish." Derek pulled at her underwear, loosening them from the wetness that caused them to cling to her labia. His fingers stroked and pinched at the fabric, sending shivers of pleasure through her body. She wiggled, trying to help. Her ass pressed against his cock and the shimmies only made her ass hotter.

The thin, moist fabric fell to her knees. When she leaned farther forward, Derek squeezed her bare pussy. Her cunt was so wet. The juices trickled over his hand and fingers.

"Your pussy is so fucking wet. I can't wait for you to wrap it around my cock," Derek kept whispering close to her ear. His breath was hot and his words hotter. She couldn't say anything.

She was frozen in the middle of this erotic daydream coming true. His fingers swept against her clit and spread her opening. Shelly held her weight on the bar across the wall above the toilet.

This all seemed so cheap but Shelly didn't care. Everything about this made her feel so alive. The desire filled her heart and added to the arousal.

She reached one hand back and began to stroke Derek's cock through his pants.

He groaned and stepped back to undo his slacks. Shelly wanted to turn around but stayed where she was. The underwear stretched across her knees. Her heels wobbled from her straining. The zipping sound filled the air of the confined space.

Shelly needed to see. Looking over her shoulder, she saw Derek tearing open a condom. She reached her hand back to grasp his hard cock.

Her eyes closed as she wrapped her hand around him. It was a nice size and bobbed while she stroked its length.

"Come on. Hurry. I want it. Give it to me, you bastard." She began to yank on his cock, needing to feel him.

"Let me put the glove on, baby."

She shook her ass before him, teasing his mind. "You wanna fuck me? You want this?"

Derek snickered. With a swish of air, Shelly felt his hand strike her ass. The loud slap echoed in her mind. A sting radiated through her. The pain took her higher.

Shelly gasped as Derek pushed the head of his cock at the opening of her cunt. The threshold of sin before her. She could stop right now and walk away. Chalk it up to a learning experience. A tease taken too far.

Shelly moaned as Derek grunted and sunk his hard cock into her pussy. The boundary crossed. She had let this temptation go farther than she originally intended, but her own pleasure took over. With each grunt and thrust, he went deeper. His hands pawed at her hips, making them ache. She heard him suck in breaths of air when he pushed to the hilt in her.

"Your pussy is so fucking tight. Fuck, you are so hot."

"Hard, fuck me hard and fast, Derek, fuck me." She was pleading for it now. With a desperate need to fulfill, she spit into her hand and reached between her legs to stroke her throbbing clit.

"Oh fuck, oh yes, yes, harder, harder." She rocked with each vicious thrust. The smacking of their skin filled the air. Shelly reached back farther and as Derek sunk into her cunt, she grabbed his balls and rolled them in her palm. She was so close but needed that extra to cross over. "Fuck that pussy, Derek, fuck that pussy, you bastard."

The moaning and lustful groans echoed in the small bathroom. Fluorescent lights flickered and the creaking of the walls filled the air. Cheap, sinful passions released through the most primitive behavior, a no-holds-barred fucking.

Shelly bit her lip as her muscles tightened around Derek's thick cock, plunging in and out of her cunt. His thrusts were slowing and she sensed him getting close.

"Shit, baby, you have me about to come. Damn, you are so hot." He had beads of sweat across his forehead. He pulled his cock almost all the way out until the head spread her pussy a bit wider then sank back in until his tight abdomen smacked against her ass.

Derek reached down around Shelly and grabbed her swaying breasts in his hands. He gently squeezed them as he fucked her. His mouth pushed against her bare shoulder and sucked in, causing Shelly to wince in pain.

He slammed in hard and deep, lifting her off the ground. Shelly felt the rush of blood flow through her. Her pussy began to tingle and the soreness of the sex disappeared. She closed her eyes tight and clenched her teeth. With all her might she tightened her pussy around Derek's cock.

"Fuck, I'm coming." Derek bit her shoulder and erupted.

Shelly held in a shriek. Words didn't need to be said. An emotional breeze whisked through her body. Her muscles flexed around his cock as they climaxed together. Over and over she felt his cock throb within her cunt. Her vaginal spasms milked him as he stopped pushing and began to relax.

Derek pulled back, falling from her pussy.

Shelly weakly stood, her knees buckling. She leaned against the wall and caught her breath. "You go get cleaned up. I need a few minutes." She looked down but had a smile on her face.

"I'll meet you out at the bar in a few." Derek reached his hand out to hers and squeezed her fingertips.

When he stepped out, Shelly heard him excuse himself so there must be other people in the bathroom. *What the fuck am I doing?*

Shelly turned to sit on the toilet. After a few minutes, the irritation subsided and she felt the urge to pee. With a heavy sigh, she relieved herself and a shudder of chills rode up her spine. The panties she had at her ankles were still wet but she needed something on and too bad for her that she didn't pack an extra pair in her purse.

Gathering herself, she stepped out of the stall. She was met by three women staring at her.

"What?" she said.

One big blonde replied, "Derek, huh? Next time use the men's room, there's only two stalls in this bathroom and the one is plugged and we all really need to pee."

The Growth Spurt

ঞ

Martin sat shaking slightly in the expensive leather swivel desk chair in front of his computer.

He had just finished his daily ritual of scanning free porn sites to whack off to during the thirty-second clips for no extra charge. The last site was a humdinger with movies of "MILF TRAINERS". Supposed studs training moms how to fuck properly. To Martin this was an odd thing because if the women in question were already mothers, one would assume they knew how to fuck. But still, he joyously jerked off to the fantasy in his mind. "This could actually happen!"

Just after he made the goofy sex face men make when coming, an ad popped up on his twenty-three-inch LCD screen. The site featured a picture of a doctor pointing his finger at an advertisement. *Primo Penis Pills. Isn't it time to be the man you want to be? Add thirty percent to the length of your penis... Guaranteed!* Below the text was a sexy couple embracing in the throes of passion.

Holy shit, he thought. "Guaranteed. Now that's something you don't hear a lot."

He'd seen these ads a million times and always just closed the window.

Just view these testimonials —

Jizm Johnny, 2005 Best Come Shot award finalist, writes, Since I've taken the Primo Penis Plus pills, my stamina has gotten gooder. And my cock — I mean, penis — has grown almost three inches. The ladies loves it much better and I can come eight to ten times a day.

The before and after pictures made Martin do a double take. The first one was of the guy with an already big cock and the after had him standing with what resembled a boa constrictor between his legs.

The more he read, the more he bought into the hype. Numerous men said how a bigger penis changed their life like a lottery ticket. Women would flock to them because they now had the cock of their dreams. Of course winning the lottery would have the same effect on women.

Something about the ad made Martin keep it open and read on. Maybe it was the doctor. Maybe it was because he felt a bigger cock would help him with the ladies. Or when at the gym, he wouldn't be so shy when showering. It was probably because of that vindictive, fucking bitch Camille Hartwood. Her heartless comments after Martin won her in a drinking game scarred him for life. He drank more beer than anyone at the football party and the prize was a blowjob from Camille.

She staggered upstairs with Martin and laughed when he pulled his cock out. He couldn't help it, he was drunk and sometimes things don't work or look the same when intoxicated. A woman fucked up enough to blow a guy on a bet was bad enough but a guy drunk enough to take the girl up on it deserved the erectile dysfunction. His cock just hung there like wet sushi. If that weren't bad enough, Camille threw up all over the front of him after drinking anything with fruit flavor and alcohol in it and then went downstairs and blew all the other guys instead.

The web page switched to the payment screen where there was the final chance to make the change in life and pocketbook. Martin paused, holding his limp, still-dripping cock in his hand. Looking down, he asked, "You know what, buddy, maybe we should try this. It might make you the big, swinging dick you always wanted to be. What do you think?"

Like most men, he stared at his one-eyed wonder worm almost expecting it to answer back. In a way it did— telepathically.

After a few extra tugs, he straightened and followed the directions on the site to receive the wonder drug guaranteed to make his penis grow "up to thirty percent bigger in length and girth". He was so excited he even paid the extra money for next-day delivery.

The next day he sat patiently for all of ten minutes then he sat like a deer in headlights. Time couldn't go quick enough as he sat watching the hands of the clock tick by. The doorbell rang and Martin almost jumped out of his chair to get it.

He swung open his door and saw two elderly women looking at him in his Hawaiian-patterned underwear and a tank top that read *I'm With Stupid* and an arrow pointing down toward his penis.

"Are you ready to take the Lord into your heart?" the one Hispanic woman asked, staring at Martin.

"Not today. I'm just waiting for my penis pills to be delivered." Martin was a desperate man. "See, they are guaranteed to make my penis grow thirty percent, guaranteed!" He pulled his shorts down to show the two unsuspecting women.

The two women stood for a silent moment. The other elderly woman adjusted her glasses, squinted then leaned toward the door and said, "God does work in mysterious ways, my boy. But he can't do every miracle." Then they both turned and walked away.

They'll see, he thought to himself. He looked down at his cock. "It's okay, buddy, don't pout," he said, and pulled his shorts back up, waiting for his miracle.

Standing in the doorway, Martin saw the delivery van pull up in front of his home. He almost came in his boxers from the joy. In fact he did dribble some seed into his patterned shorts. Hopefully the pills would help his premature ejaculation problem too.

After getting the package, Martin ripped it open and read the instructions. Everything was pretty standard except for the forty-seven possible side effects. Martin figured anal leakage and hair loss with abdominal cramps and a slim chance of losing some brain function was worth the price of having a thirty percent bigger cock. He was obviously thinking with the brain in his other head.

Take after eating, he read. Well, he had eaten a fried zucchini and banana sandwich about twenty minutes ago so he figured, why wait? He popped the first horse-sized pill and began his journey of growth.

The directions said it took time to have the muscles inside the penis grow and become more elastic to let more blood flow through them, thus making the penis larger. Martin, being the intellectual type, figured masturbating would help constrict and stretch the tissues and muscles quicker. He also figured that doubling his dosage might speed up the process.

After jacking off three or four times a day, he quickly ran out of things to fantasize about. His stable of fantasy women had dwindled down from the movie and music artists he lusted over. He was now using memories of seeing his aunts and cousins bathing in the time-share cabin they had. The boys found a hole in the wood siding and would peek in at the girls in the bathroom. That was ten years ago and Aunt Maggie's boobs had dropped from her chest to her waist.

All the masturbating was not wasted because Martin could tell things were changing right before his eyes. Or more accurately, right in his hands. It was beyond what he thought. He was getting huge. He could feel the difference. And not only physically because his confidence was growing also.

He measured himself every day to track his super-cock. The measurements were entered into a database and he made a growth graph. He was so proud. Some men needed that extra "oomph" to kick-start their lives. After the second month, Martin was ready to go back out in the real world and find himself a woman. Not just any woman though, he wanted a slut.

The night had come for Martin to free his beast. To let the monster in his pants find a cave to dwell in. Tonight, Martin was going to get laid.

After taking a shower, he posed and preened in front of the mirror naked. His pubic hair was neatly shaved off and he picked off the little pieces of tissue paper from where he cut his balls shaving them. He slipped into his new slacks because his jeans were too tight now due to his monster cock. This was the night.

While he cruised down the street, he wanted to make sure he picked the girl of his dreams. Or at least one who took a check or wouldn't charge him more than seventy-five dollars for some fucking.

He pulled to a stop at a red light and saw the perfect woman. She must have dropped something because she was bent over in a miniskirt, wearing no underwear and showing the world her goods. At first glance Martin thought she was wearing a black feather boa between her legs. He was wrong — she was just hairy.

Martin lowered the passenger side window. "Hey, baby, how much?" he yelled out the window.

She stood up and turned toward Martin. "What's your pleasure, baby? Are you a cop?" The woman looked to be in her mid-thirties, was a bit overweight with long white hair and had a face with more makeup on it than a store cosmetics representative.

"Nope, just a man with a need."

She took a long drag from her cigarette then blew it into Martin's car as she spoke. "Look, it's been a long fucking night. My feet hurt, I'm tired and my hemorrhoids are screaming bloody murder. So no anal, all right?"

"Okay. I must warn you. I have been taking some herbal enhancement pills so my cock is kinda big. That's why I wanted to try it out on a professional first."

"Don't you worry, baby. Sheila knows how to handle the biggest pricks around. Hell, I worked in Washington, D.C. and there are huge pricks wandering around there daily."

Martin followed Sheila's directions to the nearby hotel and paid for a room. He even sprung for pay movie channels in case they needed a break from all the fucking. They ironically were given room sixty-nine and went inside. Everything looked fairly clean except for the chalk outline of a man with a red stain on the carpet in front of the bathroom. Martin didn't care. It was sex time and he was ready to party.

With a thump, Sheila plopped onto the bed. She swung her fishnet-covered legs over to the side and motioned for Martin to come over. "Let's see this monster cock you've been talking about."

Martin stood at the side of the bed and tugged at his zipper. "You better lean away, I don't know how big this thing gets. I'd hate to smack you in the forehead with it."

"Don't worry. I have seen more big cocks than a chicken farmer. Lemme have it!"

With a rustle and a pull Martin's pants fell to his ankles and he leaned back to show the monster off.

Sheila sat there stunned by what was before her. She frowned then squinted as she stared at Martin's cock. "Um, sweetie, you might want to ask for a refund. It looks more like those pills changed your pecker from an outie to an innie."

"No way! I've checked it daily. My cock grew thirty-five percent bigger."

He paused, seeing Sheila squinting. "Before I took the pills it was only three inches long, now it's a little bigger than four."

The Stare

∽

Edward walked from the bathroom and sat at the stool beside the bar. His drink was still there and his nightly post as a ladies' man in Joe's Bar and Grill was intact. He staked out the bar again to see which of the lovely women would be his next target.

His eyes found the next victim of his charm. She walked in the door and was a vision of sensuality and lustful intent. Her short locks of curly blonde hair framed the face of an angel. She wore a red dress that clung to the curvature of her breasts. Small outlines of her tight nipples caused a stir in Edward. She stood a shade taller than the other women and had the one thing no man can resist. Actually a woman only needs a pussy to be irresistible but this was the added bonus. She had "the look".

Every now and then a man meets a woman who melts hearts with a stare. Something within them causes other women to become uneasy. Most of the time other women hate them. It isn't so much competition as it is the knowledge that these certain women can take any man they want. From Edward's point of view, she wanted him.

He sat, trying his best to remain cool. Nothing turned a woman off more than a spastic bucket of nerves. And when Edward became nervous, he would also get gas. Not a good mixture to impress a woman, especially after eating eggs and onions with extra-spicy hot sauce on his omelet this morning.

Edward was calm, remaining stoic and unnerved by this beauty before him. That was until she turned and looked at him. A smile spread across her lips. It was almost a smirk. Her eyes were captivating, deep and blue. Edward sucked in the trickle of drool seeping from his mouth.

All of the other guys around Edward were preoccupied with the women they had met or came to the bar with. They all had their own ways to bed women. Most guys paid the women a hefty sum to let them see their naked bodies. Then they'd lie with the details to their bar buddies as if they had really fucked them.

Edward's focus was in front of him. The woman he put on the pedestal as first prize.

She got her drink from the bartender and laughed with her friends. She whispered to one and they both looked at Edward. He now knew she had noticed him. She pulled the cherry from her drink by the stem and opened her mouth, setting the red fruit on her wet tongue.

Edward swallowed hard as he pictured those red lips wrapping around the head of his cock instead of the cherry. As she bit down, the cherry burst in her mouth and juice fell along her chin. In Edward's mind, he had exploded in her mouth, filling it with the essence of his loins. The woman licked the juice from the corners of her mouth and smiled as she wiped the rest from her chin.

To Edward she was a goddess because she swallowed.

He gawked at her as the thin strap from her dress fell along her shoulder. She wore no bra. Edward cringed because he could picture this woman naked beneath him with her perky breasts flushing pink heat and erect nipples begging for a kiss. Her long muscular thighs wrapped around his hips, pulling him deeper and deeper into her tight pussy. The gentle moans of pleasure as they made love through the night over and over again.

Edward swallowed what seemed like a watermelon. He had a hard-on so stiff he could cut steel with it. *What should my move be?* he thought to himself.

He motioned to the bartender to no avail. He too was being drawn into this woman's web of desire. Like a black widow she'd seduce the men in then eat them. Of course Edward wouldn't mind eating her.

Unless she was really hairy down there.

He had a phobia about really hairy women since high school and Bertha Schwartz. After prom he was to lose his cherry to Bertha because his parents set them up on the date. This was probably the closest he'd ever get to a sure thing. Her father worked for Edward's dad and it was sort of a way to get a promotion. It wasn't pretty and when she dropped her underwear, revealing her pussy to Edward, he could barely see it because she was so hairy and had such a foul odor, he was afraid she had sat on a skunk and it had become stuck in her.

His eyes looked up and met hers. Like a magnet he was drawn to her. She smiled and leaned back over to her friend and giggled. Her eyes thinned with her smile widening. Her eyes locked with his again and she started walking along the bar.

Oh dear Lord! She was walking toward him. His mind went into hyperdrive to think of something charming and unusual to say.

The pick-up lines all rushed through his brain.

"Hey, baby, I'm studying to be a gynecologist. Can I examine you?"

"Do you work at a sandwich shop? 'Cause I'd like to show you my footlong."

"My hands are cold, can I warm them on your ass?"

It was pathetic. He needed something dazzling. A stunner. With his mind distracted, he didn't notice her standing in front of him.

Edward sat with his boner, dumbfounded. She was even more beautiful up close. Her clothes fit like a glove. She was a Venus, a sexual goddess.

When her lips parted to speak, Edward heard the voice of an angel. "Excuse me. I couldn't help but notice. My friends and I weren't sure if you knew but you have the biggest booger we have ever seen, hanging from your nose."

The Best Men — Part Three

∞

Shelly had lived out a fantasy by having a one-night stand. Well, it was actually three different nights and a morning brunch at the local diner, but she had her little sexual escapade and life was getting more and more back to normal.

Things between her and Gabe were finally starting to click again. She was happy and hadn't seen anyone else for a while. Since it was Friday night, she wanted to go out and kick her heels up.

* * * * *

Gabe was gentle as a lamb. His mouth warm, comforting as he kissed along the slopes of Shelly's body. This was a huge contrast to the more primitive and dangerous encounters she had been used to lately. Every inch of her body was being paid equal attention and she loved every minute of being spoiled in this way.

His warm breath whisked along her skin as he turned her over. Wet lips caressing the flexing muscles of her calf. Shelly looked into those deep eyes. With a smile he kissed her ankle and ran his hand along the back of her legs. His palm held behind her knee as he continued to kiss down the length of her leg.

Her pussy was wet and craved its own attention while Gabe tortured her with the slowness of his descent between her thighs. Each second seemed like hours. He was the sort of man who was thorough. He didn't miss anything and was extremely patient when doing something.

His complete obsession to detail was one attribute Shelly loved because when he ate pussy, he ate it forever. It was a sacrifice she decided to make whenever possible.

A flash of pleasure crept through Shelly when Gabe's mouth enveloped her pussy. He kissed and suckled on her wet folds of flesh, sending sensations and tingles into her pussy. With a deep sigh she moaned, "Yessss..." Her words of approval slithered from her mouth like a snake.

Gabe groped at her ass and lifted her slightly to make his tongue enter her pussy easier. He quickly flicked it in and out of her, splitting the slippery lips. Her clit became firmer and more sensitive to his continued tongue caress. Each time he brushed against it with his nose or tongue, the pleasure rose to another height. Shelly was going insane with delight.

The tender flesh was being suckled and slurped while the juices trickled from Shelly's wet cunt. Gabe always told her how he loved the control he had when eating her pussy. It gave him a sense of complete satisfaction to feel her inner walls vibrate and her legs tighten around his head. He knew she couldn't fake that. It was also an added bonus because after Shelly came from oral sex, she would fuck him with the smoothness and care of a true lover. She wanted to bring him pleasure and there was never the burden of anything except to crash into ecstasy together as one.

Shelly turned her head to the side. A tear squeezed from her tightly closed eyes. She gasped and gripped the sheets with her long fingers. Gabe's focus on her clit caused a fireworks show in her mind. The blasts of pleasure exploded inside her body. She gasped and started to shake. He swirled his tongue around was as if he were writing his memoirs and his tongue was the pen. Thank God, he had a lot of capital letters in his writing, she thought.

All the sexual encounters flashed in her head as she started to come. She panted like a bitch in heat. Gabe sucked hard on her cunt and shoved his tongue into her, licking upward along the thin sheet of flesh covering her clit. Shelly couldn't see anything except her visions of passion and fantasies relived.

Gabe reached one hand up and rubbed her tight nipple. His tongue was constantly licking her clit. Everything finally peaked and she let go. Shelly began to squirm and all her burdens were freed, it was so intense her juices almost squirted from within her. Her eyes stayed tightly shut and she began to giggle as Gabe continued licking her, all her sensitive nerve endings now ticklish to his touch.

Shelly was smiling and relaxed and gazed down at Gabe. His mouth glistened with her juices, his hair was messed up from rubbing against her inner thighs and he had a dorky shit-eating grin on his face. With a soft sigh Shelly spoke. "That was so, well, you know what I mean, Wes."

The pause in her voice was from her own shock. She had done the unthinkable.

"Wes? Who the fuck is Wes?" Gabe pushed Shelly's legs aside and got up off the bed.

Shelly didn't know what to say. She had been caught saying another man's name in bed.

Shelly began to cry. She curled up, scared and unsure of what might happen next.

Gabe walked into the shower and with a loud slam, she knew he was pissed off.

"I don't know why we need to go to therapy, Shelly. You cheated on me and it's over!" Gabe was very upset.

Shelly remained calm in spite of feeling a bit uneasy. "I wasn't technically cheating."

"What the fuck is technically cheating?"

"Well, when you and Dave went to that strip club. And you had that girl pull the lollipop out of your mouth with no hands. You told me you weren't cheating and I let it go."

"That's different. She was a gymnast and was showing us how limber she was. She was paying her way through college. In the nude. While straddling my face. It was very artistic."

* * * * *

The doctor's office was gray and dim. *Dr. Sheila Lewis* was etched on the nameplate resting on the cherry wood desk. Beneath her name, it read *Psychiatrist*. The two of them had been talking for a while and there was a moment of dead silence in the room. Gabe was sitting and fidgeting in the leather chair. It kept making fart sounds and like a kid, he had a hard time not giggling.

The doctor rustled through a few papers and started talking. "You don't know, do you, Gabe?"

"Know what? That my girlfriend, the woman I love, has been fucking around behind my back? I know that!"

"Technically, Gabe, she hasn't."

"What the fuck is it with you women? Technically she's been screwing these guys. Okay, technically it isn't cheating when I have my dog lick nacho cheese off my balls then."

"Umm, that's a different issue we will have to go over in another session, Gabe. Now I'll spend days trying to clear that image from my mind." She shuddered and shook her head then continued. "You have what is called Multiple Personality Disorder. After your car accident last year, something caused an imbalance in your brain. It's something chemical and this imbalance causes the multiple personalities. Each one of them is active and living within you. For some reason they come in and out and you don't remember them inhabiting you. From what Shelly tells me, she tries her best not to upset them. Personally, I don't blame her.

"Now, Gabe, this medicine will keep you stable and should stop these multiple personalities from coming back. But if you quit taking them, these other sides of you will return with all their quirks and moods." The doctor ripped the prescription from her pad, handing it to Gabe.

"So you're telling me I'm a nut-job, a wacko, whatever. My marble bag is overflowing."

"No, Gabe, you're not crazy. You just need some medication to control these other people within you. Something to suppress them. They haven't hurt anyone and since you work from home, you haven't had to deal with them."

"So who are these other guys?"

"Let's get Shelly in here."

Shelly came in to the office after the doctor asked the receptionist to send her in. She was a bundle of nerves. What were they talking about in the room? What was taking so long? What was that awful smell radiating from the receptionist's desk? All these questions would be answered soon, except the source of the skunk smell.

"Please sit down, Shelly. I was explaining to Gabe about the accident and his condition."

Shelly kept looking at Gabe. She loved him but was unsure of his reaction to what he had just learned about himself. "Are you all right, Gabe? I was worried."

After a long moment of silence, the doctor piped in, "He's just confused. He's all right. This will need some time."

"Shelly?" Gabe started to talk with his head hung down, looking at his fingers as he fidgeted. "I'm going to be fine. If you still want me and can forgive me for accusing you. I should have trusted you. It was hard when you called me another man's name as you had an orgasm. That's the shit you read about in those trashy novels and stuff."

She leaned over and gave Gabe a hug. "I love you. We'll just have to work through this. We have people helping us, like the doctor here. We'll pull through, we always have before."

"I know, sweetheart. I would like to know a little about these other personalities I have though. Can you tell me how they were and how they treated you?"

Nodding, Shelly sat back and began to talk about the other men she had met in Gabe's body. "Well, Gabe, there was Wes. He was the more moody and darker side of you. He had a powerful presence about him. He would call me Sheryl. Drove me nuts. Wes was very forceful, direct and dominant. I liked that." She crossed her legs, remembering how he had fucked her over the television with the porno playing loudly in the room.

She looked over, seeing the doctor taking notes on a pad. After the pause she continued. "Then I met Derek. He called at work. I knew it was you because of your voice. Derek was a more mysterious side of you. Very elusive and the secrecy was extremely arousing. I liked him a lot too." Shelly quietly moaned with the memory of Derek and his appetite for the spontaneous and having sex in public.

"So you see, Gabe, even though I was having a lot of sex without you, I wasn't really cheating. I was actually cheating with you technically."

"Again with the technically. I guess that explains a few things. Like my dreams."

"Dreams? What dreams?" the doctor replied as she jotted down notes.

"I thought I was having all these sex dreams about Shelly. I'd wake up and my balls were sore and I'd have sticky underwear. It was weird. I guess I saw what was happening as a dream when the reality was, I really was fucking…wait a second! After all these years of me begging you to have anal, you let this Wes guy do it?"

* * * * *

Shelly stood in the kitchen. She sighed as she remembered some of the times she had spent with the other men inside her

172

man. Darker, edgier men who stirred things within her. The men who made her pussy moist with a simple look. Men who used her for their most primal needs and wanted nothing more than the physical part of her.

In a way she missed that. She really missed the sex. The meds not only kept Gabe his normal self, they slowed his libido to a crawl. Her one-time male fucking machine was now an antique car that needed a crank to get his motor running,

Gabe was a wonderful man but subdued. Her life with him would always be filled with love and compassion. He also was pussy-whipped beyond comparison and wrapped around Shelly's finger.

She stepped to the counter and pulled the medicine Gabe needed to take every night to keep him being just Gabe. Shelly looked at the pill in her hand. It looked exactly like the vitamin E gel caps she used to take for her dry skin.

A wicked grin crossed Shelly's face. She couldn't. He needed the meds to remain just Gabe. But what about her? Didn't she deserve the passion Gabe's other personalities gave her? She couldn't cheat on him after everything they had been through but she needed a man.

A man who wanted to fuck her. To have a need for her and the nasty desires only he could fulfill. Shelly wanted all three of her men rapped up into a nice little package. Actually it wasn't a little package but a nice one. Anyway, she realized she needed all three of them. She wasn't about to deny her inner slut the fantasy of a mental cluster-fuck. Even if it technically wasn't real.

Shelly reached up and took the vitamin E bottle down. She put a vitamin gel cap in one hand and Gabe's medicine in her other hand. They both looked so alike.

Standing over the kitchen sink, she closed her eyes. All she heard was the faint sound of a pill falling into the sink and down the drain. With a sigh she turned and walked to the bedroom with a glass of water and a pill for Gabe.

The Darling Husband

ॐ

Fred felt silly going to buy some of those feminine product things for his wife. But being a typical pussy-whipped male, he was out in the late hours in search of things he was afraid of.

Sharon was a spoiled woman but deserved it. At least she told Fred she did. She had everything already. Every time she'd drop a hint about wanting something, she would go buy it within a few days because she had no patience.

He was driving down the street where there was a small strip mall with a few stores open in it. There was a cute card shop and a coffee place. Maybe a gift certificate for the coffeehouse would be something nice to get Sharon. She loooooved her morning cup. It was her bitch-awakening drink. If she didn't get it, watch out.

Fred pulled his long jacket closed. He hopped out of his truck and walked toward the door of a store next to the coffee shop. With a jingle from a bell, he stepped into the neon-lit store and a burly, hairy, longhaired man snarled at him from the front counter and reopened the *DDD Natural XXX* porn magazine he was reading.

As the myth stated, the freaks do come out at night.

There was an elderly lady wearing pink furry bunny slippers and a flowered muumuu dress. Her blue hair was pulled up in a bun and she wore horn-rimmed glasses. She was looking at some packages and mumbling to herself.

Fred shook his head, wasn't watching where he was going and bumped into a man standing in the aisle. At first glance he resembled a biker. Big, hairy and bald with a sinister snarl.

"Excuse me, I'm sorry."

In a high-pitched voice the man replied, "It's okay, sweetie. No harm done." The man turned around and Fred looked down to see assless chaps on the guy. Not only was his ass hairy but he had a tattoo that read *Bobby* in a heart on it.

Fred was somewhat lost and didn't want to be stupid and ask for help. With a tap on his shoulder, Fred turned to see an attractive woman smiling at him.

"Hello, can I help you?" she asked.

Fred was a little nervous. It wasn't as if he'd asked for this before. "Yes, I'm looking for something for my wife."

"From the look of you I can see why."

"What? Nooo, she asked me to pick something up for her."

"I see. Well, what exactly are you looking for?"

"I guess something in regular? I travel a lot and she says sometimes she has needs. She didn't get what she needed last time. She said I can call her and she'd...you know..." Fred paused. "I'm not real comfortable talking about this."

"No problem. Let me show you what we have and that might make it easier."

There was a small cutout inside the brightly lit store. On the walls surrounding Fred was a smorgasbord of rubber cocks. They were in every size, shape and color imaginable.

"Holy shit. There are so many things here. What do you do with all this?"

"It all depends on your partner. There are Ben Wa balls, pleasure missiles, ribbed, threaded, glow in the dark, black, green gelled, pink rubber, flesh-toned, clit-tickler dildos. Here look at this one."

The woman handed Fred a flesh-colored dildo with a small pouch attached to it by a thin tube. "This one is lifelike in texture and actually ejaculates."

"Uh. What do you mean?"

She reached to the pouch and squeezed it. "See?"

A squirt of fluid shot from the tip of the dildo and into Fred's face. "Holy fuckin' shit. I was just, oh my God — I'm gay now — I can't believe — um." Fred licked his lips as the fluid dribbled down his cheek. "Er, this tastes like a glazed donut."

"Well, yes, we put a flavored fluid in there sometimes to add to the woman's playful side."

"What's that?" He set the dildo down and picked up a flesh-colored rubber pussy from a glass shelf.

"Oh, that's one of our new scented toys for men. It has a realistic scent of a woman's pussy. Go ahead, give it a smell."

Fred put it to his nose and jerked his head back. "Damn, that smells like shit!"

"Oh, you had it backward. Turn it around." The woman motioned to him.

"I'll pass. What else do you sell here?" Fred handed the woman the pussy and turned around.

She stepped beside him and continued. "We have anal-vaginal double-penetrating toys, butt plugs, anal beads, nipple or clitoral clamps, cock rings, battery or electric operated vibrators. Fake pussies, fake assholes, porn magazines, porn VHS tapes, porn DVDs, peekaboo shows, nudie booths, peep shows, jack-off booths, gay porn, lesbian porn, midget porn, animal porn, transvestite porn, Japanese porn, cross-gender porn, chicks-with-dicks porn. There's a variety of costumes. There's some whips, chains, genital clamps, ropes, leather, vinyl, edible, floggers, gag balls, handcuffs, branding irons, BDSM tools, S&M tools, wax-play candles, various restraints, clothespins, mechanical fucking machines and we even have the BFOM-720."

"Dare I ask?"

The woman grinned and said, "It's the Big Fucking Orgasm Machine. It has triple speeds, hooks up to any two-twenty outlet and has an automatic reset and a breaker fuse if it shorts out. It comes with fourteen attachments and a sixty-day money-back guarantee on parts and labor. It can also be used as a blender and power drill. There is a warning that it has been known to cause some vaginal trauma if left in too long."

"Does it run on gas or diesel fuel?" Fred knew she wasn't amused by his joke.

"Okay. What can I get you?"

"Well, I appreciate your help but what I really came in here for is tampons for my wife."

S.L. Carpenter

The Peeping Thomas

෨

Penny left the corner market. She was looking forward to the weekend and had picked up a few things for a nice salad and some homemade soup. She'd added a bottle of Chardonnay to relax her mood and get her drunk enough to deal with her mother bitching at her about still being single. Reminding her that the biological clock was ticking away.

A slight noise behind her distracted her from the mundane thoughts. Stopping, she looked toward the park across the street, but the dim lights didn't reveal much except the trees swaying in the breeze.

It must be my imagination.

A lot of people were jumpy these days, especially women in the neighborhood. Somebody had been sneaking around, watching women in their homes. He hadn't attacked anyone yet, but a few really furry cats had turned up all matted with semen and Mr. Jenkins' purebred Pekinese dog was missing.

The hair began to rise on the back of Penny's neck. Someone was watching her. She could feel their stare.

Reaching her townhouse, she hurried up to the door and let herself in, locking it securely behind her and looking out the peephole. She saw nothing. Once again she dismissed it as her imagination.

Feet aching, Penny walked straight to her bedroom. She set the small grocery bag on the vanity by the bed and kicked her shoes off. It had been a long day and her mind and body were in dire need of a few minutes of relaxation. Barefoot, she wiggled her sore toes in the brown shag carpet.

"*Ahh*, that feels good." So she talked to herself. Who cared?

Slipping off her clothes, she headed into the bathroom and turned on the shower, adjusted the nozzle. As usual it took forever to heat and she stood naked waiting, splashing remnants of hair and small spiders off the shower walls with her hand. Finally it hit optimum temperature and she stepped thankfully under the spray.

A shower could rinse away so many troubles. The warmth wrapped her body in a cocoon of comfort. She leaned her head back and washed her hair. Her hand grabbed the bar of soap and she gathered lather in her palm and then reached for the razor.

She hadn't been with a man in a while but kept all the private parts clear of shrubbery. The last thing she wanted was a man to finally go down on her and see the rain forest. The soap smoothed over her pubis. Each stroke from the razor reminded her that this part of her body was being way too neglected.

After shaving herself smooth, she grabbed the showerhead and lowered it to wash away all the stubble and hair. The warmth ignited her excitement. She'd had many a relationship with baths and showers in her lifetime.

They never stopped until she was done. They never made a mess and had her sleep in it. They never asked her for a beer or something to eat after satisfying themselves. Mostly they always got her off.

The pulsing water hit the exact spot she loved to play with. Penny leaned against the wall and spread her legs slightly apart. Her blood rushed downward and a flush of heat swept through her body. Oh God, it had been a long time.

She couldn't use her fingers though because they had brand-new, two-inch acrylic nails on them and they could do some serious pussy damage. So she pressed her palm against her pubis and let the water pulse against her now-swollen clit.

"Oh shit, oh shit, *ohh*..." She could feel her excitement rising with each passing minute.

Reaching up, she twisted the hard tip of her nipple between her fingers. She always loved her nipples played with during sex. They sent shock waves of pleasure right to her pussy.

Her breathing began to speed — *this was going to happen* — she felt it building. Just as she was getting to her pinnacle —

"*Aaargh*! Holy fucking-damn-shit—"

She dropped the showerhead and frantically reached for the faucet. Dancing on her tiptoes, she cussed and shivered. "How the fuck could the hot water run out? Did everyone flush their toilets at the same time?"

She stood naked with goose bumps all over and a bad case of the hornies. "Just my luck. I get so close then—ouch, ouch, shit, I've got soap in my eye. Shit, it burns." Penny grabbed her towel and quickly wiped her eyes, drying herself as fast as she could.

The white cotton robe felt good against her bare skin. She usually didn't sleep naked but the laundry had backed up and she figured one night of bare-assed sleep would do her good. Besides, sleeping in a bra sometimes hurt her breasts.

She flopped on the bed and looked for the remote. There was the grocery bag, but she was too fucking tired to put it away right now. Pulling the remote from under her ass, she turned on the television and saw the local news had just started.

"The police are still looking for the City Stalker. They have received a few tips and are following several leads, but if you see any suspicious people in your area, you are still asked to call the police immediately."

Penny turned the volume down and lay on her bed. Thoughts of a stalker around scared her. They also aroused her for some weird reason. Having a stranger watching as she slept or bathed or if she happened to be masturbating…

Masturbating, hmm.

The shower had been a complete letdown but there was always her battery-operated boyfriend. He never left her wanting. She reached over to the drawer beside her bed and moved the magazines, gloves and lotions aside. Her hand grasped the hard shaft and all her old feelings welled up inside her again. Memories ran deep for a woman who had an ongoing intimate affair with a plastic cock. "Oh, *Henry*. I need you tonight, baby."

Her hand shook with excitement. The lights were dim in her bedroom and she lay back, peeling open her robe, exposing her skin to the air. Her nipples were reddened and erect. The wetness in her pussy was a signal that she was ready for the upcoming play. Penny spread her legs apart and touched her finger between her legs, rubbing the slippery folds of flesh. She was so ready.

She bit her lip in anticipation and turned Henry on, waiting to hear and feel the familiar hum of pleasure.

With a shudder and a low murmur, Henry revealed he was more dead than alive. She held him up like a sword to heaven and felt the vibrations die in her hand.

Henry had run out of juice.

"Jesus fucking Christ! Can't a girl even get off anymore?"

Penny sat up and leaned over to check the drawer for batteries. She had everything else in there from glow-in-the-dark condoms, lube, a squeaking rubber chicken and anal beads, but no fucking batteries. Her arm accidentally hit the edge and her grocery bag fell on the bed, spilling out the contents.

Penny was getting desperate—very desperate.

She scanned the bed and saw a few things that caught her interest. "Hmm, a carrot? No, that would poke me funny. A tomato? Euuwwww. That has a visual I don't want to think about. A cucumber?" She thought for a minute, holding the hard vegetable in her hand. "Reminds me of Jamal from college, except he wasn't this thick or green." She tossed the cucumber back into the bag. "I can't. If I make a salad and my parents are here, I'll see my dad eating my pussy." She shuddered at the thought.

Just then she heard a buzz followed by a familiar chime. "Someone's calling."

She reached into her purse and took her cell phone out. The message was just another attempt by the phone company to get her to buy something. Idly, she held the small, flat, shiny phone in her palm and paused.

I wonder.

Lying back against the pillows once again, Penny held the phone in her hand and rested it on her pubis. The chill made her shiver at first. With her other hand she grabbed her landline phone and dialed her own cell number.

The initial buzzing of the phone sent a wave of excitement through her body and made her giggle. *Oh shit, it worked.*

Then the ringtone kicked in. "*Scoooooby doooooby dooooooo.*"

Not the sexiest of songs to listen to when masturbating.

She turned off the music and began to call her phone over and over, letting the vibrations shake against her clit. Each time it hummed and shook to her soul.

Thank God for technology.

Her mind began to race with erotic thoughts. She thought of the stalker watching her. Maybe he was a really good-looking man. Dark and mysterious with a muscular body and carnal needs to fulfill. That's why he stalked women. He'd watch them because he was shy. If she let him in, maybe he could satisfy himself *and* her.

Each time the call ended, Penny hit the speed redial button next to her and her cell phone vibrated and buzzed again as she pressed it harder and harder against her clit. She needed more. It was desperation time.

Penny reached over to the drawer and pulled out a glow-in-the-dark condom. Carefully she slid it over her phone. This wasn't what a typical night at home was usually like but it would have to do. She only had two hands and one was busy with redial.

She had a need and this was her way to take care of it. She carefully slid the small phone into her pussy, clenching it with her inner walls. As she lay back, she dialed the number yet again. With an electrifying jolt of pleasure, it hummed and buzzed inside her pussy. She was a genius. Over and over she dialed the phone as she tweaked her sore nipples and squeezed her thighs together. Somehow the phone had found the perfect spot and Penny could feel every single tingling vibration deep within.

One more time—and the vibrations caused her to cry out in ecstasy. "Ohh yes, I'm coming—"

With a long buzz and vibration against her G-spot, Penny came. Her inner walls flexed and tightened and the Scooby Doo theme echoed in her mind and between her legs. The constricting spasms of her pussy must have turned the phone volume up.

BANG.

Penny was jerked from her state of bliss by the sound of a loud thud and a hammering against the sliding window on one wall of her bedroom. She closed her robe around her and squirmed to the top of the bed.

Fighting for a little control, she looked out to see a man standing naked right outside the sliding window. He was struggling with two men. They turned him around and smashed his face roughly against the window. He was rather ugly and had a scraggly beard and a torn white T-shirt. She looked lower and saw he was also lacking in the cock department. She'd seen things that size in the produce department. String beans and peas were her first thought.

She was also pretty terrified so she stayed still and waited, rapidly realizing the other men were police officers. After a moment one of the cops knocked on her window, seeing her huddled on the bed.

Penny got up and walked to the door. She opened it and the most handsome guy she had ever seen stepped into her bedroom.

Where were you twenty minutes ago?

"Sorry to startle you, ma'am. We got a tip about this guy. A neighbor saw him sneaking around outside your house here. We've been looking for him."

Penny was still drooling over the cop and heard practically nothing of what he had said. To her horny mind, he was saying he'd like to fuck her all night then give her a complete body massage then fuck her again.

"I'll need to get a statement from you, ma'am."

"Umm...I...um...I need to get some things sorted out here."

"I can come back in a few minutes if you'd like. We can get this creep into the squad car. Check with the neighbors. Maybe twenty minutes?"

"Sure, that sounds all right. I need to get fixed up and decent."

"Well, give me your number and I'll call you as soon as we're done."

Penny wasn't really thinking straight because after she gave him her cell number, she stood and watched as he dialed it into his phone.

The muffled sound of Scooooby Dooooby Dooo echoed from within her. Her body shook and the cell phone dropped out, falling to the floor between her legs.

The policeman blinked a few times, staring at the glow-in-the-dark condom moving around the carpet on its own.

Then he lifted his head and looked at Penny.

A moment of silence passed. Then she said, "You ever have one of those days?"

MORE LUST

೨

The Forbidden Love

ଔ

Was she taking a younger man home to make her feel reborn? Or was it just the pure unadulterated need to be worshipped?

Marla was proud of how she looked. She had dirty blonde hair to her shoulders and her body was toned and slender. Bringing someone home from a wedding reception wasn't her style, but she needed to fill a need. She needed to fill a void. She needed to feel wanted. Needed to feel alive. Needed to feel him inside of her. Mainly she just needed to get really nasty and get laid.

She let her jacket fall to the ground and led him into the living room.

Daniel was young, strong, and handsome. He had black hair with a dark complexion and was very muscular. He seemed nervous, but had a certain confidence to his demeanor that was attractive to Marla.

"I'm going to go change, luv. Relax, and pour us a drink?" she asked, as she walked away tossing her purse and shoes on the couch. Unbuttoning the top of the gown, she walked down the hall. Daniel watched as her ass swung with each step in the tight fabric that clung to her body.

Smiling, he replied down the hallway, "No problem. You go get comfortable."

In her bedroom Marla studied her drawers, trying to find the perfect pair of underwear. There were red, green, fluorescent, furry, crotchless, edible and a bunch of thongs. She wanted to look good and feel sexy. Even though she knew her clothes wouldn't be on long, she liked being in silk and lace. She took off her dress, letting it caress her body as it slid over her breasts and torso. Marla's small trimmed pubic patch peeked out of the low cut underwear she was wearing. She slid them down her legs and decided she liked wearing nothing at all best.

Standing naked, she felt the shape of her body with her hands. Her skin felt soft to her touch, like the petals of a rose. She took some perfume and sprayed it in the air and walked into the fragrance, letting it fall into her naked flesh. She picked up her silk robe and put it on with nothing underneath.

Marla was going to enjoy this. She needed to feel this damn sexy. To have a man want her so bad he couldn't think of anything except her pleasure. This was her time to shine.

Marla stepped into the living room. The fire burning in the fireplace made the room moody and warm. He was playing with the stereo and had his shirt unbuttoned and hanging loose on his muscular frame. Biting her bottom lip, she saw his muscles flex as he moved. The warmth of the fire was nothing compared to the fire between her legs.

"You like music?" she asked coyly.

"Of course I do… WOW!" Daniel turned and stood, staring at her in the dim light.

She was captured by the illuminating glow of the fire as she walked over to the piano in the living room. Marla sat on the stool and started playing Mozart's "Moonlight Sonata".

The music was beautiful. It echoed through the empty house like a wind.

Daniel walked over and stood behind her, watching as her fingers stroked the keys. His hands touched her shoulders and rubbed them softly. Marla was trying to concentrate on her playing, but as she leaned back, relaxing to his touch, her head pressed against the growing hardness in his pants. She became a little hesitant as she felt the growing wetness between her legs.

Daniel looked down. Seeing her breasts freed from their confinement, he opened her robe with his thumbs on her shoulders. Marla slightly parted her legs when she felt a growing flow of heat to her pussy. Although her inner desires had come alive and she needed to be touched, Marla continued her piano playing.

Daniel pulled the top aside, exposing her breasts to the flickering light. Her hands stumbled on the piano keys when he moved his hands down her torso and kissed her shoulder. The space between Marla's legs widened as he cupped her breasts in his large hands. Looking down the curve of her body, Daniel saw her spread her legs apart and begin to squirm against the piano stool. The distinct scent of her passion made him lick his lips—he almost drooled over the thought of tasting her.

Marla moaned as his fingers found their way to her small patch of hair and tangled the curls. He playfully combed at it, making her laugh, and he snickered. His hand found her slick flesh and gently stroked along the length of her labia. The feeling almost made Marla want to close her legs to capture his hand, but instead she opened wide for more of his touch. The folds of skin parted under his rough fingertips as they probed the wetness just inside the lips.

Her hands held fast to the piano stool and she tried not to fall back. Her pussy was a volcano of heat and her lava needed to erupt and flow. She turned around, straddling the piano stool, and looked up at Daniel's face. She grabbed his neck, pulling him closer and the heat of his mouth brushed her cheek. Then he kissed and nibbled on her earlobe sending shivers through her. She stood up and pulled him to her mouth, kissing him deeply.

As their tongues tangled in her mouth, Marla's hand found its way to his swollen crotch. She tugged at the zipper, giving herself access to his cock. Her mouth opened wide in delight, seeing the size of it. Her head spun as she grasped the shaft in her hand. She wanted to feel him inside of her.

Daniel kicked the stool away and pulled Marla against him firmly. Her ass rested against the cold ivory of the piano keys, which chimed as he pushed against her. Her leg wrapped around his calf and thigh and her hand still firmly grasped his cock inside his pants.

The flesh of his cock was hot where she stroked it. His hands grasped her ass and her pussy melted. His index finger found the slick base of her pussy and he poked at it.

Daniel was becoming almost unglued by her overwhelming passion for him. He picked her up with his hands on her ass and laid her on the top of the grand piano like a lounge singer. Frantically, Daniel pulled his shirt off, fighting the buttons on the sleeves, wanting to be free.

Her feet rested on the keyboard of the piano and she was totally submissive to his wants. Marla's body molded to the top of the piano as she lay flat on it. Chilled by the clash of her heat and its cold, Marla shivered. Daniel tugged at her pubic hair with his fingertips as his mouth worked its way down her midsection to her pubis. A deep echoing moan came from Marla when he sank his thick finger into her. His mouth found the hot spot and licked the bud of her clit while his finger probed inside of her pussy.

Passion made her sweat and her naked flesh stuck to the smooth surface. While he focused on her pussy with his hot breath, she caressed her right breast and gently pulled at her nipple. Her other arm fell off the side of the piano as she became both overpowered and absorbed by her pleasure. His finger rubbed along the top of her inner sanctum, and she gently continued twisting her own nipple, making her body tremble with desire.

Daniel forced his tongue between her lips as his finger probed deeper. Marla jumped when he stroked the one area inside the pussy all men look for, the G-spot. He could feel the inner walls of her pussy grow and expand in rhythmic spasms while he rubbed her spot. He slipped his thumb in the upper fold of flesh and pushed up, stretching her tighter then he pulled his fingers together, pinching her flesh which made her shriek. She could barely keep her eyes open from the intensity of her pleasure.

For what seemed an eternity he touched and felt every inch of her inside. In every woman's heart there's a place of heightened exhilaration before she orgasms. Marla was there — her mouth fell open and her tongue traced her lips. She felt almost euphoric and incredibly loose. Her body seemed frighteningly relaxed then her climax hit and she stiffened. Flailing in unbridled ecstasy, her feet pounded the keys of the piano. She felt an unearthly sensation of release as she came. Daniel sucked hard on her clit while his finger drove into her. Her legs slipped off the keyboard and stuck straight out as the wave finally crested and peaked.

Feeling limp and spent, Marla lay atop the piano. Daniel played chopsticks while she recovered, making her laugh as the tune echoed through the room.

Marla rolled off the piano and grabbed Daniel's shirt. She put it on, trying to relax from the chill through her body. She walked slowly towards the kitchen and caught her reflection again. The dim firelight shone from behind them, and their reflections were outlined by the flicker of the flames. She had Daniel's large shirt open, and his saliva glistened on her blonde pubic hair and on her inner thigh. Daniel stayed playing at the piano, and she stared at the way the light danced on the walls. It made her see herself in a different way.

Daniel stood up and walked over to Marla and looked into the mirror as he wrapped his arms around her. She grasped his hands as they covered her breasts. Marla stood frozen against the mirrored wall. Her hands pressed against the mirror and she was slightly bent over. Her butt rubbed against the length of his shaft as it stood erect against the crease of her ass. She stared intently at her reflection in the mirror. Her breasts pulled away from her body from leaning forward and her nipples were taut and small from the excitement.

Daniel's hands reached around her and his shadow seemed to envelop her in a cocoon of heat. They both burned hotter than the fire of their passion. "Come on, let's go lie by the fire," he whispered.

"No, I want to watch you make love to me here," Marla replied.

Daniel unbuttoned his pants and they fell to his ankles in a crumpled pile. His cock was still hard and Marla longed to feel it buried deep inside. He stepped behind her and a wicked grin crossed his face as he held her tight. His hands moved under her breasts and gently cupped them in his palms. His thumbs brushed against nipples that ached for his attention. Her eyes closed and she felt swept away.

She looked at the mirror and could see the outline of her pussy, still wet from the excitement and anticipation of feeling him inside. She watched as Daniel kissed her neck and guided his hand down to her pubis. His finger toyed with the moist hair, and the tickling caused her to giggle. As his finger pierced the opening, she swallowed and watched it disappear into her. She licked her lips and pressed her ass against his hardened cock. Her lips dried as she breathed heavier.

Daniel pulled out his finger and brought it to his mouth. He sucked on it making a yummy sound. He pushed her over more and, fighting the tension of his penis, he pushed it down between her legs almost lifting her up from the strain as it rested between her labia.

Marla watched Daniel's cock disappear into her and felt the intense pressure him filling her. She started to feel dizzy and her body perspired from the heat of the moment. She put a hand on her knee for balance and her elbow ached as it rested on the mirror keeping her from falling. She looked back and watched as Daniel withdrew his pulsing cock and saw how the flesh of her inner lips seemed to hold it into her and how as the head almost came out the lips spread wider. Then he plunged in again.

Her eyes teared, and she was pressed hard against the mirror. Her face pressed against the cold glass as Daniel grabbed her hips and hammered furiously into her. She put her palms against the glass to steady herself from his pounding. Her hot breath fogged the glass surface, and her hands slipped down the glass as the sweat and want seeped from her. He slammed harder, muscles trembling with strain. Their intensity was ferocious. Her hand reached to stroke her clit, and she found herself caressing his cock with her own juices covering her fingertips. As he drove deeper into her, she shut her eyes and slipped off the edge of control to total abandon.

Daniel was sweating and breathing hard. Marla's breasts swayed to the rhythm of his strokes and the shirt she had borrowed was up almost to her neck from him pushing it up to grope at her skin. She saw the look in Daniel's face of oncoming ecstasy. As Daniel started shaking, Marla felt him swell and she shuddered as a rush of heat brushed over her. His cock pulsed out the heat from his loins as her own juices trickled down her leg.

Daniel collected himself and bent down to pull his pants up and Marla pushed his hands away and knelt before him, almost collapsing. Her fingers grabbed his pants and pulled them up his legs. When she reached his crotch she gazed lovingly at the sight of his penis. It was limp and still shiny and oozing from the sex. Her mouth watered and she licked it, tasting the sweetness from their lustful experience. Marla bit her lip and took what she could in her mouth and sucked it. Her eyes closed and she felt the blood flowing back into his cock, and it grew in her mouth as the saliva in her mouth covered it with heat.

She looked up at his smiling face as she slid the length of him in and out of her wet mouth. His eyes seemed to gleam and close as he filled her mouth until she couldn't take any more. Daniel's knees weakened and she let go of his pants, as she sucked hard at him and reached her hand up between his legs to grasp his ass in her hand. Fucking her mouth, Daniel held the back of her head as she pulled him into her faster and faster. She couldn't breathe and let him pop out. A bead of drool trickled down her cheek. She gobbled him back inside her mouth. Her pussy was wet again and the inner itch needed to be scratched. Toying with his penis, she flicked at it with her tongue and looked up to see his eyes shut tight.

Marla stood up, grabbed his cock in her hand and led Daniel to the couch. She leaned back on the seat and lifted her left leg up, having Daniel hold it in his hand. She looked down and grabbed his hardened cock, and she shook a little as she guided it to her intensely hot fire. Looking down she watched Daniel slide the length of his cock into her. The angle let her feel the pulsing vein of his cock sliding in and out of her.

Desperately, Daniel plowed deep and fast into her. His pace was furious and the friction made her ache as he fucked her. The passion was more then a simple fling, this was an uninhibited, primal urge taking control. He slipped out and pulled Marla up and bent her over the top of the couch. Daniel grabbed his cock and pushed it into her exposed ass, making her scream in pain and unbridled ecstasy. The pure tightness of her virgin anus made it feel as if she were being split apart, while he ground his stiffened cock into her. She came with an intense roll of an earthquake as he pulled out and spilled his juice onto her ass and up her back.

Marla's eyes were tearing as Daniel staggered backwards. She leaned against the back of the couch and slid down, feeling the warmth of the fluids on her back. Her head was spinning and she ached from the sex. To her, it was well worth it. She had a need to feel this way. She needed to feel desired, needed, lusted after. Her body twitched and quivered as a warm glow filled her inside and out.

This was forbidden love. A desire and lust not supposed to be. But, she had no remorse over what had happened.

"Well, we better get dressed before your father gets home. He's probably pretty drunk again from the wedding reception," Marla said, as Daniel got up and struggled to bend over and pull his pants up. Daniel was almost half her age and she had worn him out.

"I am so happy my dad married you last year," Daniel said smiling.

"So am I," Marla said as she felt that wetness between her legs again. "I'll make sure to tuck you into bed tonight."

The Pill

છ

Kyle rushed home to surprise his wife on their anniversary. He had it all planned and wanted everything perfect. The kids were all going to stay at a friend's house, Trudy was going to be home at precisely 7 p.m. from work and he was going to surprise her with three things.

A wonderful dinner (he was picking it up from the restaurant on the way home).

A candlelit room setting a romantic mood.

He was going to be naked with a bow on his pecker and a big smile on his face.

He looked at the clock and saw it was already 6:45. Once he had the table set and candlelight flickering on the table he decided to get out his secret weapon. A friend of his had told him of all the great effects Viagra had on his sex life. Kyle wasn't weird but did engage in some "off the beaten path" adventures with Trudy to spark their sex life. He and his wife had toys and other sex aides but neither wanted to depend on them. So he sat quietly reading the label.

"Hmmmmmmm, take one tablet twenty minutes before," he read aloud from the instructions.

He sat there in a state of awe thinking how great medicine could be, then read on. "Hmmm, sustain an erection for an uncertain amount of time from 30 to 60 minutes."

Kyle looked up at the clock above the fireplace and saw it was about five minutes before seven. Time for the medicine. The label said take 1/2 to a full tab. *What the hell!,* he thought as he swallowed down a full tablet. He walked around cleaning up the house then grabbed a beer and sat down to read. He was enthralled in his latest Hustler magazine and could see the Viagra was having a strong effect on him. He noticed it was 15 after and still no Trudy. Then suddenly, the phone rang.

"Hello?" Kyle answered.

It was Trudy. She called to tell him she ran into somebody and was going to be late.

After he put the phone down he stood up, and so did something else. *Hmmmmm.* He was fascinated with it, so he did some tests.

He hung four towels on it and still no problem. He balanced a broom on it. Used it as a bat playing softball. Put donuts on it and lastly used the force and pretended it was a light saber. After thirty minutes passed he was all worked up and hornier than a rabbit and it had become obvious his wife wasn't coming home.

He went upstairs into her closet and looked for something to wear. Though he had hidden this fetish from Trudy, he had a fascination with women's undergarments. The feel of silk always made him a little more uninhibited and was the reason he usually insisted on her wearing it to bed and even during sex. He rustled through her drawers still having a hard-on that wouldn't quit. He decided to put on her red crotchless teddy and her high heels.

He fumbled putting it on and almost gave himself a hernia from the straps against his groin. He tried not to bend his dick backwards as he pushed it out the front of the teddy's opening. Looking in the mirror he took some deep red lipstick and messily applied it to his lips.

In the corner of the closet he found a brown paper bag. As he opened it he remembered ordering it after watching Nikki Tyler in a porno movie and getting all excited and whacking off for hours about it. It was one of those fake bottoms made out of rubber and supposedly had the feel and texture of the real thing. There was even a picture of her for the pillow so you could imagine it was her you were screwing instead of a rubber attachment.

Kyle had an extreme hard-on working and didn't want to waste it, so he figured he'd practice before the wife came home. The feel of the lingerie made him horny and the Viagra had him feeling adventurous, so he placed the toy on the bed as if she was bent over in front of him and plunged his stiffness deep into the asshole of the toy. He attempted anal sex with it because Trudy didn't believe in it. He found Trudy's vibrator in her nightstand and decided to see what the big deal was so he slid it painfully into his own anus.

He was now thoroughly stimulated and felt empowered by the ultimate erection so he viciously screwed the toy. After a few deep strokes he felt a tightening around his penis. He slammed hard into the anus of the attachment and realized he couldn't withdraw himself out of it.

What the FUCK? Kyle thought and stood up with the rubber torso stuck firm against his body.

He looked at the box and discovered a warning that a hole needed to be cut at the base of the toy for disposal of the, *uhhhhhh*, fluids. If there isn't a hole, there is the danger of causing a vacuum and a vapor lock, then having to wait for the erection to go down or go to the hospital to have it removed.

Kyle was suddenly terrified. He tugged and pulled frantically trying to get the fricking thing off. The extra pulling and tugging only excited him more. No matter how hard he tried, everything he did seemed to make it worse.

"What the hell am I supposed to do now?"

As he stood panic-stricken in the living room, the door opened and Trudy looked to see her husband, holding a jar of Vaseline, standing in a crotchless teddy, high heels and red lipstick, with a 12-inch vibrator in his ass and a rubber fuck-toy attached to his penis.

"OH MY GOD?!?!?" Trudy screamed, almost vomiting at the sight.

Kyle's boss walked in after bumping into Trudy at her work. They had discussed Kyle's big promotion and she asked him to come over for dinner as a surprise.

The loud scream and thud from Kyle fainting could be heard for miles.

The hospital was able to remove the toy easily, but when he felt the vibrator embedded itself into his bowel cavity and they had to operate and do a sphincterectomy. Kyle can now fart and not make any noise. You've probably seen him on Jerry Springer.

The Long Nights, Part 1

ॐ

The long day's work made Melissa tired. She felt exhausted and her body ached. Sitting in front of a computer all day didn't help. Her eyes felt like they weighed ten pounds. She had her caramel French vanilla frappacino waiting for her as she slipped into her flannel pajamas. Then she parked herself in the la-z-boy for some premium chilling and relaxing. But there wasn't anything on TV except a few badly acted R-rated Skin-e-max movies, and the TV flickering light through the dark, quiet apartment sent her into a badly needed sleep.

Melissa awoke to a bright light shining in through her window. She rubbed her face and scratched her ass, as she walked over to close the blinds. Glancing across the alley to the cross view apartment, she saw a very well-dressed man looking into a walk-in closet and tossing some clothes onto his bed. Melissa was about to shut her blinds, when she saw him undoing his tie and unbuttoning his shirt.

Interesting, she thought.

He slid his tie up over his well-groomed, thick black hair and pulled off his shirt. His chest was tanned with not too much hair on it, and he was very muscular. Not overly buffed out but nicely cut.

Melissa found his unwitting striptease extremely erotic and entertaining. *Am I wrong to be watching this stranger undress?* As he unbuckled his belt, she knew she was doing the right thing.

His white underwear clashed with his tanned muscular legs. She was hoping he needed to change them also. He turned around and slid them down his legs, kicking them aside. The muscles of his ass flexed and rippled making

Melissa salivate. Walking to his dresser, he hung out in all his glory. Melissa grasped her crotch in a reflex, seeing something so beautiful. He wasn't hung like an elephant, but he certainly had nothing to be modest about. From Melissa's point of view he filled out his boxers rather well, especially because as he put on a pair, the tip of his cock peeked out the leg of the shorts. Melissa found herself drooling as she stood motionless in the shadowed window.

He put on a pair of sweatpants and a tank top that clung to his muscular chest and walked out of the room.

DAMN! Melissa thought. *I was just getting warm, well, wet from watching him and he left.*

A light went on in the next room and she saw him lying on a workout bench. He started bench-pressing and she watched the strain in his muscles as they flexed. He pushed the heavy weights up, making his blood rush through his body and his groin swelled. Melissa licked her lips and her pussy grew moist as the needs of the flesh took control of her.

He suddenly got up, and walked out of sight. Melissa groaned in frustration feeling cheated. She was turning away when just as suddenly he reappeared in the room and began working out again. In the doorway a tall, slender Asian woman loosed her hair from the bun on her head. Her long, silky black hair fell along her shoulders to the middle of her back. She gazed upon the man as he pushed the weights up and down. She too admired his brute strength.

The woman unbuttoned the first few buttons on her business dress and walked over to the man. She said something to him that made him smile and laugh. Melissa was not alone in noticing the swelling in his groin. The Asian woman knelt between his legs and brushed her hand on his midsection as it flexed, and then pressed firmly on his groin.

For a brief moment time stood still. Without moving her hand, the woman closed her eyes, smiling wistfully as she felt him grow. Melissa found herself swept away also. It had been a while since she had felt the pleasures of a man.

Time began again and the woman pulled down on the sweatpants, freeing the stranger's cock from its confinement. He tried to pull them back up, but she wouldn't let him. The woman's hair fell down the side of her face as she lowered her mouth towards his proud, firm shaft.

Although the woman's hair hid the sight of him being swallowed from Melissa, she still felt as if it were her that tasted this stranger. Her mouth watered and she found herself again lost in the erotic mood of the night.

The Asian woman pulled her hair aside, and Melissa stared. Transfixed, she watched the woman draw his large cock into her mouth, her cheeks puffing as it filled her. The tip of the woman's tongue peeked out and licked down the vein along the underside of his swollen hardness.

Melissa felt a twinge of frustration, but she bit her lip and squeezed her legs together. Her pussy started to ache from desire and need. As she looked out the window, she couldn't help but slip her hand into her pajamas. The darkness of the room made her invisible, but Melissa felt as if she were glowing bright red from the heat she had burning inside. She stared intently at the two strangers across the alley and imagined it was herself instead of the Asian woman enjoying this mystery man's cock.

The Asian woman stood, letting the hardened penis pop free from her mouth and pulled her dress up over her head. A black bra and thong covered the sacred parts of her body. Her black stockings were held up by a black garter-belt. The man smiled ear to ear as the woman turned away from him and unfastened her bra. She teasingly flipped it to him and covered her small breasts, acting shy. The stranger placed the lacy, black bra over his cock and leaned back, relaxing and admiring the woman. She bent over and slowly peeled the thong from between the cheeks of her ass. The woman's hair touched the ground, as she waved between her legs at him.

Melissa whimpered at the way his cock jerked at the sight of the woman bent over in front of him. She moaned at the sight of the woman's lovely, small breasts and their extremely tight nipples.

The woman walked to the end of the bench where his face was and straddled his head, so that her pussy was hovering over his face. The woman gently caressed between her legs, letting him see her finger disappear into her wet sex. The way she closed her eyes made it apparent she was getting extremely hot. She lowered herself and he slid his tongue into her pussy, while she continued to rub her clit. Her nipples protruded as she became more stimulated. She found his stiff cock with her other hand and she pulled at it, while he delved into her pussy with his snakelike tongue. The Asian woman's face was becoming more pale and awash in perspiration.

Melissa felt her own wetness burn for attention. The tip of her finger grazed against the tips of her nipples as they strained against the fabric. She became hot and beads of sweat accumulated between her breasts. Oblivious to her surroundings, she let her pajama bottoms fall to the floor, clasped her hand onto her labia and fondled the swollen tip of her engorged clit. Her mind wandered and she tried to imagine what the Asian woman's body felt. She watched her fall atop the stranger and ravage his cock with kisses and almost swallow the entire thick shaft. The extreme eroticism of her voyeuristic encounter made it feel less invasive because they couldn't see her and more sexual because it made her free to explore this fetish she discovered.

Melissa felt herself peaking as she gazed out the window. The Asian woman stood up and waddled down the stranger's slick, muscular body. His body shone with the heat from their encounter. The Asian woman spread her legs wide and lowered herself onto the erect shaft that glimmered from her saliva. She jerked and strained to not scream out, as the large, thickened shaft vanished deep within her. For a moment the woman remained motionless and only panted as she sat on top of him. Then, she looked out the window into space and smiled as she wiggled. Melissa could almost see the woman's pubis constrict when she slid up and his hardness would almost slip free from her.

As she slid two fingers inside of herself and pinched her nipple under her top, Melissa felt herself getting close. She wobbled as she stood up, struggling not fall. She grasped the curtain and leaned against the wall, as she watched the couple making love. The look on the Asian woman's face made her desperate to feel what she felt. The throbbing of a man inside of her vagina and the essence of his loins spilling and spurting and filling her with warmth.

Melissa felt her juices glide down her thigh. Seeing the lovers' intense pleasures made her close her eyes and picture herself being there, having the stranger bury his cock within her and fill the void of her needs. As her thumb pressed on her clit, she felt the rush of blood from her head and came for what seemed like forever. The burn of desire made her feel overwhelmed and naked. She collapsed to her knees and started to laugh at the trickle of juices from her pussy. She felt totally spent. Her eyes glazed over and closed from the strenuous release, then she finally relaxed and breathed slower, deeper breaths.

Her vision was blurred when she leaned down to pull up her pajamas and adjust herself. As Melissa stood up and looked out the window, she saw the weight-bench empty and the lights dimmed. Nobody was there and she found herself feeling a little uncomfortable with the effect this had on her. She felt alone now, after having shared this with the couple of strangers. It was exhilarating and yet, somewhat empty, because she couldn't feel it for real.

As she climbed into bed the inner peace and relaxation of her body made her almost drift into heaven. In her body the ache was still there. The ache for someone unknown.

The Traffic Ticket

ຂາ

Vicki was on her way home and in quite a rush. She sped through traffic paying little attention to the speed limit, let alone the stop signs. She looked into her rear view mirror and saw the flashing lights.

"SHIT!" she whispered, as she pulled the car over to the side of the slightly deserted winding road.

In the side mirror Vicki could see the officer sitting in his police car, writing something and punching information into his computer. She rustled through her purse trying to find her license and insurance card.

Tap, Tap, Tap. The policeman rapped on the car window. "Excuse me ma'am, I need to see your license, please."

She sat up and looked out the window at the policeman's rather large crotch. "Boy that's a big gun you have there, officer," she said. "I'm sorry, but I can't find my license or any identification. I must have left them at home."

"Step out of the car, please, ma'am."

Her heart racing with adrenaline, she stepped out of the car. The policeman had a muscular frame and was extremely handsome. He stared at her in awe.

She was statuesque with long blonde hair and wore a short skirt and halter-top with no bra and high heels. She always dressed to accentuate her looks—she always got out of sticky situations with them.

"Ma'am, there was a car stolen earlier this evening matching yours. Do you have anything to prove ownership or your ID?"

"No, I'm sorry," she said, gazing into his eyes and smiling devilishly. "There's got to be some way we can work this out."

He looked sternly back at her, obviously not impressed with her actions. "Now listen, the person we're looking for is armed and dangerous. I'm going to have to search your car."

He found nothing but a couple roaches in the ashtray and a pair of expensive red lace underwear under the seat. While he searched, Vicki looked at him and flirted openly, leaning over to show her large breasts in her loose fitting top and giving him a good look as they brushed against his arm. The cool night air made her nipples hard. They jutted proudly out, showing through her top.

"Well there's nothing in here but I'm afraid I'm going to have to search you also," he said raising an eyebrow.

They walked to the other side of the car away from the road, and she leaned against the side of the car in the standard spread-eagle position. He moved his hands from around her ankles, up the sides of her muscular calves to her strong thighs. He stopped as his search confirmed she wasn't wearing any panties.

"I'd better make sure this is a thorough search for any concealed weapons."

He ran his large hands against the cheeks of her ass and pushed her against the car. The cold steel excited Vicki. The icy cold against her chest accentuated the fire in her backside. He spread her legs apart farther to continue his search. His hands pressed against the puffy mound between her legs, and Vicki moaned while he stroked it with his fingers.

"What kind of gun do you carry out here in the sticks?" she mumbled, as he rubbed harder between her legs. "A .38?"

As he yanked off his belt and pulled his pants down, she reached back and grabbed onto his gun. "Oh, that's definitely a .44 magnum."

He grunted as he mercilessly drove his gun into her. Every thrust had her slamming harder and harder against the hood. The icy chill sent electric shocks through her as her breasts pressed against the cold steel. He reached under her shirt and grabbed both of them in his hands and squeezed hard, as he pulled her against his hardness. He pulled up her top, exposing her large heaving breasts and slammed her chest hard against the frigid hood. Increasing the tempo, he reached up to her shoulders and furiously pounded against her hot fire. She felt him swelling inside her. His grunts became more intense and louder, her skin flushed and her pulse quickened towards the peak of her excitement.

When her orgasm started, she leaned down and grabbed onto her knee to keep from falling as he rammed into her like a jackhammer. He stopped with a hard, deep drive into her. Ecstasy swept through him and he exploded into her with his hot fluids. His knees weakened and he staggered backwards.

Just then another police car showed up. He pulled up his pants and Vicki adjusted her clothes, as the other policeman got out of his car and walked up.

"Jesus Dave, you had us worried. We've been calling and you didn't answer."

The officer looked over to Vicki who was leaning against her car with her head spinning. "You know, Dave, if you're going to meet your wife for dinner just ask. You don't need to make a scene."

The Cheating Bitch

℘

Norm decided to surprise Brandy at home one day. He was always so busy with work and running around, he wasn't what you would call attentive to her needs. Not as much as he could have been anyway. She stayed home alone waiting for him to get back from work, then they'd sit and talk about his day. She was still in good shape, but the way they used to go on trips and run around were now just a memory. She was actually getting kind of lazy just lying around the house.

So as Norm pulled up in the driveway, he laughed to himself thinking how surprised Brandy would be if he went in through the back of the house.

As he approached the back gate to the pool area, he heard a grunting sound. He ignored it, not even imagining what it might be, while he reached for the gate latch. Looking around the side of the house, he admired the large backyard.

Stunned, he stared blankly. Over by the hot tub, he saw something he couldn't believe…

Brandy was kneeling over and some dude was humping away at her!

How could she? Norm couldn't move. He was astounded at the sight of her doing this. He had never seen this guy before and didn't know what to do. The betrayal, the deceit, tore at him. His perfect world was crumbling.

Should he kill the bastard and take care of her after? Should he just leave and confront her later? What if she caught something and gave it to him? What if she got pregnant? How long had she been doing this behind his back?

The tears swelled in his eyes. His emotions took over and the memories flowed through his mind. All their trips together, all the times they stayed up late watching TV and eating pretzels and just kicking back. She would even watch football with him without complaining.

Everyone called them a perfect match.

Now it was all over. His trust was shattered by a single moment of passion.

His heart broken, he decided to end this now. He furiously kicked in the gate. Charging into the yard, he spotted the water-hose and turned it full blast on Brandy and her stud.

Brandy looked up shocked and tried desperately to get away. Her partner growled, angrily glaring at Norm. With a loud "POP" they parted, and he leapt at Norm.

Norm turned the hose full force on the big, black Labrador. The dog yelped and scurried out the gate drenched, and Norm turned to look for Brandy.

As he turned the hose off he saw Brandy hiding under the patio table. He walked up and looked deeply into her dark brown eyes. His heart melted and he forgave her. "I can't stay mad at you girl," he said.

Norm patted her on the head and said, "Damn girl, I didn't know you were in heat. You're a purebred. Tomorrow we're going to the breeder to get you bred!"

The Knight in Distress

🎜

The brave knight looked across the meadow. In the distance he saw a castle. His quest was almost a reality, and he didn't even know it. It was said that he would taste the forbidden fruit of passion on his twenty-first birthday. It would be the fruit of a princess and he would marry her after a fortnight.

He had waited and waited to fulfill this quest, he had dreamt and fantasized about it, and now it was finally upon him. But since the sheep ran away from him now, he hadn't had the practice he so desperately needed.

As the knight approached the castle he saw a patch of wildflowers and decided to pull some for the princess. He knelt to pick the flowers and breathed in their scent.

"Ewww, these smell like shit!" he exclaimed. Then, he looked over and saw his steed plopping a load of horse droppings next to him. He chuckled and stood up only to see a tree limb hit him square in the face.

After the cobwebs cleared and his face stopped bleeding, he saw a vision.

"Am I in heaven?" he asked the beautiful young woman over him.

"NO! You have picked flowers from the royal garden, and for that you shall pay!" With that she picked the tree branch up again and hit him in the nuts.

After blacking out from the pain, he came to again, sore and speaking in a higher voice. He saw the lovely maiden standing over him again, so he quickly covered his balls with his hands as a reflex action.

"Fair Maiden, I will not let you abuse me thusly. I am Sir Fredrick and I have come here to fulfill my destiny."

She bowed her head, greeting him. He saw a crown upon her head and knew she was the princess he had journeyed far to find.

Fredrick groveled for quite a while to apologize. Then he explained his situation to the Princess. She was very taken with his candor. He too found her very appealing and she had a nice ass also, but that was just an observation… She had nice breasts too.

The day went on as they walked through the courtyard and talked. Time was of no concern as the two of them seemed to be made for each other. They held hands and laughed. It was a perfect time and a perfect day.

The afternoon turned to evening and Fredrick grabbed the princess' arm, pulling her to him and kissed her softly. After slapping him sternly, she grabbed him and kissed him back. Their embrace was erotic but fumbling as both of them were inexperienced in the courtship rituals. Yet they knew they were destined to be together.

As they got back to the castle, the princess, whose name was Eden, placed his hand on her heart and said, "This is where you are and belong." She then put his hand on her pubis and said, "This is where I want you tonight." Taking his hand in hers, she led him down a long darkened hallway quietly to the door of a bedroom chamber.

The chamber was dark and extremely large, lit only by the moonlit night sky through floor to ceiling windows. A canopy bed, draped in red silk, beckoned from the center of a long wall covered in picturesque tapestries. The pillow covered mattress seemed inviting and warm.

Eden led him to her enormous bed. He stood before her seeing in her the fulfillment of his journey. She was truly a vision of beauty to behold. She beckoned him to kneel before her. He got down on one knee and watched in wonderment as she unwound the ribbon in her hair and let her hair fall beyond her shoulders and to her waist. She shook her head and her hair rippled like rivers of woven silk. He cast his eyes down, burning as if he had looked into the eyes of an angel sent from heaven. She took his face in her hand and smiled, looking longingly into his eyes, wanting his complete attention focused on her.

Eden's fingers trembled as she tried to unfasten her dress. Fredrick stood up and moved next to her. He grasped her trembling hand in his and kissed each knuckle as if it were her knees and licked the soft skin between them as if it were the softness between her thighs. He moved behind her on the bed. As he unbuttoned the back of her dress, Eden's breath quickened and she closed her eyes, lost in the moment. Every button freed her soul from the cage it was in. Soon her passions would be freed and she would become a woman.

Fredrick grasped the top of the dress and moved it away from her shoulder, pressed his lips against her soft skin. Eden shivered at the brush of his lips against her bare skin, as he slid the dress off her arms. As he kissed her neck Fredrick breathed in the fragrance of her purity and was almost overwhelmed (either that or his pants were cutting off circulation to his John Thomas).

She stood facing away from him and let her dress fall to the floor. To his amazement, she turned around and revealed her beauty to him. Her breasts were small, pert and flushed. The small, tightened nipples stood out and her hair cascaded along the lines of her body. And lower was a small pair of silken white underwear drenched with lust.

The slightest hint of her blonde pubic hair was visible, and as Fredrick touched the area above her panty line, her tummy flinched. Fredrick kissed her firm tummy and felt her heart pulse hard and rapid. His hands trembled as he reached around and pulled her underwear down her ass. She moved her legs back and forth making them fall to her feet.

Now he understood where the saying "Garden of Eden" had come from. This was a sight of unparalleled beauty and a place where temptation seemed to take over common sense.

Eden put her hand on the top of his head running her fingers through his hair. She caressed a breast and nipple with the other. The aroma of her wanting was so intoxicating that Fredrick became drunk with desire. He kissed just above the hair of her womanhood. She closed her eyes and let her head fall back as she pushed down on his head, begging him to go further. Her breathing became deeper and she became lost in the sensations. As his tongue outlined the outer lips of her untarnished sanctuary, her legs weakened.

Fredrick lifted Eden's leg up and rested it on his shoulder. Being a virgin himself, his only knowledge and feeling was to kiss her lower lips as if he were kissing her mouth. The kisses between her legs became deeper and more forceful as Fredrick tried to please her. He slid his tongue out between her lips and Eden moaned. Fredrick knew he found her weakness and the taste and heat from deep within her told him that Eden was close to losing control.

She pulled hard on her nipples, causing her eyes to tear. The intensity of his tongue exploring inside of her and the growing feelings in her body made her feel like she was more alive then any other time in her life. More and more she wanted to feel him inside of her and she imagined him thrusting deeper. Letting her passion take over, she surrendered to the intense pleasures and pressures inside her begging to be freed.

Fredrick savored the taste of her, licking the juices that seemed to pour out of her soul. As Fredrick pulled his head higher to see her, his tongue stroked against her swollen bud and she cried out. So he did it again and again, feeling her body shudder. Her hands pulled at his head to continue until a brief moment of stillness before she climaxed. Waves washed over her body while the orgasm rolled through her. She collapsed and fell to her knees before Fredrick.

She regained her composure and beamed, gazing into Fredrick's eyes. She slowly got up and lay on the bed. He undressed before her and she put her hands behind her head and admired him, watching his muscles flex as he pulled the numerous layers of clothing off. His shorts bulged tight against his swollen manhood and showed a hint of wetness from his obvious expectations.

Eden sat up and softly touched his skin with her fingers. The roughness was a contrast to her soft untarnished flesh. She pulled his undergarment down and looked into his eyes. Her hair brushed against his skin, and she watched as the beating of his heart made his penis pulse. She kissed the tip softly tasting the small deposit of his anticipation. Then, she slid her lips down the shaft, slowly taking as much of him as she could into her mouth. Fredrick closed his eyes and sighed in pleasure as her fingernails raked his chest and up the back of his legs as his cock slid in and out of her mouth.

Fredrick was in heaven. He had finally found his princess and was becoming her prince. The continued attention to his penis was making him crazy. Being a virgin to all but sheep, he hadn't felt the pleasures of a woman or her mouth. He became excited beyond all expectations, finding himself straining to hold back what was building in him since birth. He moaned softly and she felt his manhood grow impossibly harder and felt the strain of his balls tightening against his body.

She stopped and held him tight against her. Looking into his eyes, she said, "I need to feel you deep within me," then lay back on the bed and opened her legs to him inviting him into her purest self.

He climbed on top of her and rested his weight on his hands being afraid he might crush her. He looked down her body and was in awe of the beauty before him. Her breasts were flushed to a soft pink and her nipples still tight and aroused. He kissed each one softly.

She held him tightly and whispered, "Be gentle," then she raised her leg up and wrapped it around his lower torso.

216

He slowly penetrated her and pierced the opening making her wince in pain from never having had anything inside of her before. Except a few candles and maybe a carrot or two. He stopped and tried to withdraw but she pulled him back into her with her leg until the base of his hardened manhood pressed against her pubis.

The incredible tightness made it almost impossible for Fredrick to hold back. He held her tightly waiting for her heavenly channel to adjust to him. He kissed her gently and pulled back slowly and her natural lubricants helped make his slow strokes glide freely in and out. Fredrick kissed her and the taste of her own juices aroused her. She looked down and could see the length of his thickening manhood disappeared into her over and over, deeper and deeper.

Fredrick had a tear in his eye because the sheer pleasure of the moment was more than he ever imagined. His breaths became short and she opened her legs wider, pulling them upwards, and met each of his thrusts. Eden felt him swell inside of her. She tightened around him and she came again. He moaned loudly almost yelling as his fluids erupted inside of her over and over.

His arms weakened and he rested on top of her.

Eden smiled knowingly. She had both become a woman and had made Fredrick a man.

As they lay there together embracing, the moon full shone through the window and lit the room in a silvery glow. They both fell asleep with their bodies entwined basking in their love.

The next morning Fredrick awoke alone in the room and dressed. He had his morning bowel movement then announced he wanted to see the King.

He had an audience with the King. Fredrick paid his respects and pronounced his intentions to marry the princess as soon as possible. The King was overjoyed. He would now have a rich landowner for his dear daughter and they would both prosper from the marriage.

In a few days the arrangements were made and Fredrick's family joined him at the castle. His side of the cathedral was empty except for his mother in her beautiful gown, his father, drunk and wobbling in his seat. Also there were his big brother Ferdinand and his six sisters. Betty, Bertha, Beatrice, Beth, Brianna and the little one, Jane, all sat smiling. Lord, they looked pathetic. Except little Jane, she was all pretty and sitting quietly picking her nose and sticking things on the seats.

The wedding was beautiful. A flock of doves fluttered heavenward as the princess and her court walked into the cathedral. The bridesmaids and bride came down the aisle in their veils and gowns. Fredrick was so happy. He was afire waiting for his bride.

The ceremony started and the King lifted the bride-to-be's veil…

Now there are ugly people and there are butt-ugly people. This woman was worse then butt-ugly. Short brown teeth, small pimply nose, matted light brown hair, dark brown crossed eyes and a triple-chin. This was one ugly bitch.

At first Fredrick's eye twitched. Then a loud booming rumble echoed through his stomach. In a state of horror Fredrick looked up and asked the King "Wh-whhhhooho is this?"

"This is my oldest daughter Princess Eunice," the King replied, "Is there a problem?"

"Well, DUHHH. This isn't my destiny! This is my nightmare."

Surveying the cathedral one of the bridesmaids looked up and lowered her veil, "I am her younger sister, Eden."

In a desperate attempt to save himself and save face, Fredrick looked upon his family for help. His dad wobbled and burped up some wine and crackers that oozed down his chin and his mother was crying. Ferdinand was picking up the boogers Jane had stuck on the chairs and was eating them. Inspiration struck.

"How do you feel about a double marriage?" Fredrick asked in a panic-stricken voice to the King.

The Kind consented and the rest is history. Fredrick with Eden and Eunice with Ferdinand lived happily ever after.

* * * * *

In a small side note to this story, Ferdinand and Eunice had some incredibly ugly children.

The Bridesmaid

ဆ

As the night playfully ran its course, Christi, as maid of honor, was having the bridesmaid's party at her apartment. Dana was getting married next weekend. This was her farewell party to freedom and they were all drinking wine and having a great time. She'd decided to have one of those Pleasure Parties with the girls to embarrass Dana with the toys and stuff.

All the boxes and displays were opened by the hostess. The girls giggled and laughed at the dildos and vibrators in various shapes and sizes. They turned out the lights for a demo of glow in the dark toys. They even had a condom blow-up contest that Leslie won. This was no surprise to most, being she was by far the slut of the bunch with a reputation for an infatuation with giving blow-jobs. The oils and creams were the most interesting. They applied them to each other and felt the textures and feeling of the lotions.

Then the midnight hour approached, much to their dismay. One by one the women began to leave.

Dana was staying with Christi all week to get everything ready for the wedding. They had been friends since college and experienced a lot of each other's lives. They had seen each other blossom and grow as women and watched each other have sex with boyfriends. Once they even engaged in a threesome with Dana's boyfriend. Christi wouldn't let him to screw her, feeling it might hurt their friendship but masturbated as she watched them and touched their bodies as they made love.

The two of them cleaned the apartment. After finishing they grabbed some fattening junk food and kicked back on the couch. They were both relaxed from the wine and all the evening's laughter. Christi stretched and yawned. It was getting very late so she told Dana she was going to hop in the shower. Dana gave her a hug, thanking her for the party. Christi grabbed Dana's hand and kissed it as she left the room.

Dana had a cute figure and was about 5'5" tall with average-sized features and still trim. Her dark hair contrasted her fair skin. She took care of herself and it showed. As Dana went to get undressed for bed, she couldn't help but look into the open bathroom door.

Christi was still in the shower rinsing her long, dirty blonde hair. The curves of her body and the way the water caressed her olive colored skin aroused Dana. She was absolutely beautiful. Christi took the bar of soap and lathered her hands up and slowly rubbed her body. To Dana, it seemed as though she paid particular attention to cleaning her breasts and the small patch of pubic hair on her pubis.

Dana crept closer to see through the transparent glass shower door. Her curiosity was being piqued and her arousal was growing more intense. Christi reached between her legs and rubbed her labia as the water trickled between the lips. The party had obviously triggered her inner desires and releasing this pent-up frustration had become a need. She reached to the shelf in the shower and grabbed a long cylindrical object. Dana tried to see what it was but didn't want Christi to see her, so she stayed where she was instead of maneuvering for a better view.

Christi put one leg up on the small indention for a seat in the shower and looked down as she glided the small toy into the wet opening between her legs. Dana sucked in a deep breath and felt a rush sweep over her. Biting her bottom lip she watched Christi slowly fuck herself with the unknown object. Christi threw her head back, engulfed in a moment of passion. The water from the shower filled her mouth, spilling out along the sides of her neck.

Dana couldn't stop staring. Warmth crept over her body as she felt a sudden rush of adrenaline. She noticed her nipples becoming extremely hard and even the nightshirt pressing against them made the tips ache. Her hand found its way to her fire and she cupped her swollen muff in her hand. The heat within her seemed to seep out and the flesh of her pussy was wet and very sensitive to her touch. As she watched Christi play with her toy in the shower, Dana's finger found its way into her wet sex. She slid her hand under the silk fabric confining her and closed her eyes. Dana lost herself in the moment, in the feeling of her finger probing her engorged pussy, forgetting for the moment about Christi. Looking over again she was shocked to see Christi staring back at her, enthralled and wanting Dana to continue.

In a sort of mental truth or dare, Dana pulled up her shirt high enough for Christi to see her finger darting in and out of her pussy. Christi rolled her eyes and smiled. She grasped her breast in her hand and moaned while watching Dana. Dana looked at Christi and silently urged her to continue doing herself.

Instead, Christi giggled and stepped out of the shower, then grabbed the towel from the rack. Christi's breasts shook as she dried her hair and walked towards Dana. Frozen with unknown fear, Dana let her shirt fall and stood there dumbfounded. Christi reached out and touched her cheek like time was running in slow-motion. Pulling her face closer, Christi kissed her ever so gently. Dana got lightheaded and dizzy. They had played a little in college but just for fun, never for real.

Christi took Dana's hand and led her to the bedroom where she lay her down on the fluffy bedcover. Terrified and almost helpless, Dana submitted herself to Christi's advances. Dana's hand shook as she touched Christi's smooth skin. Christi took her hand in hers and kissed the palm. Leaning forward she kissed her lips gently as she guided her hand along the line of her body. As Christi looked at her, Dana rolled over and pulled her shirt off, letting her breasts free. Dana unfastened her hair-tie and her long dark hair cascaded down her shoulders to her chest.

Christi, still damp from the shower, felt sleek and hot between Dana's legs. Desire added a sheen of sweat to her already moist skin. Her pelvis rocked against Christi causing her labia to spread, engorged and sticky against her damp panties. Wetness seeped through the flimsy lace and Christi felt the heat against her abdomen. She brought her hands up the length of Dana's legs astride her body. Christi's long fingers traced Dana's body's creases and found their way to the frilly lace of her underwear.

Christi looked into Dana's eyes as she slid her hands under her thighs gently lifting her bottom up off the bed. Christi leaned over and kissed Dana's flinching tummy. The soft texture of her lips caressed the silky smoothness of her flesh. Dana moaned softly, feeling Christi's tongue follow the indention of her muscles. Christi's tongue slid into Dana's bellybutton as she placed her palm over Dana's steamy sex. Dana's legs strained to prop her hips upwards as Christi followed the line of her underwear with her wet tongue.

Christi slipped her finger under the tight elastic of the band and slowly tugged the underwear down her thighs. The fabric was wet and clung to her pussy until Christi pinched at them to loosen them away, touching Dana's incredibly vulnerable sex. Christi watched Dana struggle as she pulled the soaked underwear down her calves. Dana rested down and Christi lifted her leg up taking the underwear off her feet. The light shimmered on her moistened pussy.

Christi rolled onto the bed next to Dana. Dana's apprehension was washed away by the feelings of her heart. The warmth of their bodies when their skin touched almost burned. Christi reached over, touching Dana with her fingertips. Like stroking the keys of a piano she played a symphony on her skin making her fingers touch each key in perfect tone.

Dana was frozen and wanted Christi to release her more and more from her torment. She wanted and needed to have this feeling. Nobody ever made her feel this good by just kissing and touching her. Looking down she saw Christi lean over against her and licked her lips. Christi sat up and rested her arm across Dana's body propping herself up above her.

The swelling of her breasts and her rapid breathing made Dana scared and desperate at the same time. Feeling unsure but watching Christi's mouth kissing her skin above her stomach, Dana arched upward, begging for her lips to kiss her aching nipples. Christi moved up and cupped Dana's full, flushed breasts in her hands. Dana's eyes closed and she breathed in deep feeling the sensations race through her body. Christi molded Dana's breasts in her hands letting the taut, erect nipples stand firm between her fingers. While she grasped her breasts, her fingers closed and pinched against Dana's nipples. Dana's hands grasped the bed, tugging in a desperate attempt to maintain control.

Christi's wet lips brushed around Dana's areolas feeling the small bumps and contours of her breasts' form. Dana squirmed and squeezed her thighs together containing the fire she needed extinguished. Shocks of electricity shot through Dana's body to her clit as Christi bit on the sensitized tip of her nipple. Her murmur of pleasure made it clear to Christi she had found a weakness. Mercilessly Christi sucked on each nipple while cupping the heaving breast in her hand. She would pull up until the tip would pop free from her lips.

"Please stop torturing me, please," Dana pleaded as a tear trickled down her cheek. She wanted Christi to deliver her into ecstasy.

While her mouth and one hand continued to play gently with the nipples and areolas, Christi's other hand slid down Dana's tummy to the tuft of hair between her legs. The curls of hair were slippery and a warm, slick juice covered the area. Christi put the finger to her nose and breathed in her friend's scent. Dana bit her lip and stared at Christi, watching her suck the fingertip and close her eyes.

Christi took her wet finger and drew across her bare chest. The shimmer of light made the image flicker. Dana teared up again seeing the glow of a heart drawn on Christi's chest.

Christi kissed Dana on the mouth. Dana reached to hold her but Christi pinned her arms above her head and brushed Dana's lips with her tongue. In that moment Dana felt like she was floating. The softness of that kiss was nothing like any man's kiss. It was sensuous, erotic and full of feeling. She was paralyzed and so full of stirring emotions she became overwhelmed.

Desperate, she tried to stop herself from giving into this insatiable hunger. Christi straddled Dana and slowly moved down her body letting the tips of her nipples drag against her. The feeling of another woman's breasts touching her skin made Dana shudder with pleasure. All down her body Christi slid, her flesh blazing against Dana's.

Christi knelt over the end of the bed and looked at Dana's wet pussy. A deep needy moan echoed through the room as Christi's finger parted the opening of Dana's wanton pussy. Like an unbridled horse Dana bucked and shook, while Christi teased the labia and stroked around the opening, not yet venturing inside. Moving closer, Dana opened her legs wide, letting one dangle off the bed. She could feel Christi's hot breath against her pubis. Lost in the abandon of lust, Christi stretched her labia wide and exposed Dana's hardened bud. Then she gently circled Dana's clit with her fingertip.

Dana stared at the ceiling and clenched her eyes tight against the blinding flash as Christi's tongue flicked her clit. Her body became one big erogenous zone as everything became responsive to every touch. Christi sucked hard at Dana's clit making it pulse. Christi had never tasted the sweet flavor of a woman but enjoyed the way the silky flesh melted to her tongue. Now she understood why some men craved the feel and taste of an aroused pussy. The increased stimuli and deepened desire made Dana's muscles loosen and her juices flowed heavier. Dana reached down and ran her fingers through Christi's hair as she suckled at her pussy.

Christi grabbed Dana's hands and moved them up to her own breasts. Christi looked up and licked the length of Dana's pussy. Dana cupped her breasts and began fondling them as Christi continued her assault on her pussy. The way Dana pulled and squeezed at her breasts while Christi sucked her pussy made her remember the ecstasy she felt from going to forbidden places and taking unconventional chances to explore herself.

Dana's rush peaked and she was swept away in a flood of emotional ecstasy when Christi finally slid her fingers inside. Dana felt Christi seeking the perfect spot. Her long slender fingers knew exactly where to touch. In a moment frozen in time Dana felt Christi hit her g-spot and suck hard on her clit and lost control. Her body shook and spasms overtook her. A flush of heat flamed through her as she came.

She had never felt like this and wanted it to last forever. A kind of abyss she fell into and didn't want out of.

Dana's body was flushed and her skin seemed hot as Christi kissed her pubis and rested her head against it. Dana pulled Christi back up onto the bed. She flopped and scrambled to the edge of the bed and reached to her overnight bag on the hope chest. Dana opened the bag and dug a large rubber dildo out of the bottom. It had a head on both ends and had every detail colored to make it seem more realistic.

Dana laughed as she playfully sucked on the end of it pretending it was a real man. Desire and a touch of jealousy ignited Christi's curiosity. She moved across the bed, grasped the other end and looked down its length into Dana's eyes as she too sucked it as if it were real.

Christi's hand crept between her legs and fondled the wet folds of her pussy. Her clit was throbbing as she finger stroked against the swollen, protruding hood. She became a little lightheaded as she sucked on the end of the large dildo and imagined the thick length satisfying her lower craving.

Dana stroked Christi's cheek, bringing her back to reality. She gently took the toy from Christi's hungry mouth and replaced it with her slippery tongue. Dana traced her face with her fingertips enjoying the softness of her skin. Christi moaned as the feel and taste of Dana's tongue caused a darkened want inside of her.

Dana lay back and slid the toy between her breasts and along her torso until it reached her pubis. She was transfixed by Christi's expression while she painfully pushed the large tip between the lips of her pussy. Her eyes fluttered and closed, as the length of it filled her. Her hands shook, so Christi took hold of the other end and moved it slowly in and out of Dana's pussy. She leaned down and kissed Dana's belly, then moved lower and tasted the juices seeping from within her. Christi slid the toy deeper into her, causing her to sob. Scared she had hurt her friend, Christi tried to withdraw the monstrous shaft but Dana grabbed her hand and forced it deeper as if daring to take all of it.

Christi's own needs took over and she moved herself around and positioned herself between Dana's legs. She pressed the other end of the rubber cock against her own wet opening. Gasping, she watched as the tip stretched her labia apart. It seemed to slide in easier than with Dana but the feeling of the fullness made her shudder and almost cum.

Dana cried blissfully with pleasure. Their bodies seemed drawn together and in a smooth motion they ground against each other as if making love. Christi tightened her inner muscles to grip the toy and fucked Dana with it. They rhythmically thrust apart then together, feeling their bodies come alive and flush with passion. As the toy probed each of them simultaneously they felt their heated passions growing. Wanting Dana as much as the toy, Christi reached out and grabbed Dana's ass and pulled her closer. Their tangled legs became handles to draw them even closer still. As Dana shook and jerked violently in another orgasmic rush, her legs tightened and their pussies met with the toy buried to the hilt in each of them.

Her head spinning, Dana pulled the toy out of herself. Moving down on the bed she took the toy in her hand and slowly slid it deep into Christi. Dana's mouth was hungry for Christi's taste, so she kissed her breasts, then licked her nipples. Never having been with any other woman she wasn't sure what she did was pleasurable, but knew that this is what she liked having done to her.

As Christi tried to sit up Dana pushed her back down and licked her protruding clit, grasping the end of the toy and twisting it back and forth inside of Christi which made her grab the blankets and pull them loose from the bed. Her back arched and her legs pushed her ass up off the bed against Dana's hot mouth. Her breasts reached up, pleading for someone to touch them and suck the aching, taut nipples as Dana unmercifully twisted the half of the dildo buried in Christi.

The inner walls of Christi's pussy stretched and expanded, making her entire body more responsive. The heightened sensitivity made her feel like she was being ripped apart. In desperation, Christi grabbed her breasts, pulling the nipples hard. She felt Dana sucking at her clit again and felt her body lift off the bed and crash back down as she climaxed violently. She couldn't open her eyes because the tensions made every muscle clench tight. She shook uncontrollably and when Dana pulled the toy out she came again.

When she had relaxed enough to focus on what happened, Christi felt content and fully spent. With Dana lying against her side a warmth and comfort filled her heart. The experience made her know that a true lovemaking session could fulfill even the deepest needs.

They spent the night lying wrapped in each other's arms and sleeping in an altered state. The warmth of their bodies, the steady rise and fall of their breath made the bed seemed like an island oasis. It all seemed so right.

The morning sun shone in the room and Christi awoke to see Dana gone and a single flower on her pillow. The smell of bacon filled the apartment as Christi got up. She streaked across the room to take a pee then searched for a robe to put on. In the kitchen Dana was cooking away wearing a long T-shirt. As she bent over, Christi saw she had nothing on under it as her ass peeked out. They both smiled and started giggling as they chatted. A relaxed feel filled the room. They both knew their incredible experience didn't hurt the friendship that was so precious. They loved each other, like best friends do, and this new path only intensified their feelings.

Knowing she would soon be married, Dana felt she should talk to Christi about the previous night. In an awkward voice Dana stuttered through saying, "Uh, Christi, last night, uhhh, wonderful, ummmmmm, orgasmic, uhhh, I'm getting married and shouldn't have, uhhh…"

Christi took Dana's hand and kissed it, "Relax, we just experimented in something we've both been thinking about since college. I love you, Dana, and I always will. You know that. We always were open and tried things, now we're past it and we won't let it happen again."

* * * * *

They spent the next four days in a deepening sexual state. They took each other to heights and experienced things no man (except maybe Antonio Banderas) could show them. They explored each other and found new ways to use the vacuum cleaner and kitchen whisk. The rolling pin could be used for a completely different kind of kneading and who would have known that a corkscrew was shaped like that for a reason? They had a wonderful time but it was pervaded by a wistful "never again". Within a few days Dana would be marrying Jacob and would revert back to being just friends.

Christi helped Dana get ready for the big day. She did everything bridesmaids were supposed to do. They went to the spa and had their make-up and hair done. Then had an expensive, extremely rich lunch all the while trying to hold back their feelings. They drank champagne and had their pre-nuptial pictures taken. Christi smiled and pretended to be overjoyed for her friend but the whole time she was crying inside, knowing that this was the end of a part of their friendship she had just discovered.

* * * * *

As they stood at the altar listening to the priest reading the sermon, Dana felt Christi's raw and weeping presence behind her. Her heart ached in sympathy with her friend. Thinking about Christi, her heart grew heavy with doubt. Questions filled her head. Was she gay? Was she unsure about Jacob? Why were wedding dresses so tight across the bust?

Before the priest started the vows, he called out, "If anyone here knows why these two people should not be married let them speak now or forever hold their peace."

A silence filled the room. Dana looked over her shoulder to see Christi's watery eyes and couldn't speak.

Suddenly a quiet voice said, "I do." Pete, the best man, looked at Jacob and said, "I can't let you marry her, Jacob. I love you. We've been lovers for two years and I can't hide my feelings anymore." Pete stepped up and kissed Jacob passionately. The saliva from their tongues slimed across the front of Jacob's white tuxedo.

Shocked, Dana slapped Jacob and jumped into Christi's arms. They laughed and ran from the church. Christi smiled and Dana cast off her veil and grabbed a candlestick someone was holding outside the church. The two women giggled and got into the limousine and sped off.

The Watcher

Those eyes…those deep blue eyes.

Clyde sat there gawking uncontrollably, drooling at the vision before him. He didn't even know her except from seeing her from afar. Never in his wildest fantasies would he believe a woman this fine could want him.

They had nothing in common except they were both 5'4" tall. She was 110 pounds and he weighed 175. Her measurements were 38-25-36; his were more like 37-40-38. She liked rock music and he loved the blues. He was a John Wayne movie buff but she liked Julia Roberts' comedies. He graduated from high school and married and went to work while raising a family. She was a 22-year-old junior at Yale studying psychology and drama.

But he did know what turned her on: she loved leather. She was an exhibitionist and he loved to watch!

He sat there patiently watching her, as she stood bent over a chair wearing black stiletto heels and a leather peek-a-boo bra. She stared back at him with that nasty little smile on her face and those piercing blue eyes. Moving over to the bed with its satin red sheets, she lay down on her stomach with her left leg pulled up ever so slightly, accentuating her ass. She lifted her chest to reveal her perfect breasts and her red curly hair flowed across her neck and shoulders. Then she rolled over to her back and dripped yogurt onto her nipples and smiled devilishly as she smeared it around her areolas.

God how he wanted to help her! He even stuck his tongue out but she wouldn't let him…yet. She moved over to the doorway and grabbed onto the top of the frame, revealing her entire body from her flaming red hair to her painted fire red

231

toenails and all her other absolutely perfect attributes in between.

He longed to touch her, but he couldn't. He was slowly being tortured by the longing in his heart and the yearning in his body.

She moved back onto the bed wearing a sapphire blue robe. She closed her eyes and opened herself for only his eyes to see. She had an incredible looking pubis with the red pubic hair trimmed back revealing everything a man could want.

Clyde wiped the sweat from his forehead and licked his lips. He hungered to taste this Venus before his eyes.

She pulled back the outer labia beckoning him to delve deeper into her velvety vice.

Clyde couldn't take it anymore. This was too much for him, too much for any man. He unzipped his fly and tugged feverishly at his manliness trying to free it. Suddenly:

Knock, Knock, Knock!

"Did you fall in?!? Dammit, Clyde. Every first Monday of the month you get that Playboy magazine in the mail there's no getting you out of the frickin' bathroom! You're gonna go blind doing that!"

The Desperation

ॐ

The candles burned hot and the flickering lights cast the silhouettes of two lovers against the wall. A trail of clothes were thrown randomly across the floor and the smooth sounds of jazz played quietly in the background, interrupted only by the harsh breaths from the lovers as the intensity of their passions reached a crescendo.

She was beautiful, riding him and throwing her head back as she felt her orgasm approach. Her full breasts rose as she gasped and her muffled cries of passion only made him drive harder and she rocked back and forth on his cock. She traced his lips with her fingers and he nibbled on them. Trying desperately to keep upright, she felt weak and almost ready to collapse against him. She knew she couldn't stop she was too close.

He caressed her tummy gently then grasped her hips. Tilting her forward, he drove deeper inside. She felt like a balloon about to explode. She pulled her long hair back with one hand and held herself up with the other hand, digging her nails into his chest. She clenched her teeth, closed her eyes tight and jerked hard like an earthquake as she came. Over and over the ripples of the orgasm rolled through her body making her muscles flex around his swollen hardness.

"Oh my God!" he moaned, as she quickly pulled him out and slid down to wrap her mouth around his engorged manhood. She could taste her own juices as she sucked down the length of his penis. He shook and then froze, tightening his muscles and stretching out so hard that his toes curled. He then erupted like a volcano and his lava ran down the sides of her mouth. She continued milking the fluids built-up deep inside of him until there were no more.

"Damn. It's been so long, babe," he said quietly.

She stood up and smiled back at him, wiping the stream of cum from her chin as she walked to the sink to spit it out. After she brushed her teeth, the gargling of Listerine warbled through the bedroom. "Well, you're the one that got me pregnant. I didn't want you poking the kid in the eye."

"Well thanks for giving in. I appreciate it."

"SHIT!" she said desperately. "I go to all the bother of having sex even though I don't feel like it because they say it makes you go into labor and *nothing*. SHIT!"

"Well I hope you enjoyed it a little?"

"Ya right that's how I got into this mess." *BUUUURRRRRPPPP! Pftttttttttt.* "Damn, I got gas now. Move over, my back hurts and my hemorrhoids are screaming. And don't snore so loud tonight, it's pissing me off."

Lying in bed together, they looked at each other smiling.

"I love you."

"I love you too." she whispered.

Then they both farted and rolled over.

The Advice

❧

As guys will do at work, the topic of discussion was sex. Vince's sex life or lack thereof to be exact.

"Man, I tell ya, all she wants to do is shop or watch the television. It's enough to drive ya crazy!" Vince said.

With a semi-sarcastic smirk on his face Lee replied, "You have to add a little spark in your sex life or the woman will get bored. You do, you know, satisfy her, right?"

"Hey man, when we do have sex I give it to her good! None of that three strokes and a squirt shit, I give her the big 'O' and then it's my turn!"

"Of course you do. Why else would she rather watch Home Shopping and Jay Leno every night when she could be having sex with you?"

"Ya!!!… Hey wait, what the hell are you saying?"

"Let me tell you something and don't ever say anything to my old lady or I'll nail your balls to my boat. Last night my wife and I had the most incredible sex. I mean, like this is the shit you see in the pornos." Lee sat down and began describing the previous evening. His eyes were big and he was very animated.

"After work I gave my wife a box with a note attached to it that read, 'You're the boss tonight.' Inside I put four red lace ties, a blindfold, a small bottle of scented oil and a feather. Damn! Just thinking about this is giving me a hard-on!" Vince moved his chair over a little as he listened intently. "Anyway she tied me to the bed, blindfolded me then rubbed that oil all over my body and on my jimmy. And I'll tell you, man, she was like possessed or something because she screwed me like a hooker would screw her best client. I probably only had three hours sleep and had to drink two liters of water to replenish the fluids in my body. It was by far the best sex we'd had in years... No, I take that back, the time in the elevator was better...but that's a different story." Lee wiped the sweat from his brow and told Vince, "You should try something like that with your wife, dude. She'll love it, trust me!"

Vince rushed home and bolted into the house. He tripped and fell over the stupid poodle his wife bought last month because she found it cute and (she knew it would piss him off if he knew how expensive it was). Since he had never wanted a dog, he truly detested it.

"I hate you, you damn mutt and you hate me too. Get the fuck outside you dumb bitch!" he yelled as he kicked the yelping dog out into the backyard.

When his wife Louise finally came home, she found a small box with a note from Vince on the kitchen table. She read the note. 'You're the boss, you can do anything you want tonight!' She opened the box and found four leather straps, a scarf, a bottle of chocolate syrup and a rubber glove. She giggled and walked into the bedroom to find candles burning and Vince stepping out of the bathroom with his robe on.

"Did you feed the dog? She hasn't eaten all day?"

"Hey, this is the only *dong* I'm worried about feeding!" Vince said grabbing his crotch.

"You think you can handle anything I want?" Louise slyly whispered, looking at him with a fire in her eyes he hadn't seen since she saw a 50% off sale at Nordstrom's. "Take off that silly robe and get into bed, *NOW*! Take off those stupid silk red bikini underwear too."

Louise walked over and grabbed onto his *dong* and smiled devilishly, and said, "Don't move." Then, she unbuttoned her blouse and unsnapped the clasp holding her expensive, implanted, 44D breasts inside of her bra, and they burst free from their confinement. As she reached to tie his wrist to the brass bed, she pressed her swelling breasts against his face, causing his cock to stiffen with anticipation. The sweet scent of the $100 an ounce perfume she ordered from France made him dizzy with need. While she tied his ankles to the end of the bed, she dragged her flaming, red acrylic fingernails along the inseam of his legs. His shaft throbbed from the almost erotic images flashing through his mind.

Now Louise had total control and she *enjoyed* control.

"Come on baby, anything you want. But make it quick, I'm going insane here." Vince silently begged her to continue with this domination and submission game.

"Shut-up asshole, I'm in charge now," Louise barked.

More aggressively still, she wrapped the scarf around his face making him blind to what she was doing. Now he could only hear and smell what was happening. He heard her slipping out of her clothes and giggling.

"Wait here. I've got to go into the kitchen," she said nastily. "Oh that's right you can't move."

He felt her run her finger along his body and flinched as her nails dug into his legs. She placed her lips over the top of his cock and slowly lowered her mouth around it letting her tongue slide along the vein down the side to the base. Then she wrapped her tongue around his swelling cock completely like a snake around its prey.

"I'll be right back. I need the chocolate syrup…" Louise kissed his mouth deeply then walked away.

This was the most incredible thing Vince had done in a long time. Because Louise was always working or shopping, they never got time like this to explore. Giving her control had positive advantages. She could let her passions take over. She could do anything she wanted and Vince knew she liked the taste and feel of semen. She thought it was a natural way to get protein.

Being tied up had its disadvantages also. He couldn't see anything. He couldn't touch his throbbing cock and the sound of her footsteps on the kitchen floor were really driving him crazy. All he could hear was her footsteps across the floor. The back door opened. "What the hell is she doing? Probably feeding that fuckin' dog," he thought aloud.

"Did you miss me?"

"Hell yes!" Vince blurted out.

The sensation of the cold syrup against his flesh was an indescribable pleasure, surpassed only by the feeling of Louise flickering her tongue to lick it up. Next to the joy of her mouth against his big dong was her naturally wet, perfume-enhanced pussy against his mouth as she slipped into a 69 position. He couldn't bury his face or tongue deep enough. His pleasure was heightened as she sucked on his cock and he flicked his tongue into her sex.

Vince nuzzled deeper and rested his chin against her clit. The vibrations of his humming the Alphabet Song sent chills up her back. She almost jerked his penis loose as her mouth sucked hard and she sat upright gasping for air. Vince lapped up the juices coming from within her. Louise's hand furiously stroked his cock and fondled his balls as she sucked the tip. She then sat upright forcing her pussy to press against his mouth as he relentlessly ate her out. She tugged and stroked the length of his cock with her hand. His penis was red from the friction.

Louise sat up and threw her head back lost in pleasure. Her pussy seemed to gel against his face. She rotated her hips, grinding her cunt on his eager tongue. Vince mumbled and made yummy sounds, tasting her dripping juices in his mouth. Louise squeezed Vince's cock as she felt herself peaking. All her muscles tightened as the tension built within her. She was so far gone that she forgot she was holding him.

Vince felt like a stress toy and the head of his penis bulged as she squeezed relentlessly.

She came with such a force that it took his breath away… Though that could also have been from her pushing on his stomach to keep herself from collapsing from weakness or the fact she almost ripped his penis off. He was so into her that he didn't hear the phone ring. She sat on his face and pulled on his hair to continue his journey and oral exploration of every crease and crevice of her womanly cavern.

"Damn Vince, it's been a while, babe. Lee's wife Denise just called and told me there's a sale at Macys and they close in an hour, so I'll hurry back to finish. You told me I could do anything I wanted. Thanks, you are the best. You just wait right there!" she said gleefully not waiting for his reply.

Louise hurriedly dressed and took all the money from Vince's wallet with her as she scurried out the door. She was so happy.

"But, but, what about, you know, SHIT, what next?"

All Vince could do was lay there with a hard-on. His cock was covered with chocolate syrup and Louise's spit.

The hungry, mean dog jumped onto the bed and growled at Vince. The dog sniffed the air smelling the syrup and growled ferociously at her tormentor. Vince struggled to get away. He yelled at the dog and it leapt at his groin with teeth bared.

The screams of unearthly pain could be heard for miles.

The Other Man

✍

The slow steady drumming of the rain outside the door was drowning out the moans inside. Looking in through an open window, all that Dave saw was a fire, two half full glasses of champagne, a silver bowl of strawberries and another bowl of cream. That simple tranquility would have been broken by a whimpering cry of deepened ecstasy ringing from the room if Dave could have heard it. Clothes were strewn across the furniture. A wet dress, red brasserie, and a pair of trousers lay on the floor along with a striped button up shirt. Dave pushed his face against the window, his breath fogging the glass as he tried to see what was happening.

He believed his wife Tami was cheating on him. She had become more distant, more secretive. What he saw here would be his proof. He brought a camera to take pictures, then he would tell her their marriage was OVER. The cold rain drenched his trench coat and Seattle Mariners baseball hat. Still, he stood in the mud determined to find out…tonight. He crept in the shadows along the wall of the house to the next window. There, he stared through the camera into the dimly lit room and saw something moving. Through the lens he saw a woman's head moving up and down.

Dear Lord, it's Tami!!!!!!

He could barely see her face but it was definitely Tami. In horror, he watched his wife as she held onto another man's penis, giving him a blowjob like the ones only hookers give. A tear came to his eye as he saw Tami throw her head back. A bead of drool trickled along the corner of her mouth and she smiled wickedly. She still held fast to his enormous hard cock glistening with her spit.

Tami's flowing black hair hung across her face as she leaned forward to take the head into her mouth. Her tongue circled the tip moving farther and farther down the shaft. She seemed to moan and abruptly pulled up and stood before her lover. Dave saw she was wearing his favorite thong, the white one with a frilly lace waistband, and no bra.

Tami cut the thong waistband with a pair of scissors and tossed them aside, as her lover sat in front of her with an incredible hard-on. There was wickedness to her tonight, a side Dave had not seen in quite a while—a kind of dirty, naughty, frisky, "let's fuck" attitude. As she straddled her lover in the chair (Dave's favorite chair for football), she reached down and grabbed his cock in her palm and guided the hardness into her opening. The cock twinged and flinched in her hand, as she first just spread her labia with its tip then drew the swollen head into her. As if possessed she slid down the length of it, and screamed in pleasure so ecstatic Dave could almost feel the scream vibrate through him.

Strangely, Dave was aroused seeing his wife fucking another guy. He watched as she grasped her lover's wrists and showed him how she wanted her breasts touched. Her nipples taut from excitement, she moved his fingers against them. Dave remembered touching Tami like that and he was overcome by the fear of losing her to this man.

When she reached her limit, she firmly pinned her lover's hands against the back of the chair and slammed against his torso making his head jerk forward from the sheer force. She seemed almost desperate as she reached down and frantically rubbed her clit while she fucked her lover. Dave could see that her fingertips were wet from touching the entrance to her desire. She took her fingertip and rubbed the juices from her sex along the lips of his mouth, dipping a finger into her pussy and touching his lips again. She then kissed his mouth and her hair fell forward, covering their faces. Her chest had sweat on it from her non-stop rhythm of their sex. She slammed her pussy frantically onto his hard cock. She rode his cock with abandon.

Her mouth opened wide and her eyes strained to stay open as she shivered. She was so close. With an abrupt thrust that buried her lover's cock to the hilt, she looked up to the sky tears flowing from her eyes and she collapsed and shook in a deep orgasmic climax that seemed to last forever. She flipped her hair to stare into her lover's eyes. Her face was blank, though her body still jumped from the spastic contractions on his still rock-hard cock inside her.

In a jealous rage Dave broke in the door and rushed into the living room. Tami grabbed a blanket to cover herself. Dave was crying as he pointed the gun at her. How could she do this to him after everything they've been through?

He couldn't do it. He screamed at the stranger to stand up. But he remained motionless. Dave was a volcano of emotional pain. He then erupted and shot the lover in the back of the head three times. Tami screamed as the plastic scattered out across the floor and into the fire which hissed and spit, then settled again. The quiet was deafening. Shock took over both of them and a hissing noise echoed through the room.

Dave stood there dripping wet from the rain, crying, thinking he had killed a man out of sheer jealousy.

In fact, he'd murdered…a mannequin.

Seems Tami had been secretive lately because she was feeling unfulfilled. Her friend Joan had purchased her a "boytoy". It was a life-size rubber doll with attachable anatomy in various sizes. She had picked a large (Dave was definitely a medium). The jumbo looked like it was for elephants.

She told him how being alone a lot had made her search for alternatives and she couldn't bring herself to cheat on him. So this was the next best thing. Her biggest problem was that she had fallen in love with the boytoy, or "MEAT" as she lovingly called him. He was always there when she needed him. Stamina had never been a problem and the premature ejaculation problem was never there. He never complained about her housecleaning. Never nudged her in the ribs with morning breath, wanting sex. Didn't eat everything in the refrigerator and didn't like sports. He actually listened when she talked. Never told her to lose weight. He made love on demand and always satisfied her and her friends when they stayed the night. He didn't get jealous. Didn't fart in public and blame her. Let her go out with her friends. He even cuddled with her as long as she wanted after sex. His only joy was being there for her.

He was the perfect male.

The Long Nights, Part 2

ဆ

The night was long and Melissa didn't sleep very well with the visions of the stranger and the Asian woman rushing through her head. Her body still ached for the touch of a man because it had been a while. The opportunity had arisen but the men she attracted were after one thing. She was attractive and a very sensuous woman but her career and time weren't on her side. After college she rushed into the proverbial rat race and became another rat.

Melissa awoke to the numbing buzz from the alarm clock at 5:30. Blinking her eyes rapidly, she stumbled to the bathroom hitting the nightstand with her foot. The shower water covered her in warmth. She relaxed and closed her eyes. She rubbed the washrag along the slick curves of her sore muscles and smooth skin. The water caressed her flesh. Her hands wandered on her body and as she closed her eyes she saw her strangers again. Not wanting to scare the visions away, she kept her eyes shut tight and envisioned the man in the shower with her.

A sudden warmth filled her as she rubbed the washcloth along her pubic bone and the frill glanced off her pussy. She clenched her eyes tight, grasping her breasts, but in her mind it was the stranger that grabbed them. The taut nipples flashed shock waves straight to her clitoris as the water streamed on them and trickled off the erect tips. Her body was on fire and the wetness of the shower couldn't stop the burn.

A deep moan echoed in the small glass shower as the stranger's tongue rubbed against her clit and Melissa leaned against the ceramic tiled wall. The surface was slick and smooth against her face as the rough wetness dug into her pussy. Leaning over to give the tonguing freer access, she felt the water trickle along the cheeks of her ass.

She breathlessly envisioned the stranger's long hard shaft penetrating her opening. Sliding two fingers into her pussy, she pressed her breasts against the wall while reaching her other arm up over her head. The wet, smoothness of the wall made her feel as if she were being pushed against it as the stranger drove into her from behind. There was a slow drumming spatter of water as it slid down her back and fell from her hand as it pushed her finger ever so deeply into her convulsing hole. Her desire was taking over and she became flustered, forgetting where she was. Moaning loudly, she almost cried from the sheer pleasure of these fantasies of her heart.

She moved her other hand up to her breasts and pulled hard at her nipples, making them ache. As her climax approached Melissa found she was unable to hold herself up. She turned and faced the showerhead. Her mouth filled with water and she gasped.

Grabbing the showerhead off the hook she sat in the shower and pressed the force of the water against her pussy. Vigorously she rubbed her clit as the water washed the flesh of her pussy. When she came, she slammed her back against the wall. She sat motionless and weak, while water gushed along her thigh, washing her clean.

The morning flashed by and at work Melissa was a little more relaxed than usual. Stretching her sore muscles, she walked home. As she strolled up to the stairs to her apartment, she saw the stranger and Asian woman approaching their complex across the way. They walked up to the set of mailboxes right outside the door and stopped to talk to someone on the walkway steps. Melissa saw the Asian woman open the bottom right mailbox and check her mail. Then the couple went inside.

Being curious, Melissa walked across the street and looked at the mailbox the woman had opened. "Tony and

Kayla" she read off the mailbox. *So that's who they are*, she thought finally putting a name to the images in her head.

The next few nights flew by and every night Melissa would check the window to see if they were there. Thursday on her way home from work, she passed a pawnshop and saw a pair of binoculars in the window for fifty bucks. An evil grin crossed her face and she stepped in. A few minutes later after a little bartering she had the binoculars and 40 dollars less money. Now she could see Tony and Kayla up closer and more personal.

She went home and took a long shower, then strolled into her living room to watch "Sleepless in Seattle" again when she saw the binoculars on the table. She giggled and picked them up, then walked over to the window and looked out. She could see the park now. It was down the road and she could never really see it from the apartment. She saw the lights of the city flickering. She spent a while just gazing out her window seeing other buildings. There was a woman walking her dog, two men kissing on a bench and a couple fucking in a convertible.

A light shone out from Tony and Kayla's apartment so she turned to face it. The binoculars put her almost inside the room. She saw the reflection in the hall mirror of someone running across the room. It looked like they were fighting about something.

Should she watch? Should she turn away? Melissa was torn again but continued to watch. She felt drawn in to watch them, even if she was invading their privacy. Tony and Kayla were face to face yelling and she could make out the words "Fuck you" more than once by reading their lips. Suddenly Kayla slapped Tony's face and jumped on him, smothering his mouth with her tongue. She pushed him hard against the wall causing the hanging picture to crash to the floor. Tony reached out to touch her and Kayla slapped his hand away.

Desire burned inside of Melissa. She was transfixed by Kayla's power over Tony.

Kayla pulled at his shirt, tearing it open. Reaching over, Kayla grabbed the letter opener on the desk and shredded the hole in his T-shirt, then pulled it loose from his chest leaving the strands to hang. Tony tried to move forward and Kayla shoved him against the wall again. Kayla was in total control.

Melissa's bathrobe opened as she stood staring at the couple. The slight coolness of the room made her body chill even as her own feelings warmed her. She rushed into her bedroom and pulled out her pocket rocket toy and rushed back into the living room, not wanting to miss anything. Melissa moved a chair over to the window and sat down, refocusing her eyes on the couple.

Kayla was tugging at Tony's belt and slung it from the loops. She hung it around his neck and undid his pants, unzipping the front. She reached her hand in the flap of his underwear, wrapping her hand around his growing cock. Melissa looked closely through the binoculars at how Kayla was biting his nipples and squeezing his large cock in her hand. Tony's eyes were closed and he looked like he was enjoying everything. Kayla knelt down before Tony and slid his underwear down his flexed thighs.

Kayla showed no mercy as she took the entire length of Tony's cock deeply into her mouth. Tony stared skyward and grasped her head. Kayla stood up and slapped his hands away. She turned his face against the wall and slung the belt from around his neck, making him flinch in pain. She cruelly wrapped his hands behind him.

Melissa's view with the binoculars had her almost in the room, feeling the heat between them. She found herself stroking her thighs with her toy. The humming vibrations of the toy became less distracting and more exhilarating. She stared as Kayla knelt down against the wall in front of Tony. She grabbed his ass as he fucked her mouth.

Melissa's pussy was afire and the toy seemed destined to explore her heat.

Kayla grasped Tony's thigh and pulled him towards her more vigorously. Melissa moved to the corner of her window to see Tony's cock slide in and out of Kayla's mouth. Her view became clear and she saw Kayla pull her skirt up and reveal her trimmed pussy. Tony would slide his hard cock into her mouth and Kayla massaged her pussy at the same time.

Melissa had seen other women masturbate, but Kayla stirred her. The way she manipulated the lips of her flesh seemed so sexy and natural. Melissa found herself copying the movements and she became a little distracted from her vigil. Melissa became a little overwhelmed as the sanctity of her moment was broken by a sudden primal urge to satisfy her desire. Her toy made its way to her wetness and now hummed against her clit. She plunged two fingers deeply inside the walls of her pussy. The tightness around her fingers made her dream it was Tony's stiff rod instead of her fingers.

Melissa watched as Kayla moved both hands to Tony's ass and saw him strain and flex as he struggled to keep composure. She almost heard him yell as he came. Kayla stood up against the wall and wiped the dripping essence from the corner of her mouth as she held Tony tightly. Melissa licked her lips wanting to taste the salty seed from Tony's cock.

Melissa lost herself in the desperate need to feel Tony fucking her. She dropped the binoculars and put her leg up over the arm of the chair. She plunged her fingers in and out of her pussy as the pocket rocket massaged her clit. Her wet hair hung loosely as it fell against her body and the orgasmic feelings washed over her in a hurricane as she began to come. The steady vibrations against her clit caused her body to tremble and shake. A pleasurable smile widened on her face as she laughed.

She gathered herself and stood up. She moved the chair back and leaned over to pick up her binoculars and took another peek. When she looked over to Tony and Kayla's apartment she saw them standing by their window looking back at her through their own binoculars.

The Transplant

℅

"Mr. Jones? Are you awake? Mr. Bob Jones?"

"Huh, what happened? Where am I?"

"You're in the hospital. You were involved in a freak snowboarding accident."

"Is everything okay? I mean, how bad was it? Good Lord, I can't feel my legs. I'll never walk again! I'll never be able to play baseball! I'll never…"

"Sir, calm down, you're fine. But I must inform you that you've lost…how to phrase this, your, uh, ummmmm, leg."

"The right one?"

"No," the doctor muttered.

"The left one?"

"Uh, no. The other leg," the doctor muttered again.

"You mean…?"

"Yes, the middle one."

"AAAAAAAHHHHHHHHHHHHHRRRRRRRGGGGG GHHHHHH!!!!!!" screamed Bob and an echoing rumble issued from the hospital room and filled the corridors.

After Bob awoke from passing out, he contemplated what to do next.

"Is there anything you can do? I'm getting married in four months! I just couldn't bear not having a…you know."

The doctor paused, thinking to himself and said, "Well, there is a new operation that's performed with crazy glue, viagra, silicone, fiberglass, duct tape, a bunch of ointments, parsley and a lot of prayers. I'm not sure it would work for you. In the only successful case, they attached the guy's own

249

penis and yours is, well, an owl took yours and fed it to her nestlings and all that's left is this." The doctor held up what looked like a small chewed up piece of bacon.

"What about transplanting someone else's on? Can you guys do that? I'm desperate!" Bob asked.

"Hummmm, interesting possibilities," the doctor said, contemplating the idea.

After consulting with the other doctors and trying frantically to find blood and skin matches to the existing stiffs (no pun intended), they came up with three potential donors.

"Well, we think it can be done but we need your consent. And we want you to choose your new weapon." The doctor handed him four pictures of the other men's genitals.

"This one here is Arthur, an accountant from Brooklyn." The picture was of a penis with a telephoto shot really close up. For size reference it was next to a color crayon and still looked small.

"Too small. Boy, he must have whacked it daily…look at all those stretch marks!" Bob said, while pointing at the picture.

"Vincent here, a yuppie from Queens, is probably our best candidate."

The doctor mentioned that the penis had a little bend in it. It actually looked like a question mark.

"Are you kidding?! Look it's all bent to the right. And I at least want what I had, if not more." Bob motioned like he was holding a large pepperoni.

"Lastly there's Tyrone. He was a Semi-pro basketball player and a bouncer at a couple local nightclubs." Bob looked at the pictures with half a cock in each one. "You need to put both of those pictures side by side. We couldn't fit it on only one Polaroid."

"Now that's the one for me!" Bob shouted excitedly as he found his sword of choice.

"Sir, other than the obvious color difference there may be some problems. I can't really recommend…"

"I don't care, I want this one! Boy, what a honeymoon surprise this will be!"

The operation went well and the swelling went down. There was no infection and everything seemed to be great. Bob was now a new man with a new and improved tool. Wanting to christen it like a new bass boat, he decided to not whack off or do anything to himself until the wedding night. He wanted to be like a virgin again.

The big day finally arrived and Bob's wedding was upon him. Everything was beautiful. The bride, Jennifer, was dressed in a white satin gown with lace trim and a hand-embroidered train done by her mother. Her blonde hair was up, her skin was tanned and she was simply stunning. The day, Jennifer, the ceremony were all exquisite.

Bob stood proudly and anxiously at the altar through the procession. He adjusted himself a few times not being used to something dangling below his boxers. He stood staring while she approached to join him and exchange their vows and pledge their eternal love. All Bob could think about was the honeymoon night and showing her his surprise.

Finally, after exchanging the rings and saying their vows, they both said, "I do." They kissed then ran through the crowd. Trying to remain calm, Bob smiled forcibly having pictures taken. Then came the crying and kissing by family members, the typical father-in-law talk and all the while he watched Jennifer glow. Finally they jumped into the limousine and sped off to the reception.

The reception hall was decorated in the blue and white colors of their wedding. Bouquets of flowers accentuated each table and the white tablecloths. Everyone was cheering as they walked in hand in hand. Except Bob's dad. He was very drunk and flirting with a tree. Otherwise it was very touching.

When the special dance started, Bob and Jennifer took the floor and danced romantically to Shania Twain's, "From This Moment". Jennifer held Bob tight and kissed his neck. Then she whispered, "I can't wait until tonight... There's a little present in your pocket from me."

Bob gulped and as they danced he reached into his pocket to get a handkerchief because he suddenly felt hot. He wiped his brow and a distinct scent filled his head. He looked and saw it was her white panties he was using to wipe his sweat. He breathed in the aroma that was soaked into her silk panties, and he felt a twinge in his pants.

As the song was ending, she ran her finger down his cheek to his chest and winked saying, "I just shaved, too, and it *itches*."

The stripper's theme played, and the disc jockey pulled a chair out for Bob to remove the garter belt. Bob's buddies all whistled as he picked her foot up and slid his hand up her leg to her garter to pull it off. He smiled as he looked up at Jennifer and then up her dress. The shimmer of wetness was on her pink flesh. She smiled wickedly at him knowing what he was looking at.

Suddenly, Bob was *hungry*.

He tried to concentrate the best he could. At the reception table he sat next to Jennifer and they chit-chatted with the others. Jennifer's mom walked up. While Jennifer listened to her mom talking, Bob slid his hand onto her leg and slowly moved it up. Jennifer sat up quickly and chirped as his finger touched close to her pussy. She told her mom it was gas and continued listening to her. Leaning forward she blocked any view her mom had and parted her legs ever so slightly. Bob took her invitation and kept eating with one hand and toyed with her labia with the other one.

"Are you okay, dear?" Jennifer's mom asked. "You look warm, and you're sweating."

"I'm fine, it's just warm in here." Bob's playful flicking of her clit made her want the impending sex even more. She was wet and feared the juices dripping from her pussy would stain the dress.

She excused herself and took Bob into the corridor. Outside the door she grabbed his butt and kissed him deeply almost smothering him.

"I have waited four months for sex. Other than my vibrator, nothing has touched my pussy, and *now* you decide to be naughty. This isn't fair!" she wailed.

Bob looked down the corridor and saw a maintenance closet. He grabbed her arm and pulled her into the room. The room was dark and full of chairs and folding tables with a few silverware carts.

Jennifer tugged at Bob. "No, no, no. We need to get back before people notice we're gone."

Bob grasped Jennifer with his strong hands, pulling her abruptly against him and kissed her deeply. Feeling the heat from her body, Bob became inflamed with desire. Succumbing to his passion, she held him with her arms around his neck. Bob kissed her neck and eased her down onto her back atop a room service cart. He unfastened the clasp of her gown and lowered it down past her shoulders. He kissed her chest until it flushed to a rose hue.

"No Bob, we can't. Not until tonight," she moaned, not really wanting him to stop.

Bob wanted to respect her wishes but needed at least a taste of her. He pulled her dress up and his mouth watered at the sight of her clean-shaven pubis. He knelt before Jennifer and kissed up her legs to her thighs. He saw her labia open, beckoning him on, to what he knew she really wanted. He almost swallowed her outer lips as he voraciously nuzzled between her legs.

"Oh, Bob, the dress. We'll ruin the dress!" she wistfully whispered in a desire-induced hysteria.

Bob looked around and grabbed a folded napkin. She raised herself up with her legs so he could put it under her bottom. As she lifted her hips, Bob buried his extended tongue into her. Jennifer closed her eyes and moaned loudly. He looked up her body and watched her tummy shake as he licked inside of her. Her breasts almost popped from her gown as they swelled with need. The excitement and fear of getting caught only made Jennifer more aroused and desperate for Bob to take her.

Bob held a cheek in each hand and he kneaded her ass like a breadmaker. He had always loved her ass. His thumb found its way up to her pussy. He flicked against her clit with the tip of it, making her moan. She could feel her excitement as it was building. Bob pressed his thumb into her as he drank from her well of desire. Her sweetness made him growl. He pursued her orgasm deeper and more vigorously attacked her clit.

A sudden rush filled Jennifer's head. She shrieked, stiffening her back, and came while Bob nuzzled her clit. He sucked on it, making her gyrate and shake. She smiled and giggled, as he flicked his tongue across her lips promising more to come later.

They straightened themselves up to get back to the reception. When they opened the storeroom door, they heard scattered applause from the dozen or so guests standing in the hallway. Bob bowed and they went back in the reception area.

The flight to Hawaii seemed to take forever. After the accident and surgery, they had decided to wait until their wedding night before actually having sex to make it just that much more special. Now all their anticipation would be released in an incredible night of passionate lovemaking. After about 10 orgasms they would be completely spent. Then fall asleep in the comfort of each other's embrace until the next morning.

Jennifer softly kissed Bob and slipped her tongue between his lips ever so slightly. She bit on his bottom lip and quietly whispered to him. "I've been waiting for you for so long. I can't wait to have you." Bob gulped as she smiled devilishly. "After your little gift in the reception hall this may get a little rough." She grinned mischievously then slipped into the bathroom to get ready.

Oh boy, now I get to try out the new equipment, he thought to himself. Just for this night he thought he'd really do something different for her. He took out a red lace ribbon and dropped his pants down. He reached down by his knee and tied the ribbon around the tip of his enormous cock and made a nice little bow on the end.

Jennifer stepped out of the bathroom wearing a silk mini-robe, and nothing else. She took one look and jumped back, screaming "AAAAAARRRRHHHHH, WHAT THE HELL IS THAT?!?!?!"

"It's my transplant," Bob said while standing there naked with nothing on but a red ribbon on the end of his new fourteen-inch penis.

"Damn! You said you had some surgery after the accident, but... My goodness it's...it's...fuckin' huge!"

Jennifer was astounded and excited all at once at the prospect of having to deal with this *THING* for the rest of her life. She was actually incredibly turned on by it because she had always fantasized about having sex with a black man. She loved Bob and wanted to tell him that the *THING*'s blackness and size excited her but feared his reaction. So, she bit her lip and said, "Well cowboy, let's give this horse a new rider!"

She walked up to Bob, untying her robe and opening it up with each step closer. She pressed up against him and reached down to grasp his *THING* in her hand and slowly stroked it. With her other hand she grabbed onto the other half of it.

"Um, honey, are you turned on?" she whispered into his ear.

"Oh, ya!"

"Um, then why is, uh, it so soft and not hard?"

"I don't know! The doctor said I was in perfect condition and everything was fine. It's all there in my chart." Bob wasn't going to be denied and wickedly said, "Okay, baby lay down and I'll see how this stick shift can handle your curves as I drive it into the tunnel!"

Jennifer giggled and jumped onto the bed. Licking her fingers she slipped them between her pussy lips and opened herself to him. He climbed on top of her and positioned himself and rammed his body onto hers and moaned, "How about that?"

"Um, honey, do you know what an accordion is?"

Bob nodded yes.

"Well your penis just turned into an accordion."

The entire night became an experiment in frustration. No matter what they did nothing worked. Oral sex, doggy style, honey, masturbation, her on top, him on top, porno movies, the sheep, the hand puppets, nothing they tried helped. At about 3:30 in the morning Jennifer had given up. She was exhausted and frustrated. Her ultimate fantasy turned into a fucked-up, twilight zone nightmare.

"Baby, I don't know what's wrong. Maybe it's just because of the transplant. Hand me that chart in my briefcase." Jennifer handed him the medical records and he was reading through them when he came to the release forms that had been signed by Tyrone, the organ donor. As he read the charts a look of horror struck his face.

"What is it?" she asked.

Bob handed her the chart and she began to read aloud, "Tyrone has, by far, the worst case of impotence I have ever encountered in my thiry years of experience. No treatment, medications or surgery has helped him. My best recommendation is for him to become a monk."

The Cross Dresser

෨

"Hey, how about going out for a drink after work, Marsha?"

"No, Eric. It's been a long day and I just want to go home and crawl into a hot bath with a bottle of wine," she said. Marsha acted overly tired so as not to hurt his feelings since it was his first week.

Eric shrugged off the refusal then smiled after her comment. "Need any help?" Eric asked, pepping up quickly.

"Ha, Ha," she replied while walking away.

Marsha undressed from work while she looked into her closet for something comfortable to put on. Amongst her vast array of business and formal wear was some men's clothing she had gathered from past boyfriends and overnight liaisons she'd met and basically used for companionship and sex. She slipped out of her heels and let her skirt fall to the ground. *Damn that crap is so uncomfortable.*

She wiggled her toes and gazed at a sport coat hanging in the corner. As she put it on she could still smell the faint fragrance of cologne in the fabric. *Nathan, this was Nathan's,* she remembered fondly as she smiled and licked her lips. It fit loosely, but it looked rather stylish. So she tore through her closet and drawers looking for something to match the jacket. *Good thing brown is an easy color to match,* she thought.

She stared into the mirror and thought, *Shit, I look pretty damn good for a guy!* The sports bra held her breasts tight to her so with all the layers she could pass for being a guy.

There was something missing. *Oh yes!* She rolled up a couple socks and tucked them into her pants to give the illusion of being a man. Of course, the bulge in her pants reminded her of a man she knew. He had a HUGE bulge, and knew how to use it!

Damn, keeping this thing straight is a bitch! No wonder guys are always adjusting themselves. The finishing touch was a Stetson cowboy hat with her hair tucked in. Then, never being one to shy away from a new experience, Marsha was out the door to the local hot spot to see if she could pull this off.

At the club Marsha blended in nicely. Probably better than expected. At the end of the bar was an attractive woman staring at her. She was very tall but slender with shoulder-length hair and wearing a sporty dress and cowboy boots — pretty cute. She looked like someone she might have seen before shopping or something.

Now she'd never thought about this situation. At first Marsha was a little uncomfortable but at the same time it was a little exciting.

"You wanna dance?" the woman asked.

"Uh, sure," Marsha replied, trying to lower her voice.

After a couple of line dances and a few Jack Daniel's, 'Mark' was feeling a lot better. As the 'Boot Scoot Boogie' ended they started to play Toby Keith's new slow ballad and the woman, whose name was Erica, grabbed her to slow dance. She grabbed her tightly to keep the charade going but wasn't sure if the woman would notice her otherwise female features.

God, this woman is attractive and smells so good.

"You don't talk too much, do you Mark?" Erica whispered.

Marsha couldn't help but hold tighter to this woman as she thought about being with another woman. She wasn't a lesbian or anything, but the thought had crossed her mind before. Like when one of her male friends was making love to her and she needed something to fantasize about other than the guy's hairy ass.

Suddenly Erica grasped her ass and kissed her on the neck right below the ear.

WOW!

She slowly moved her hand around the front and grabbed hard onto the sock. Erica whispered into her ear, "Let's get out of here." Then bit on her earlobe.

Oh man, what do I do? she thought, ideas racing through her mind.

Back at her place, Marsha set out some wine, turned the lights down and put on some soft music just like all her boyfriends had done. Also, it gave her time to think of how to explain to Erica about what was going on. She glanced over and saw the firelight faintly flickering on Erica's face making her look that much more attractive. *How the hell am I going to pull this off?* she thought to herself. *I am going to tell her I was curious about dressing and acting like a man. And that I am so sexually motivated by her that I want to...no, I can't.*

She handed Erica a glass of wine. Sitting down across from her, Marsha smiled shyly.

"Uh, Erica, uh, I'd like – ," she stuttered.

"Don't be shy, Mark. I'm a big girl," Erica said as she slid off the couch and sat in front of Marsha between her legs. She set her hands on Marsha's legs, and moved them slowly up to her sides. Gently grasping Marsha's neck, she motioned her to come closer until their mouths met. She slightly parted her mouth, barely tracing Marsha's lips with the tip of her tongue. They were so soft. Marsha was almost euphoric with pleasure as she opened her eyes.

"I need to tell you something," she said as Erica leaned her back in the chair.

Marsha couldn't move as Erica slowly kissed her neck and licked the perspiration beading up around her neckline. There was no turning back now. Intense excitement built up inside her. Erica slowly unbuttoned the shirt exposing Marsha's breasts. Looking surprised, Erica wickedly smiled.

She was amazed at the way Marsha's breasts firmed to her attentions and buried her face into the cleavage and pulled the bra up with her teeth.

Marsha's chest heaved with every deep breath, and she couldn't help but want Erica to continue. Every touch sent electric shocks straight down to the scalding fire burning between her thighs. Ecstasy drove all thought from Marsha's mind.

"Please, release me!" she begged. The intensity just kept building.

"Lie down and close your eyes," Erica asked.

Erica could see what she needed and lay Marsha down on the rug. She pulled her shirt and pants off. Erica painstakingly massaged Marsha's body starting at her chest, caressing her breasts. When she gently rubbed on Marsha's tight nipples, Marsha felt tingling sensations down to her bucking pelvis. As Erica removed her anticipation-soaked panties Marsha couldn't control her thrusting. She needed to explode from this pent-up sexual frenzy.

Erica moved her hands in a circular motion towards Marsha's pubis and slipped her finger between the outer lips of her vagina. The juices were beckoning her to explore deeper so she slid her index finger inside. Marsha moaned deeply, raising her hips to pull Erica's finger in deeper and her muscles drew it in and held on tightly. She grabbed onto the carpet beneath her and clenched tightly as another finger was forced into her. Erica moved her fingers in a tight rotating movement, stroking against Marsha's engorged clitoris. Marsha's pussy was so supersensitive that nothing else even mattered—her entire focus was on that one spot.

Erica reached underneath her ass, picked up her pelvis and dove face first into her muff, forcing her tongue inside. Marsha melted. It was as if honey were poured onto her pussy. Erica spread her fingers apart exposing her clitoris, then lashed it with her tongue. The way she licked the hood and length of her clit made Marsha almost pass out from the desperate need to climax. Erica slid her finger deep into Marsha's wetness and, finding her G spot, plunged repeatedly harder and deeper against it. The glorious and riveting pulses rushing through her body only added to the intensity of her orgasm when Marsha finally let go and shook uncontrollably.

Marsha's legs were like Jell-O, so weak and limber from all the tension released. Her shaking was still very apparent and uncontrollable. She was still lying on the rug with only the light from the fire shining on her glistening sweat when she said, "My god, I've never been with a woman. I don't know what to do but if you tell me...is there anything I can do for you?" She really wanted Erica to show her. "What do you want me to do?"

When Erica didn't respond, Marsha rolled over to Erica and kissed her and moved down her body to her skirt. She slowly pulled up her skirt to her crotch and saw something distinctly peculiar: men's underwear wrapped with an Ace bandage. Confused she looked up at Erica with a "HUH" on her face.

While Marsha lay there, Erica took off her wig—she was really Eric. Actually he made a pretty woman and not that bad-looking a guy.

"You know, the next time someone asks you out don't be so hesitant."

"I thought there was something familiar about you," Marsha said.

"Next time you shouldn't wear boots with a long skirt."

The Plane Ride

&

Debra was trying unsuccessfully to put her briefcase into the upper compartment, struggling obviously, when Jim stepped up beside her.

"These things can be a bitch. Let me move mine out of the way then yours will fit in there."

"Why thank you," she said, checking out his ass as he reached up to put her bag away.

"I'm sorry. I always bring more than I need for these long trips, thinking I'll get some work done. Hello, by the way. I'm Jim."

"Debra. Nice meeting you." She shook his strong hand noticing his long, thick fingers.

Debra was an extremely successful businesswoman with a Fortune 500 computer company. But being a workaholic, she never had much time for any kind of relationship or recreation. A corporate takeover was the only reason she had taken this trip. Because she was a good-looking blonde, people envisioned her sleeping her way up the company ladder. The reality was she fought hard to keep her reputation intact. She was a bitch.

Jim was flying back to LA for a job interview. His family still lived there, but he had moved away for a job in Detroit that fell apart. He wanted to get a job back home in California and this was his big chance.

After listening to Sade's new CD on the headphones and downing martinis, Debra was feeling pretty mellow. She and Jim started talking and pretty soon she was flirting with him, unbuttoning the top two buttons on her blouse to reveal her large, completely paid for breasts. They were talking about themselves and sex eventually popped up. Jim had "popped up" too, so he adjusted his swelling growth in his trousers many times. Being a little embarrassed, he requested a pillow from the stewardess.

Debra was telling him about some of her more elaborate fantasies and how having sex in public places really turned her on. But, then the drinks or all the rain outside the plane made her need to go to the bathroom. So she got up and leaned over to him saying, "Don't go anywhere, I'll be right back," giving Jim a complete view of her breasts. Her hand accidentally fell into his lap...accidentally. She raised her eyebrow at the length of Jim's hardness.

"No problem," he said, adjusting his crotch again.

She stepped into the bathroom. Her head spun a little as she sat down. Suddenly there was a cracking sound. The plane jolted and the lights started flickering. She stood up, quickly pulling herself together, and opened the door.

As Debra stepped out of the restroom she yelled, "What the hell is—???" and before she could finish the question Jim was in front of her.

Jim forced her back into the bathroom and switched on the occupied sign. Debra looked into Jim's eyes and saw his desperation.

"Don't say a word," Debra ordered.

With their end in sight they had nothing to lose. Debra violently tugged at his pants, while Jim tried to unbutton her expensive blouse. As the turbulence increased so did their fury. He slammed her back against the wall and ripped open her blouse, scattering the buttons everywhere. He buried his face in her bosom and licked her cleavage hungrily. She unbuttoned his pants and forced the zipper down, unaware he wasn't wearing any underwear. Jim's scream was excruciatingly loud. After the initial pain subsided, he tugged and tore at her underwear shredding them from her body.

He grabbed her hands and shoved them against the wall. With one hand he lifted her backside up. The other held her leg at his hip. No words were said as they stared deep into each other's eyes. He plunged into her letting out a deep moan. There was also a loud sucking sound. Her ass was pressing against the flush button on the bathroom wall. The turbulence from the plane increased and the vibrations shook the walls.

Debra closed her eyes and wondered when the plane would crash. *What's going to happen to my family? How long will it take them to find us? Won't it look kind of funny if they find our bodies in the plane bathroom? My father's gonna have a cardiac. I hope they bury me in that pretty dark blue pantsuit I just bought. Who the fuck is this guy I'm having sex with? At least he's pretty good at it.*

The plane violently shook, bringing Debra back to reality. She could feel her climax building. Pushing her feet against the wall and leaning back, Debra spread her legs wider, almost touching her knees to her shoulders. Licking her finger, she then rubbed her exposed clit. Her pussy was on fire. Jim watched and held her ass up, continuing to ravish her. She saw the veins pulse on his cock as it sank into her pussy. Closing her eyes ecstatically, she felt the ripples in her vaginal walls as they tightened around his swelling cock. She moaned and shrieked loudly, banging her fists on the wall. The end was nearing for both the plane and for her. Debra pulled his hair, bringing his face to hers. Their lips met and she forced her tongue deep into his mouth.

Jim was like a jackhammer, slamming deeper and faster into her, then it happened. They screamed together. The climax was so intense they felt the walls shaking and moving. They came together knowing they were crashing toward the ground.

The stewardess looked down on them as they tumbled out of the bathroom. Jim fell to the floor on his back and Debra toppled out the door on top of him. Dizzy and breathless,

Debra looked up. Jim couldn't see anything because Debra's crotch was on his face.

"I'm sorry I opened the door...but with all the screaming and crashing about in there, I was concerned someone might have gotten trapped," the stewardess said while trying to keep a straight face. "Could you please go to your seat? Please madam, could you tuck that boob in."

"But, the plane... I thought it was crashing???" Debra asked while straightening out her clothes as best she could.

"No, we were just having some major turbulence over this nasty storm. Uh, sir, could you please put that thing away?"

"Mummmbble, mum, mummble," Jim fumbled with his trousers as his dick stood out like a flagpole.

"Oh, sorry Jim. I'll get up." Debra giggled while sliding off of his face.

They both gathered and straightened up their clothes. While walking back to their seats the other passengers applauded.

"So," she said trying to compose herself, "where was this interview going to be?"

"It's at a company called 'Compute-graphix.'"

"Uh, is your name Jim *Johnson?*'

"Why yes, it is."

"Oh, um, I'm Debra Carlson. I'm supposed to interview you tomorrow but this, um, preliminary interview has told me enough. You seem to have met all my requirements and criteria. You're hired."

The Dancer

ৰু

The air in the club was thick with smoke and the ringing sounds of beer bottles and glasses echoed through the dim light. Paul sat at the barstool drinking his sixth beer and waited patiently for his girl. He was a smaller, slim man, powder-gray hair and had a large bulge in his pants that the topless waitress snickered at.

"Happy to see me?" she smiled.

With a snarling growl, Paul burped and replied, "I'm waiting for Mona," then pulled a large wad of dollar bills out of his pocket reducing the bulge.

The music thumped through the onlookers' bodies as they drooled uncontrollably at the dancers. Paul glanced at his watch and knew it was her time to perform. He pushed and stumbled to the front table, wanting to be close. He was always her most enthusiastic fan. He had been in the club a few times before and one night caught Mona's show. Since then he had been a regular patron whenever she performed.

The lights dimmed to a spotlight and the slow groove of Madonna's "Take A Bow" pulsed out of the speakers. The stage was dark and empty except for the spotlight. Mona eased her arm out from behind the curtain. Her white full-length gloves covered her skin and she pulled them off, revealing her blood red fingernails. She exposed her leg all the way to her smooth thigh then stepped out onto the stage. She was wearing a white thong, white stiletto shoes and a black silk wrap around her body. Paul smiled wide as his Venus looked upon him. The chatter quieted as the other men caught a glimpse of this vision of unbridled passion.

To Paul, she was his. She was his angel. She never expected anything from him except admiration. That and a few bucks to let him nuzzle between her large, full, real breasts. Even though most men become attached to strippers after a lap dance or two, he didn't want it to be something cheap or perverse. He was truly smitten with Mona. He never crossed the line, even though he had thought of asking her for a private dance. He respected her and her artful way of dancing. Mona had become his ultimate fantasy. She was all he ever wanted in a woman and more. He had followed her to all the local amateur nights in the airport district strip clubs.

A trickle of drool ran down to his chin. Her body seemed to flow like a wave as she moved across the stage. Everything was fluid. It was as if she floated across the stage on a breeze. Every time she turned, the wrap would reveal a little more of her perfectly tanned body. She saw Paul and smiled wickedly and winked at him.

The wrap fell a little more, revealing her large natural breasts. The men all smiled as she looked nastily at them. She grasped her breasts and licked each nipple, teasing their minds. She walked up to the wanton men and pressed her large breasts around their faces. One by one she pulled the dollar bills clenched between their teeth.

Paul jerked at his pants trying to get his money out as she pranced around the stage, giving the men a good look at her breasts and letting them nuzzle between them. Paul, feeling excited, pulled out a handful of ones, when she came over to him. Mona giggled and had him slip the money in her thong and nuzzled his little head between her huge breasts, letting him breathe her perfumed body in. She gently kissed his forehead and smiled.

Paul was in heaven.

The wrap was almost completely off and the crowd wanted to see more. Mona bent over giving everyone a clear shot of her ass and the tightening of her thong against her wet lips. A loud moan came from the crowd as her glory was revealed. She threw her hair back and shimmied daringly, pulling her thong down her legs and over her heels. She gyrated and rubbed the fabric between her legs.

Mona licked her lips and smiled as she walked over to Paul and handed him her underwear in exchange for a twenty dollar bill. Paul closed his eyes and put the panties over his face to breathe her passion scent in. His pants almost ripped loose at the crotch at the smell of her. When she bent over in front of him showing her pussy, Paul lost it.

He stood and knocked his drink over with his stiffened cock. He could feel his pants sticky and wet against his crotch, as he leaned forward and buried his face in her muff. His tongue darted out and licked deeply inside of her. In shock Mona stood up grasping his face between her butt-cheeks. Paul grabbed her hips and frantically pulled back. Mona's high heels tangled with her wrap. She lost her balance and all 462 pounds of her wobbled, fell off the creaking stage and crashed onto the floor atop Paul's head. Paul's neck snapped from the force of the fall and his head got wedged into Mona's anus.

It took three men to pull his head out of her ass.

When the EMT's arrived, they found Paul lying face up with a smile on his face and covered in feces.

"Oh My GOD!" shouted a paramedic, "that's the Congressman! Where's my camera?!?!?"

The front page of the next day's *Enquirer* had his picture plastered on the cover with the caption "Congressman finally pulls head out of ass at local strip-club."

The Hangover

℘

Nicole's head pounded loudly and she rolled over in the bed. The constant throb of a hangover was obvious. She wanted to keep her eyes closed against the light and never open them. Instead she rummaged through the clothing thrown across the floor trying to find her underwear.

Last night was a blur. She tried desperately to remember what happened but it just became fuzzier. Her last memory was the beautiful wedding and reception at the Hilton. She had a vague image of dancing and talking at the bar with a guy. Her best friend had gotten married and she had been a bridesmaid, again. The old cliché, "Always the bridesmaid never the bride" fit her perfectly. She had been a little down about that.

Nicole squinted, trying to keep her head from pounding. She wasn't sure where she was but could see clothing lying over the chair and her gown hanging up on the closet door. A light shone from under the bathroom door and the sound of the shower echoed in the background.

She sat up, wobbling dizzily from the evening's leftover spins. Her eyes began to adjust to the dim light and she looked around the room trying to focus on things. She noticed a strange discomfort as she sat on the edge of the bed. Her ass hurt a little and she suddenly thought why. She vaguely remembered having her face buried in the bed and engaging in anal pleasures. She glanced at the floor and saw a pair of boxers and four glow in the dark condom wrappers. She grinned at the wetness between her legs. Too bad she didn't remember anything!

Her mind started spinning as she put her head in her hands. Feeling nauseated, she sat on the edge of the bed again.

Nicole felt the strain of her bladder—she needed to pee. She stood up and staggered towards the bathroom. Tripping over champagne bottles and flowers, she barely kept her balance and had to use the walls of the hallway to support her.

The bathroom was brightly lit. Nicole squinted as she opened the door and slowly wobbled in.

The steam from the shower helped to clear her head a little. She sat on the toilet farting loudly. The steady release from her bladder made her sigh as she tinkled. "Ahhhhhhhhh!" Nicole trembled as a chill of relief swept through her.

"Is that you, hon?" she heard a female's voice from the shower.

Her stomach quivered and she let out an abrupt hissing fart that burned her sore anus. With that, she sobered up abruptly, wondering what the hell had happened.

"Don't flush dear, I'm almost done here. Unless you want to join me?" the voice giggled.

"Uhhhh, just a sec." Nicole considered what she knew as she jiggled her ass above the toilet getting the last drips of wetness off her. *What should I do? Where did the condoms come from? How drunk was I last night? Is this why I have this aftertaste in my mouth? Am I gay now? Why does my ass hurt? Is the woman pretty? Does she have bigger boobs than I do?*

Nicole was torn and also curious as to what had happened last night. She had never done anything of a lesbian nature. Feeling that whatever happened last night happened and she couldn't change it, Nicole decided to just go with the flow.

"You were incredible last night," the mystery woman said. "I hope you had fun too. You certainly seemed to be enjoying yourself."

In a desperate attempt to seem like she had a recollection of what happened, Nicole just agreed and sat on the cold porcelain toilet. Her pussy was sore from whatever happened the night before and it irritated her when she urinated.

"It was a new experience for me, that's for sure," she finally said, trying to be convincing.

"Are you coming in here or not?" the mystery woman asked in a playful tone.

Nicole stood up and took a deep breath. She closed her eyes collecting her thoughts. She breathed out, pulling herself together and opened the shower door.

As she stepped into the shower the woman faced away from her. She had long blonde hair and a nice shape to her. Her ass was firm and rounded like a teardrop. The small tattoo on the small of her back was petite and feminine. She stood about 5 foot 5 inches tall and had olive-toned skin.

"Can you wash my back? I'd appreciate it," she said, handing Nicole the puff cloth. "After all," she said slyly, "it's your fault I hurt it. "

Nicole, felt lost and confused. She crossed a line she wasn't sure she was ready for. Mostly she felt uncomfortable but still curious. She couldn't help but stare admiringly at the woman's body while slowly rubbing her back with the cloth and watching the bubbles trickle down to her ass with the warm water. Nicole felt a sense of closeness and moved the woman's wet hair to the side and pressed against her body.

The woman turned her face to Nicole and leaned against her body. "Hello again lover," she whispered.

Nicole saw her face again for the first time. She had a very pretty face. Nicole felt compelled to wrap her arms around and wash her perky, small breasts with the puff cloth and soap. The feel of the slippery flesh against hers became more arousing as the seconds passed.

Nicole understood how she could have been attracted to this woman the previous night. She had a deep sensuality to her. Maybe there was more to this. She could never stay in a long-term relationship with a man. She always seemed to be able to talk to women more easily than men. But, she did LOVE the feel of a man's hard cock inside of her. That was one thing she could never do without.

They kissed gently as the woman leaned her head back, letting Nicole feel her breasts. She tasted the inside of Nicole's mouth with the tip of her tongue. Nicole seemed almost to mold to her. As the heat rose, her inner desires and the unknown boundaries excited her in more ways than she had ever imagined possible. Thoughts of another woman's body rubbing against hers. Thoughts of a knowing woman suckling her pussy the way men can't. The images shot through her mind, as she kissed this beautiful woman.

The woman's nipples were erect and the water trickled off the tips like a waterfall. Nicole's fingers followed the colors and textures of the mystery woman's breasts and nipples. She breathed a long drawn-out moan of pleasure.

Nicole ran her finger against the woman's nipples and was aroused by the deepened moaning. She noticed the moaning was coming from both of them. This made it clear that the feelings they had were mutual. Nicole had never touched another woman like this before but it seemed almost natural to her. As the woman reached back to grasp Nicole's ass, Nicole slowly moved her hand down the front of her crossing a boundary she hadn't crossed before, at least not while she was sober. She knew what her own pussy felt like and having a man touch her made her almost cum from a simple flick of a finger.

She felt the small patch of hair and twisted it in her fingers and kissed her shoulder. Nicole began to salivate as she pictured plunging her finger into the woman's slick pussy, how she could rub the folds of flesh between her fingers and feel her clit swell. She was being sucked into this real life fantasy.

At first she wasn't sure what she felt so she grabbed it again. Either this woman had something stuck inside of her or Nicole had her hand on a rather large penis.

The woman moaned in pleasure and Nicole grasped harder. The woman turned around and Nicole gasped as she looked down to see an enormous erect penis pointed at her.

"What the fuck is that?" Nicole shouted.

"Well it's clearly a penis," the woman answered, obviously amused. "Don't you remember? It was in every orifice you have last night...you didn't seem to mind then."

"Good lord! I must have really been drunk last night. What happened?"

They both dried off and Nicole sat listening to Samantha, Sam for short. It seemed Sam was a she-male and a friend of the groom.

"Last night I sat talking to you at the bar. You were drinking and picked me up at the wedding. I told you I was a she-male and you dared me to show you my penis. You led me to the room and had every kind of carnal pleasure known to man...or woman...with me."

Nicole's pounding headache returned and she felt extremely ill. "Please tell me nobody knows about this. My family wouldn't understand," Nicole begged.

"Well, you hiked up my skirt and gave me a blow job in the cab after leaving the reception..." Sam paused seeing Nicole sweating. "But only your sister and some guy named William saw it."

The Pits

ॐ

The crowd was enormous and violent, while the music blasted at a deafening level. It was by far the best Linkin Park concert I'd been to that year.

I glanced over into the mosh pit below me and couldn't believe my eyes. *What a goddess!* I had to get a closer look. So I thought, "What the Hell?" and dove off the bleachers and into the crowd.

After a few minutes the blood stopped and my headache was dulling a little (the bottle of Rum helped too).

Now my only problem was to find *HER* amongst this mass of bodies thrashing around me. After about three songs I spotted her going around the outside circle of the mosh dancing and bashing about. She was a vision.

I could tell that she was really into fashion. Spiked ruby red and bright yellow hair shaved on one side with the word "BITCH" buzzed in, a nose ring of a skull, lip ring, six or seven earrings with one attached to a chain connecting to her other nose ring and black lipstick. The barbed wire tattoo around her neck and the other tattoo on her arm of two roses intertwined around the words "FUCK OFF" only accentuated her petite frame. She was wearing a leather peek-a-boo bra that only partially covered her large, slightly sagging breasts with two nipple rings that looked like handcuffs, a puke green miniskirt, black fishnet stockings ripped to shreds and red cowboy boots. My god, she was beautiful!

I figured the easiest way to get close to her was to join into the inside circle of the mosh going in the opposite direction and speak to her whenever we would meet. The only way to get over there was to go over the top.

I screamed at the drunken skinhead in front of me, "DUDE, I need to get into the middle of that mosh!"

"BODYSURFER!!!!!" the idiot shouted and three guys picked me up and threw me into the air.

Now surfing over a crowd can be a very painful experience. I had my balls grabbed six times, my eyes poked, ass pinched, wallet stolen, shirt ripped before I was dumped into the mosh headfirst and my headache came back. But it would be worth it if I could talk to her.

The inside of a mosh pit is a very violent and scary place with all the pushing, punching, flying elbows and head-butting. But that wasn't going to stop me. I was on a MISSION!

The first go around I saw her coming around and yelled out, "Hey Babe, you look fuckin' hot!" I smiled and reached out my hand. She glared at me and snarled. I didn't see her fist as she clipped my cheek with a right cross that made my face feel like it was gonna cave in.

She must work out to be that strong, I thought as my cheek throbbed in pain.

Maybe it was my delivery?

Maybe it was what I said?

Well I'll get another chance.

The second round I blurted out "Yo, Goddess, what's your..." Before I could finish my sentence, she kicked me on the shin with the point of her cowboy boot, sending a lightning bolt of pain screaming up my leg and blood streaming down to my socks.

I guess she didn't care for that line too much either, I figured when I stopped hobbling in pain.

Now I'm pissed. No more Mr. Nice Guy. Maybe that's what she needs. To be told what I want and that I won't take any more shit from her. Sometimes love is a bitch! She is obviously attracted to me because she has touched me in a passionate way twice. So now it's either put up or shut up!

As she came around again I limped over and grabbed her by the nipple rings and said, "Listen, *BITCH,* I feel intense passion for you. So let's stop playing stupid fuckin' games and get down to business. NOW!"

The last thing I remember was her grabbing my crotch and digging her sharp black fingernails into my cock, then head-butting me.

The doctors have assured me that the operation was successful. They assured me that there are a lot of men that have fathered children with only one testicle. The reattachment went well also and if John Bobbitt can do it I should be able to also.

The Anniversary

&

A full moon lit the night sky. Two silhouettes danced ever so closely while Bill Medley sang "Unchained Melody". They softly kissed and hugged each other tightly as the music slowly faded away.

"A last toast to finish off this special night… To my wife, ten years of marriage and the love-light still shines in our hearts. I love you!"

"Oh, honey. That was sweet," she said and hugged him hard against her.

They had been sweethearts since high school and during their first year of college they got married in the old fashioned way, in Las Vegas on a hot June night. That November the first of the three children were born.

Together they scratched their way into the middle class. Like the rest of us, they worked long hours, hating their jobs, seldom finding time for even an occasional passionate moment together. They hoped this weekend would help re-ignite the fire that used to burn so hot. Those nights of drive-in movies, parents' couches and the fear of getting caught, they all seemed so long ago. Actually they were long ago.

Tonight was going to be their night to remember.

"Let's take this bottle of champagne up to our room and really celebrate."

"Rupert, don't drink too much. 'Cause you know what it does to you."

"Tonight is a special night, babe, and nothing is going to ruin my bliss with you. Let's go upstairs and get naked."

"OOOH, how romantic." She laughed as they hurried to the elevator. It was broken, so they had to use the stairs and got winded by running up them in the rush. When Rupert twisted his ankle slipping on some spilled beer on the stairs, Delilah had to carry him to the room.

No amount of money had been spared for their night of unbridled passion. The room was very dimly lit by candles on both nightstands and the neon MOTEL 6 sign that flashed outside their room. There was a roll of quarters by the candle for the bed vibrator. The red and blue flannel sheets were pulled back, beckoning these two lovebirds to enter.

On each side of the bed were their nightclothes. She planned to wear a red camisole with black lace on the edges, a red garter belt with black stockings and a sapphire blue silk robe. His attire was a pair of white satin boxers with "Home of the Whopper" inscribed on the front and a Hugh Hefner style green robe. Love clothes, to say the least.

"Rupert, I want to take a shower and get ready. I have a little surprise for you…"

"Anything you want Delilah, schnookums."

Zip, snap, drop, rustle, rustle. Rupert was ready to rock.

"Where's my Old Spice, babe? Oh, nevermind, where's the stupid remote control? Let's see what's on the tube. Cool, a porno channel!"

While Rupert was watching *Blond Beach Bimbos Door To Door Dildo Salesgirls*, Delilah got herself ready for a night of unbridled sex.

The shower had relaxed Delilah some. She slowly dried herself off and slipped into the camisole. After tucking, pulling and sucking in her stomach, she squeezed her large breasts into the nightwear. She looked over into the mirror and caught a glimpse of herself. When putting on her ruby red lipstick, she noticed there were no wrinkles under her eyes. She felt her face and the skin was still soft. She slowly started caressing the rest of her body with her hands. She still had firm breasts that only sagged a bit from having three kids breastfeeding from them. Her hips hadn't widened too much, in fact hardly at all compared to most women that have had kids. She turned around to see her ass and even that still had a nice shape to it.

The years have been pretty good to me, she thought.

Basically, she was rather proud of her looks. Except of course for her size 12 feet.

She slipped on her new robe, turned off the light and stepped into the room. Rupert's eyes were transfixed...on the TV.

"Hey Stud, what do you think?"

"Incredible!"

"No, me! Not the TV. How do I look?"

"Oh, that's nice dear," Rupert said distractedly.

Not to be deprived of the attention she deserved, Delilah stepped in front of the TV and stared at Rupert.

"Babe, you look absolutely incredible." He winked and smiled devilishly, "Please turn around so I can see everything."

Delilah felt very sexy and playful because this was something he hadn't said to her in years. She turned around slowly and had her back to him while she wiggled out of her robe.

"WOW, you are so damn hot! Now bend over a little and spread your legs apart."

"RUPERT!" she said shocked and a little mischievously.

Delilah faced away from Rupert and closed her eyes bending over. The tightness of the camisole pulled the fabric taut against her pussy. She felt that deep warmth creep through her and she pulled her hands up her torso and grasped her breasts. "Just a little more..." Rupert whispered. Delilah bent over a bit more giving him a full view of her ass.

"Yes, that's perfect! Now I can work the remote control!" he said as he changed the volume.

"I can't believe you! We come over here for us and you sit here watching porno movies!" Delilah turned her head to the side and leaned over a little further stretching the fabric tighter still on her moist pussy, looking at the movie. "GOOD LORD, look at the size of that thing!!!!" She stood there watching a petite blonde, no bigger then a hundred pounds take a monstrous member in...all twelve inches of it. Wincing, Delilah stepped back next to Rupert.

Delilah, still being a little upset, hopped on the bed. She noticed Rupert was sporting a woody and really paying attention to the movie.

"Rupert, does this stuff really turn you on? More than I do?"

"No way! Babe, you are an incredibly attractive woman. You're sensual, sexy, extremely pretty and my best friend. Sometimes watching something like this is just to get my creative juices flowing and with the kids around we couldn't have something like this at the house. Besides there are some things that you wouldn't do to your best friend."

They both stared at the screen watching the ELEPHANT man (or whatever his nickname was). He had the little blonde straddling him and riding on his cock like a bull rider.

"Rupert, would you like to do some of those things with me?" Delilah asked worrying he'd be shocked or scared to ask her.

"I don't know honey. Sometimes I'd be a little afraid to ask. HOLY SMOKES, would you like to try that?" The guy had the woman turned away from him and laying atop a desk as he hammered into her from behind.

"Sorry honey, it'd take two times what you have to even attempt that! Why don't you turn that TV off? Let's make some of our own stuff up as we go along...stud."

Delilah stood before Rupert and pulled his face to her bosom. He breathed in her sweetly perfumed breasts. They strained to be free from the camisole. She took his face in her hands and licked his lips with just the tip of her tongue and fell forward drifting onto the bed with him. Straddling him, Delilah felt his cock's firmness lying under her wet pussy inside the lingerie. She slid her hand down and inside the fabric feeling the slick juice of her want. She pulled her wet finger out and rubbed the juice along Rupert's mouth. He licked his lips tasting the essence of her inner sanctum.

RRRIIIINNNNNGGGG!

Angrily Rupert answered the phone, "Hello? I told you kids not to call us unless there was an emergency!" He sat up, his voice becoming concerned. "What do you mean the baby won't eat dinner? Well you're not supposed to feed her chili beans and anchovies! You feed her baby food. She's only one year old!" Becoming more angry and frustrated he barked, "Where's the baby-sitter? What do you mean she took our bottle of Dom Perignon, a can of whipped cream and the dustbuster into our bedroom with two boys and locked the door?"

Delilah was becoming scared and upset from the situation and sat up.

"Where's that music coming from? The bedroom? You guys stay downstairs and we'll be home in a little while."

Rupert shielded the mouthpiece and whispered to his son, "Hey, flick the switch in the closet next to our bedroom, it activates my bedroom camcorder. Don't tell anyone about it!"

Rupert slammed the phone down angrily.

"Should we leave?" Delilah asked looking disappointed and somewhat concerned.

"Hell no! We've been planning this for months. I want to be with you. Come here, woman!" he growled.

Rupert moved behind Delilah and slowly caressed her shoulders then kissed her softly on the back of the neck. He moved his hands along her sides creeping them slowly toward the front of her. He longed to be the camisole that clung ever so tightly to her body, caressing every part of her.

Delilah reached behind her and held the back of his head. She thrust her chest out exposing her cleavage to his eyes.

"This outfit is driving me crazy."

"Does it turn you on?"

"I like to see you in anything, but mostly in nothing at all!"

Rupert forced his hands into the bust of the corset and grabbed her breasts.

"Uh, honey, my hands are stuck," Rupert said, struggling to get his hands free from the front of the outfit.

"What? Ouch, that hurts! I can't put my arms down!" Delilah cried, feeling confined and awkward.

RRRIIIINNNNGGGGG, RRRRIIIINNNNGGG!

"Shit, I can't answer the phone!" Rupert yelled.

"Try unzipping it! The zipper is in the back. Use your teeth." He was behind her but his hands were stuck in front and over her shoulders. So he did his best contortionist maneuver and stretched his neck down and grabbed the zipper in his teeth.

"Ahhhh! Ouch, I just chipped my tooth and the latch on the zipper broken!" he screamed as blood trickled from his mouth.

They tried to break loose from their odd situation but they lost their balance and Rupert slammed against a small table. The lamp fell and broke, scattering porcelain all over the floor. The table dropped onto the floor with a loud thud. To top things off the small candle on the table caught the carpet on fire.

About this time the motel manager was making his rounds and walked by their room. He couldn't help but hear the screaming and thrashing about in the room, as Rupert frantically tried to free his hands. The manager, assuming the worst, banged on the door and since nobody was answering he unlocked the door. From the doorway he saw Rupert bent over with Delilah in front of him and his hands locked in her camisole. To the manager it looked like he was choking her, so he rushed up behind him and pulled at him, freeing his hands.

They fell back with Rupert cracking his head on the coffee table. Delilah's breasts popped out and the camisole ripped a seam.

At the police station Delilah was booked for prostitution, Rupert's head received twelve stitches and the *Enquirer* interviewed the hotel manager.

When Rupert finally came to, he explained to the judge what was going on. After the laughter subsided, the judge made him pay for damages and ordered him to go home. When they finally got home the kids were all in bed sleeping, the house was clean (even their bedroom), and the babysitter was doing her homework (Biology of human sexuality).

"What a night!" Rupert told Delilah as she was taking off her make-up and standing in front of the mirror wearing her old, beat up flannel robe.

She jumped into bed with her green mud mask and told Rupert, "We don't need a motel room, we've got this old bed and we've made magic here for 10 years! I love you Rupert... Rupert?"

"ZZZZZZZZZZZZZZZZZZZZ, snort, huh?"

They snuggled up next to each other and fell asleep in each other's arms, just like every other night.

The Apartment

છ

Linda had just spent a four long weeks away on business and had taken the red-eye flight home. She was exhausted and wanted nothing more than to get in her own bed. She had a headache and slight hangover from airline drinks and her luggage seemed to weigh a ton as she dragged it towards her apartment.

After what seemed an eternity of stairs, she walked in without even turning on the lights and headed straight for her bed. When she went in her bedroom, she saw a pair of pants draped over a chair in the darkened room. *Carl must be here,* she thought to herself. Not even bothering to shower or take off her make-up, she stripped naked and slipped into her bed. *Oh, it feels so nice to be in my own bed,* she thought to herself. It had been so long that she barely recognized it—it felt so much better than she remembered.

As she lay there in an extremely relaxed state, Carl rolled over. He put his big strong arm around Linda. His warmth soothed her as he hugged her tightly, softly kissing her on the earlobe.

"I missed you," he whispered while slowly stroking her soft skin ever so delicately.

"Mmmmmm, that feels nice," she whispered back, leaning into his body.

He rolled her onto her stomach and climbed on top of her. His large hands began rubbing and massaging her back.

"God, it's been so long since you've done something like this to me," she softly said. "It feels great!" Linda began to melt to his touch, her body relaxing and molding to the curves of the bed.

It was very stimulating and quite a turn-on to have someone baby her like this. Time stood still for her as he painstakingly massaged every inch of her back and slowly moved his hands around to feel the sides of her breasts. As he cupped the smooth fullness of her breasts, Linda moaned into the bed feeling herself falling into bliss. She felt so relaxed and it was almost dreamlike. As Carl moved down to her rear end and legs, he stopped briefly to softly kiss the small of her back and her thighs. He ran his tongue along the creases of her body, along her backside and hips to the center of her back between her shoulders. *Damn I am so fuckin' turned on,* she thought to herself enjoying her arousal.

Carl moved his hand between her thighs and felt her wetness. His fingers slipped between the labia and felt her pussy heat to his touch. When he kissed her back and the curve of her ass, Linda almost came. His mouth followed the crease of her ass, and she leaned face down into the coolness of her pillow as his head moved behind her. His finger poked deeper into her, making her squirm, and when his tongue reached the opening of her pussy she couldn't help but moan in pleasure. He pulled his finger out and sucked on it like a lollipop. Grabbing her legs, he pulled to the edge of the bed and knelt on the floor. He nuzzled his nose to her ass and licked the length of her hot sex. The tip of his tongue swept across the opening. The juices from within her trickled down her inner thigh mixing with the saliva from his tender eating of her sanctuary.

The gentleness of his seduction became more intense from the taste of her. His deeper desires started taking over. His hard-on was aching to probe her and the taste of her sweet juices spurred an animalistic desire in him. Standing up behind her, he put a hand on her back and reached under her with the other one, lifting her up and plunged deeply into her wet cavern.

She could not believe how good it felt. The hard thickness of her man plunging into her with reckless abandon. The smacking sound of his stomach against her ass making her body shake. It had been so long and he felt so different than before.

He grabbed onto Linda's hips and started driving deeper and harder into her. His own grunts and moans were becoming savage. It was glorious. She felt the swelling passion inside as she clenched the sheets in her hands and bit on her lip.

Oh, what a feeling!

When he reached forward and slid his hands up under her breasts grasping them firmly in his strong hands, goose bumps trickled across her body and she started screaming.

Linda stood up on her knees and Carl bit hard on her neck. She reached back and grabbed onto his ass frantically pulling him towards her shrieking, "Dammit Carl, don't stop! Harder...HARDER...don't stop! This is fucking incredible!"

Stopping abruptly, he reached over to turn on the light and said, "Carl? Who the fuck is Carl?"

"AAAAHHHHH!!!! Who the hell are you!" Linda shrieked as she pulled up the blanket. She sat there staring at a naked stranger, and looking extremely dumbfounded with his doinger hanging out.

"I'm John. I live here. Who the FUCK are you?"

"Linda. *I* live here."

"Wait a minute, I've been living here with my wife for five years. Apartment 28B on the fourteenth floor, don't tell me I don't live here."

"Fourteenth floor? Uhhhhh... I'm sorry... I live on the fifteenth floor."

The Home Movie

മാ

Jim and Nancy had been married for almost ten years. Their anniversary was next weekend and Jim felt compelled to do something a little extra to spice up their love life. The passion still burned between them, but it didn't ignite as often as they wanted. Life's little turns took their toll on their quality time together. Meaning, they weren't having sex much. Kids, work and the ordinary calls to family life were coming between them.

So in an attempt to add a little flavor to things, Jim had purchased a new camera and tripod. He planned to send the kids to his in-laws for a night and spend the night fucking like rabbits in a cage. Of course, there would be a little more room than in the back of his Volkswagen when they were dating, but he still hoped it would rekindle the fire.

* * * * *

When a very tired Nancy came in from work, the house was dimly lit with a trail of candles leading to the kitchen. She slowly followed the trail toward the light in the kitchen, glowing brightly against the darkness of the rest of the house.

Her curiosity drove her forward toward the unknown. When she stepped into the kitchen she saw a bowl of fruit, a black silk blindfold and a note on the table. She grinned devilishly at the note, in Jim's handwriting which read:

My dearest soulmate,
The kids are at your parents, we are all alone,
Time will go back ten years, back to our start.

Take off your clothes, get comfy and warm,

Because tonight we will free the beasts in our hearts.

A scorching heat filled Nancy's body as she unbuttoned her blouse. She looked down her body as she ran her hands over her breasts and down the muscles of her tummy. She unfastened the latch of her skirt. Her fingers slipped inside the elastic waistband of her underwear and she pinched the fabric between her legs to peel them off her wet pussy and felt the heat rising within her.

Another set of hands grasped her waist and Jim pulled her close and whispered into her ear, "You will be my nourishment, like you always have. Let me devour you and feast on your bounty."

Nancy's knees weakened from the brush of his lips against her ear. She closed her eyes and felt her pussy warm to a fire. Jim reached to the table and took the blindfold in his hand. He tied it across Nancy's eyes snugly, but not too tight. Just tight enough to ensure she couldn't see what he was doing. His hands cascaded along the fabric of her clothing, sliding her loosened shirt along her arms and off. Jim kissed her shoulder as he moved the bra strap aside and down her arm. He kissed the back of her neck and shoulders and removed the other strap.

Her skin was pale and pure but her chest flushed pink as her heart started racing with excitement. His lips kissed the side of her neck and down her shoulder blades. He undid the hook of her brassiere causing Nancy to shudder. She leaned forward exposing the flesh of her bosom and the rosy hardness of her nipples. Jim slid his hands back around to her tummy and pulled her back against his shirtless chest. The heat of his skin warmed Nancy's chills. His hands ventured upwards as he cupped her full breasts in his hands. He bit into her neck teasingly as Nancy's body melted against his. Jim's hands caressed her breasts and wandered all over her fragile frame.

Jim tugged at the loosened skirt with one hand, making it fall down her legs to the floor. The red lace on her panties always made him crazy. His finger toyed with the frill as he outlined the shape of the fabric against the curves of her hip and inner thigh. Her clean-shaven labia swelled with anticipation as the utter darkness behind the blindfold accentuated the fury of her growing passion. He put his hand over her pussy cupping it in his palm. The silk fabric was wet and slippery from her growing excitement.

"Lie down on the table," Jim instructed her.

Jim took her hand and led her to the table and she blindly hopped onto it and shrieked, "AHHH, this is cold!"

"It'll warm up in a minute," Jim commented. "The warmth from your pussy could heat up an igloo."

Again she felt nervous because she couldn't see him. She had no clue what he was doing or what he had planned.

She didn't know that Jim had set up his tripod with his old camcorder to film this encounter to show her later.

Nancy lay there, surrounded by fruits like a model for a Renaissance nude. Jim dragged his fingers over her body as he walked to the end of the table where her head was. When she reached for him, Jim grabbed her hand and kissed her palm.

Nancy used her other hand to search for his pants. Her blinded fumbling for him aroused Jim. She grabbed at his sweatpants tugging the strings, trying to release his swollen cock. She pulled at his pants, drawing him to her, then scooted to the edge of the table, letting her hair fall off the edge. Her head hung over the edge and the tip of Jim's cock was inches away from her mouth. She deftly took his shaft in her hand and flicked the tip of it with her tongue.

Jim looked down upon her blindfolded head and watched as she inched him into her mouth. The skin of her lips tightened as his cock slid against them. He saw her neck tense and cheeks puff out as he got drawn fully into her mouth. He closed his eyes and felt her mouth wash over him. She sucked hard on the tip and breathed in the smell of his body.

Jim reached his hand down between her legs and slid his finger between her shaved wet labia. Nancy spread her legs apart and encouraged his explorations. As his finger dipped into her, she sucked his penis deeper into her hot mouth. His stomach tightened as she used her tongue to follow the vein along the bottom of his cock and feel the pulse of his heart from it. She took her hand and caressed his testicles as she wrapped her tongue around his cock like a snake coiling its prey.

"I can't handle this," Jim said stepping back, not wanting to lose control too quickly.

After pulling his sweats over the hardness of his penis, it protruded out like a cannon, still seeping fluid from the incredible sensuality and feel of her mouth. He took a lace ribbon and tied her hands together and pulled them over her head and to the chair at the end of the table.

The confinement along with the black darkness of the blindfold left Nancy totally at his mercy. Jim knocked the bowl of fruit from the table, scattering everything and scaring Nancy. She squirmed on the table as she heard Jim open the refrigerator door. She heard things rattling but couldn't free her arms or see what he was doing.

Jim moved between Nancy's legs and parted them wider. He pulled her pussy closer to his end of the table. Her arms ached from having them stretched high above her head. Jim licked his lips and a strawberry into some whipped cream and rubbed the smooth coolness across her pubis causing Nancy to shiver from the cold. Playfully he rubbed the cream on her erect nipples and licked it off sloppily.

Teasing her more he took a bite from the strawberry and slipped the rough dimpled texture in and out of her pussy and across her swollen clit. He dabbed the strawberry into the cream again and slipped it between her labia. Twisting it like a screw he pushed it a little deeper. The rough dimples rubbed against her pussy making her opening part and then close as he pulled it away. The sweet cream only lubricated her pussy more, even though she didn't need it. Being a gentleman, he continued by licking the remaining cream from her shaven lips, only darting his tongue inside of her to make sure he didn't miss anything.

Nancy ached to grab Jim. She was panting and almost breathless as she was beyond excitement. Her body was so alive and sensitive to everything Jim was doing. The blackness of her blindfold was a match lighting her fire.

After letting Nancy have the last bite of the strawberry, he grabbed another piece of fruit. Jim's mouth hovered over Nancy's engorged labia. She felt his hot breath against her wet pussy. Her mind burned with ravenous desire. He bit on a peach and the juices ran down the sides of his mouth to his chin and dripped onto her pussy. Jim licked the sweet juice from her pussy lips and took another bite, letting it flow over her again. She squirmed and tried to close her legs but Jim held them firm as he teased her relentlessly. His cock was thumping against his abdomen as his heartbeat caused it to throb.

Pulling his sweatpants off, he stumbled getting his shoes off. He moved to the end of the table and climbed onto it and straddled Nancy in a 69 position. He moved down and his chest rubbed against her tummy. Nancy felt his cock brush against her cheek and she searched for it with her tongue. She found it and guided it into her mouth, sucking so hard Jim winced.

Jim grabbed the banana from the scattered fruit across the table and tried to concentrate on what he was doing as Nancy sucked hungrily on the length of his shaft. He leaned over to lick her pussy and get it ready for the new toy. Nancy moaned as the tip entered her. She made a desperate attempt to cry out with Jim filling her mouth. The vibrations shot through his balls and staggered him.

As Jim slid the banana deeper into Nancy, her hands contorted and her fingers flexed. The insanely intense pleasure from the firmness and the bend of the banana pressed directly against her G-spot caused her to almost split apart. She let Jim go from her mouth and moaned deeply as she felt herself orgasm. As her feet dug in the tabletop, her lower torso elevated off it as if she were floating. She shook as Jim peeled the skin from the banana, spreading her lips wider, which caused her to lose control. She fell to the table and climaxed again from the increased pressure on her clit.

Feeling rather proud of himself, Jim was on all fours above her and he pulled the banana the rest of the way out and began to eat it, when he felt the warmth of a mouth caressing his penis.

Nancy slowly stroked him with her lips as he hung above her blindfolded head. She couldn't touch him with anything but her mouth. So she embraced the feel of his cock within the sanctity of her in her lips. She took more of him in her mouth savoring, the taste of his pre-ejaculate.

Jim's knees weakened as he slowly made love to her mouth. He closed his eyes and leaned down to kiss the wet lips beneath him. Her pussy was warm and sweet to his mouth.

She squirmed and continued to suck on him. She sucked hard on the tip, almost daring him to pull it out.

His own desires to release were becoming desperate and he felt the primal urge to fuck. Jim was crazed as he pulled up out of her mouth. He jumped off the table and rushed to her legs. He dragged her toward him, stretching her arms higher above her head. Nancy felt faint from the pain as he spread her legs apart, holding an ankle in each hand. Her pain faded to bliss as his cock found her pussy.

As he felt her wrap around him, he was like a jackhammer slamming harder and deeper into her. His demeanor had changed and he was almost violent in his fury. The way he had control of her and how she made him crazy with desire lit a bonfire in him. He was sweating and his neck tightened and he came inside of her. Like a dam breaking loose from built up pressure, he poured his essence into her again and again.

When Jim caught his breath he pulled out and rested his cock on her pelvis. It dripped the inner essence from their sex as it moved. Jim lay on top of her and felt her heart beat with his.

Nancy's hands were aching from being tied and she had bruises from the lace. Jim reached up to untie her hands. Seeing the bruises, he kissed her wrists gently. The bruises were a reminder of his deep desire for her. She unleashed passions in him that had been pent-up. He loosened the blindfold and stared into her eyes.

When she looked up she saw the camera on the tripod. Looking confused, she asked him, "What's that for?"

"Well, I wanted to record us and watch it some other time. After this, I see it was a good idea," he said as he laughed.

A few weeks passed. They planned to have another night together and got everything for the kids to stay at grandma's again. They scurried the kids out with all their necessities and Jim tried to rush back home so they could watch their movie.

Nancy had cooked some fish for dinner and had a bottle of wine chilled. They sat in front of the TV to watch it while eating and the movie started to their anticipation. After the opening scene started they looked at each other in shock. "What the fuck is this?" Jim yelled. "This is Veggie Tales? This is the kids movie, how did this get... Oh my God!"

As Nancy reached for the phone, it rang. She answered it and her mom talked slowly to her and said, "The kids had wanted to see their Veggie Tales tape. Instead of the children learning about the food groups, I had to explain how mommy eats with her pussy."

The Long Nights, Part 3

ဢ

Melissa spent the next few weeks—after discovering Tony and Kayla had been watching her too—working long hours. She had little time or energy for herself. Her Friday was a day from hell and she was beat up by the day's tensions, so she went to the corner bar to have a little dinner and unwind. She sat alone in the corner booth and ate and looked out the window, watching people pass. She took a small sip from her Strawberry Daiquiri and closed her eyes, savoring the quiet and the cold smooth flow of the drink.

She felt a gentle tap on her shoulder and looked over to see a man's crotch. Looking up the body, she saw Tony's face. Awkwardly she smiled and said, "Hello Tony."

"I didn't know you knew my name. I've seen you many times and in many ways but I don't know yours." He smiled as he sat down in the booth with her.

"My name is Melissa," she said, feeling nervous and once again excited by this chance meeting. They talked and both of them laughed at the situation and how watching each other made them feel aroused.

Tony was a handsome, muscular man and had a very powerful confidence that drew Melissa in. She explained to him that she had worked hard to get to where she was. She told him that she hadn't had a relationship in a long time and was somewhat jealous of his and Kayla's.

Tony told her that they were a very open couple. They loved each other but wouldn't confine each other. Sex to them was for pleasure and sharing it with her and knowing she watched them made it better. They were both exhibitionists, so it fulfilled a need for them.

Their talk made Melissa a little aroused. In fact, she remembered seeing Tony naked and she became *very* aroused. Her squirming didn't go unnoticed by Tony, so as he ordered another drink he set his hand on Melissa's knee. Her leg was warm to the touch. When she didn't pull her leg away from his hand, Tony pulled his hand away and got out his wallet to pay for the drinks. Then he put his hand on her leg again only higher up on her thigh.

She looked into Tony's deep brown eyes and desperately longed to kiss him. But she wouldn't cross that line.

As he sucked down his bourbon, his hand slid up Melissa's thigh and rested against her underwear. She didn't refuse his advances. In fact, her eyes glazed over and she parted her legs wider as his fingers outlined the labia of her wet pussy. She held the edge of the table and bit her lip to keep from moaning; his finger tugged her underwear to the side and his fingertips slipped along the ridges of her lips. Watching Melissa's pleasure flash across her face, Tony slid his finger inside of her tight opening, then looked into her eyes deeply and leaned in and kissed her.

Melissa closed her eyes and enjoyed the little shocks of pleasure she felt from Tony's fingers probing into her. She felt a passion she hadn't known in a long time. Undeniable lust and new, strange emotions washed over her body. His gentle assault on her pussy made her almost beg for more.

At an almost climactic moment Tony stopped and said, "Check please."

Melissa tried to compose herself as they both left the bar. She was very anxious and her desire was becoming a blazing need.

"Would you like to come up?" Tony asked.

Melissa was torn. Should she fill this burning need she had or respect the relationship he had with Kayla and take it slow?

She made the decision to take it slow.

* * * * *

The decision lasted almost four minutes.

Melissa threw her head back, reveling in the fullness of Tony's cock spreading her insides and filling her cavern of passion. Her mouth opened wide in ecstasy as he pulled down on her thighs. He forced himself into her until his abdomen pressed against her pubis. Her pussy adjusted to the size of his cock like a hand to a glove…he fit perfectly.

Melissa hadn't had the pleasure of a good hard cock in a long time. Filled by a man instead of a plastic battery-operated toy or a piece of fruit… He made her feel alive! All the fantasies she had after seeing Tony and Kayla were being fulfilled.

Tony's muscles rippled as he thrust into her again and again. Melissa looked up and pulled her hair back in through her fingers. His massive hands clutched her breasts and he pulled them to his mouth to suckle on the nipples. She saw her apartment window and it reminded her of them watching her. The remembered voyeurism excited her still more.

Their breathing deepened and she heard a third moaning sound. Melissa opened her eyes and saw a reflection in the mirror. It was Kayla holding a camera. She had her hand in her panties, stroking the lips of her pussy as she filmed them. Melissa froze for a second and looked up at Tony. Ecstasy overtook him and bliss showed in his face.

Kayla walked over and kissed his shoulder and looked over him smiling, as she watched him slide in and out of Melissa's pussy. "Damn she's beautiful, Tony. Even prettier than we saw in her apartment window." Then Kayla winked and massaged Tony's shoulders, as he painfully held himself motionless inside of Melissa and kissed Kayla on the cheek. "Mind if I join you?" Kayla asked.

Tony pulled out of Melissa and sat at the foot of the bed. He lay back and watched Kayla pull her sweater off over her head, exposing her strapless black bra. She guided Melissa over to the foot of the bed, where Kayla directed her to face out towards her and straddle Tony. Kayla kissed her cheek and moved over to gently kiss her mouth. The fragrance of Melissa's hair and the taste of her tongue as Kayla outlined her mouth made Kayla moan.

Melissa lowered herself down onto the length of Tony's cock, shuddering as he reentered her.

Kayla reached back to unsnap her bra. Melissa put her hand on Kayla's hip to unzip her skirt on the side and it slipped down her legs. The black thong she had on barely covered her small patch of hair and the bottom was pulled to the side from Kayla touching herself.

Kayla leaned forward and kissed Melissa as she knelt down in front of her and Tony. Tony was stiff inside of her and thrusting his hips up and down slowly, making her juices cover his crotch and trickle down his testicles. Kayla grasped Tony's balls and kissed Melissa.

Melissa held Kayla's face in her hand and they explored each other's mouths with their tongues. Melissa stifled a moan when Kayla massaged Tony's balls and he jerked up into her. Kayla's mouth was luscious and savory to Melissa, her lips were deep red and they pursed out when Melissa kissed her breasts. She loved how Kayla felt.

Tony filled Melissa's inner walls and his cock was so hard and strong that she wanted to ride him forever. He made her feel so sexy. Melissa hadn't dreamed this experience could be so heavenly. Being the center of attention between two people was empowering. She loved it.

Kayla felt the slippery juices from her own pussy and fingered her mouth like Tony was slipping in and out of Melissa.

Melissa's eyes closed as she felt herself being swept away by her own awakening into a sexual awareness she never thought existed. This was total abandon, utter ecstasy. As Kayla kissed down Melissa's torso, Melissa pushed on Tony's knees and fucked him with more vigor. Her pussy swelled with need.

Kayla licked at Melissa's nipples and pushed her back. Melissa felt as if she were falling into oblivion. Tony grasped her waist and back so she was propped up but loose. His stiffness was sliding against her clitoris. Her eyes glassed over and as Kayla's tongue licked against the length of his shimmering cock and her swollen clit, she cried out. A tear trickled down her cheek as she came. Her body became strained and shook as her orgasm enveloped her.

After the spasms subsided, she fell back into Tony's body. Tony popped free from the slick lips of Melissa's pussy and lay her down on the bed.

Kayla's mouth found Tony's cock. As if he were nourishment, she licked and sucked on his stiffness. Melissa's juices covered it and Kayla licked her lips. "Mmmmmmmmmm, you taste wonderful, Melissa. I want a little more of this."

Kayla leaned over the bed and between Melissa's legs, focusing her attention on her pussy. Kayla licked at the wetness seeping from her. Kayla appreciated the taste of a woman and dipped her tongue in and out of her pussy, lapping up her sweet juices.

The first waves had subsided from Melissa's orgasm and she felt another one quickly building. This was a deeper orgasm, as if coming from her soul. She closed her eyes and let her melted mind wander as she felt totally frail and totally exposed to her emotional nakedness.

Kayla's skin was smooth to Melissa's touch. Her fragrance filled her lungs and the feeling of Kayla's breasts and hardened nipples against her thighs was so erotic. Kayla pulled and fingered her own pussy as her needs overtook her. Her fingers rubbed her clit and her labia became engorged and puffy waiting for attention. Tony sat up, hearing Kayla's needy moans.

Melissa desperately grasped the sheets on the bed and pulled them loose as Kayla continued to lick along her clit. She glanced up and saw Tony kiss Kayla. Tony stood up from the bed and stood behind Kayla holding his stiff cock in his hand, admiring the two beautiful women exploring each other. Kayla was bent over and Tony slipped his cock into her sweltering fire. Melissa looked up and Kayla's salivating mouth fell open and she smiled devilishly with passion filling her eyes. Pure passion like this was overpowering, and as Kayla slid her two fingers inside of Melissa's pussy, she came again.

Melissa moved over on the bed. Kayla fell onto the bed and rolled over. She spread her legs and pulled Tony on top of her. Grabbing his stiff cock in her hand, Kayla smiled saying, "Let's show her what fucking is all about," and guided him into her. Tony thrust hard into Kayla, making her whimper and she wrapped her legs around his hot, sweating ass. Tony smiled and they began a furious pace of beautiful fucking…they were true mates.

Melissa caressed Kayla's chest and smoothed the small beads of perspiration between her breasts. Her hands were her guide as she was released from her constraining shell and now freed to explore the inner desires. She touched Tony's chest feeling the burning heat of his skin. His veins bulged in his neck and down his chest as he tried to hold back his ultimate release.

Tony grabbed Kayla's ass and lifted her up and plunged into her with a fury, taking long, hard strokes. Kayla's breasts shook as Tony hammered hard into her. Her eyes closed tightly, she panted as she felt him hit against her pelvis.

Melissa caressed his abdomen and groin area and his cock popped out of Kayla. Melissa leaned over and sucked his length into her mouth and tasted the sex from all three of them. She quickly licked the sticky fluid from the tip, making Tony moan. His cock strained upward, extremely stiff and shiny from the juices on it. She held it in her hand and guided it back to Kayla's hot pussy.

Tony looked down and watched it slowly disappear into Kayla's pink flesh. He moaned loudly from the hot tightness of Kayla's pussy. Kayla felt Tony tighten and strain. Her deep feelings for him made her feel his pleasure. Her body flexed and tightened and Melissa stared in joy, watching the two lovers come together.

The three of them fell asleep in the large bed entwined like a pretzel. Melissa awoke—Tony snored loudly!—and carefully got out of the bed, gathered her clothes and sneaked out the door. Back in her living room, she looked out her window to Tony and Kayla's dark apartment and a feeling of warmth crept through her. She finally found a part of herself long thought lost.

* * * * *

A few days passed and life took control of the three of them again.

Kayla came home from work and was exhausted and worn out. Tony was away and she felt lonely and bored. She kicked back in her comfy chair, kicked her heels off and sipped the glass of wine she had poured. She glanced out the window into the night and saw the lights go on in Melissa's window. The blinds were closed but she knew someone was home. Kayla thought about calling her or even stopping over for a little surprise to talk about the evening they spent together. The memories still stirred her.

Watching out her window in her darkened apartment, Kayla saw Melissa open her blinds. Melissa leaned against the window for a second and looked across and saw Kayla through the dim light in her room and waved. She opened her blinds all the way and Kayla saw Melissa wasn't alone. There was a good-looking, blond man there with her.

Kayla watched as Melissa and the man kissed and started dancing. Kayla became aroused by her own curiosity as she watched them. Melissa then sat on the top of her couch and the blond man knelt in front of her and began eating her out.

Kayla frantically looked for her binoculars and scurried back to the window. Melissa was lying back on the couch and the man continued to savor her pussy.

Kayla scanned up Melissa's body and as she saw her face, Melissa opened her eyes and winked, smiling ear to ear knowing Kayla was watching her. In her own way she was repaying Kayla and Tony for sharing their long nights with her.

Also by S.L. Carpenter

ဆာ

Betty and the Beast

Broken

Dark Lord Origins

Dark Lust

Detour *with Sahara Kelly*

Haunting Love Alley *with Sahara Kelly*

In the End

Learning to Live Again

Partners in Passion 1: Eleanor and Justin *with Sahara Kelly*

Partners in Passion 2: No Limits *with Sahara Kelly*

Partners in Passion 3: Pure Sin *with Sahara Kelly*

Slippery When Wet

Toys 4 Us

About the Author

✷

S.L. Carpenter is a born and raised California man. He does both writing and cover art for novels as outlets for his overactive libido and twisted mind. His inspiration is his wife, who keeps him well trained. Writing is his true joy. It gives him freedom and expression for both his sensual and humorous sides.

S.L. Carpenter welcomes comments from readers. You can find her website and email address on her author bio page at www.ellorascave.com.

Tell Us What You Think

We appreciate hearing reader opinions about our books. You can email us at Comments@EllorasCave.com.

Why an electronic book?

We live in the Information Age—an exciting time in the history of human civilization, in which technology rules supreme and continues to progress in leaps and bounds every minute of every day. For a multitude of reasons, more and more avid literary fans are opting to purchase e-books instead of paper books. The question from those not yet initiated into the world of electronic reading is simply: *Why?*

1. *Price.* An electronic title at Ellora's Cave Publishing and Cerridwen Press runs anywhere from 40% to 75% less than the cover price of the exact same title in paperback format. Why? Basic mathematics and cost. It is less expensive to publish an e-book (no paper and printing, no warehousing and shipping) than it is to publish a paperback, so the savings are passed along to the consumer.

2. *Space.* Running out of room in your house for your books? That is one worry you will never have with electronic books. For a low one-time cost, you can purchase a handheld device specifically designed for e-reading. Many e-readers have large, convenient screens for viewing. Better yet, hundreds of titles can be stored within your new library—on a single microchip. There are a variety of e-readers from different manufacturers. You can also read e-books on your PC or laptop computer. (Please note that Ellora's Cave does not endorse any specific brands.

You can check our websites at www.ellorascave.com or www.cerridwenpress.com for information we make available to new consumers.)

3. *Mobility.* Because your new e-library consists of only a microchip within a small, easily transportable e-reader, your entire cache of books can be taken with you wherever you go.

4. *Personal Viewing Preferences.* Are the words you are currently reading too small? Too large? Too… ANNOYING? Paperback books cannot be modified according to personal preferences, but e-books can.

5. *Instant Gratification.* Is it the middle of the night and all the bookstores near you are closed? Are you tired of waiting days, sometimes weeks, for bookstores to ship the novels you bought? Ellora's Cave Publishing sells instantaneous downloads twenty-four hours a day, seven days a week, every day of the year. Our webstore is never closed. Our e-book delivery system is 100% automated, meaning your order is filled as soon as you pay for it.

Those are a few of the top reasons why electronic books are replacing paperbacks for many avid readers.

As always, Ellora's Cave and Cerridwen Press welcome your questions and comments. We invite you to email us at Comments@ellorascave.com or write to us directly at Ellora's Cave Publishing Inc., 1056 Home Avenue, Akron, OH 44310-3502.

erridwen, the Celtic Goddess of wisdom, was the muse who brought inspiration to story-tellers and those in the creative arts. Cerridwen Press encompasses the best and most innovative stories in all genres of today's fiction. Visit our site and discover the newest titles by talented authors who still get inspired - much like the ancient storytellers did, once upon a time.

Cerridwen Press

www.cerridwenpress.com

Discover for yourself why readers can't get enough
of the multiple award-winning publisher

Ellora's Cave.

Whether you prefer e-books or paperbacks,

be sure to visit EC on the web at
www.ellorascave.com

for an erotic reading experience that will leave you
breathless.